# Digging Stars

A Novel

## NOVUYO ROSA TSHUMA

**W. W. NORTON & COMPANY**
*Celebrating a Century of Independent Publishing*

Revised portions of this work appeared in short form in *McSweeney's 52* (2018), *Ploughshares* (summer 2019), *A Lesson in Englishness* (UK: Atlantic Shorts Series, 2019), and *Dear McSweeney's: Two Decades of Letters to the Editor* (2021)

For information about permission to reproduce selections from this book, write to Permissions, W. W. Norton & Company, Inc., 500 Fifth Avenue, New York, NY 10110

For information about special discounts for bulk purchases, please contact W. W. Norton Special Sales at specialsales@wwnorton.com or 800-233-4830

Manufacturing by Lakeside Book Company
Book design by Chris Welch
Production manager: Lauren Abbate

ISBN 978-1-324-03517-6

W. W. Norton & Company, Inc., 500 Fifth Avenue, New York, N.Y. 10110
www.wwnorton.com

W. W. Norton & Company Ltd., 15 Carlisle Street, London W1D 3BS

1 2 3 4 5 6 7 8 9 0

# Part I

He came late to pick me up at JFK airport, my father. In 2005, after the terror of 9/11, parents were pretty scared to let their children fly by themselves under the care of the airline— except Mama, of course! I had been on two connecting flights from Bulawayo, first at O. R. Tambo in Jo'burg, where I'd wandered off and the plane had almost left me, and then at Gatwick in London, where the British Airways stewardess in whose care I'd been put dumped me in a room full of candy, where I did what any sensible eleven-year-old would do and stuffed myself silly, crunching through M&Ms and Oreos and Cadbury chocolates and Belgian creams like a Pac-Man on steroids.

And then we were gliding over New York City, and I felt the thrill of being an astral thing. I tried to make out the Big Dipper or the Little Dipper in the early morning darkness as we descended into JFK, but the stars were outdone by the skyglow of man-made constellations winking up at us like cyborg kin from the cosmos below.

The next moment, I was on solid ground, my sneakers squeaking across dull parquet floors, blinking back tears under the blunt lights of the airport, my father nowhere to be seen. I must have felt the abysmal terror of being without him even then, unable to locate his face. It was a wondrous thing, that face, a solid, pecan vista on which I could trace my own button nose, with its fleshy alae, and plump lips that, when he smiled, revealed, just as my own did, a constellation of pearly teeth dipping into a galaxy of wine-dark gums.

I looked up at the dour-faced airport officer in whose care I'd been put, and then bent over and vomited a sludge of candy right onto his polished shoes.

He leapt back, his lips upended in dismay. "Why, you li'l n—"

And then, there he was, ambling down the airport corridor in black jeans and a tan leather jacket, the gold rims of his oval specs catching the light. I fluttered my eyes at him. I had not expected to feel so shy. He seemed impossibly tall, his gangly legs launching him in lofty strides. I remained standing beside the angry officer, next to a dark curio store with feather headdresses and wooden Indian dolls pressed against the glass, watching first his face and then his approaching feet.

"Hello, missy," he said in English.

*Hello, missy.*

I smiled through my tears. We had always used English together, he and I.

He gave my cheek a gentle tug. And then he frowned. "What's the matter?"

The officer, who had quietened down, began to speak real fast and aggressive again, gesticulating at me and then at the gooey mess at his feet. My father, too, began to speak, his voice rising to a dangerous pitch as he yelled, "She's just a child, a child!"

I beamed, basking in his celestial warmth. He turned to walk away, and I followed him, slipping my hand in his. Together we were swept up by the sea of airport strangers, the surly officer rapidly fading into an insignificant spec.

It was the first time it was just the two of us, together like that. I could not remember when he had last visited home. We wrote each other often; he had started writing me letters from the time I could read and write, sharing stories from his childhood, which sounded like fables, for I could not imagine him, this colossal, hopelessly cosmopolitan man, now a professor of astronomy, as a half-naked rascal once-upon-a-time slinking away from the evening fire in his father's homestead to crouch behind the cattle kraal and study the night sky.

There he would remain for hours, the garlicky scent of aloe vera filling his nostrils, the cicadas a resounding orchestra, somewhere in that blue-blackness the click-click of the bats, and above all this, a glittery panorama stretching in all directions, kissing the heavens and the earth, with the umThala, the Milky Way, arching across the sky like the patch of hair left on an infant's head after the rest has been rubbed off.

Here, his sentences would become loopy and self-indulgent. I would read in one long exhalation, gasping for breath, about the marvel of isiLimela, the Digging Stars, Pleiades, the first of which winked in the eastern night sky in September, hot-blue fireflies heralding the spring rains. My father would track them, crouching with his lanky, eight-year-old body held taut, trembling, emitting a sigh when he was finally able to pin-point a shimmering light one night, and then two the next, and then four, and so on, until six, sometimes seven glow-worms hovered overhead, webbing the obsidian sky with their blue, gossamer light.

Then he got a scholarship to attend the village school run by the

Catholic missionaries and stopped rising with the Digging Stars to latch a pair of oxen to the plough, catching the last of them disappearing in the western skies as he and his siblings trudged barefoot across the crumbly soil headed for the fields, the star so crisp and hot-blue he would instinctively stretch out a gangly arm as though to pluck it. Instead, he began to rise to the regiments of an alarm clock, a red, plastic, screeching thing gifted him by Father Pius.

Years later, as an adult, while trudging through a snowstorm in downtown Manhattan, or just after one of his lectures to a stuffy room full of ambivalent freshmen, or entombed in the gloomy subway, he would look about, dazed, as though he expected to find himself out in the Sahara bush under the infinite expanse of a bespangled night sky. He would jerk up, startled to find himself where he was, a smothering weight crushing his chest. Once, he whispered, "What am I doing here?" and a scraggly homeless man yelled back, "Why don't you go back to Africa!" This rejoinder was so unexpected, so strangely percipient, that he burst out laughing. The homeless man, too, began to laugh. They laughed together, like that, for a good, long minute.

I did not know what to make of this. I was too young for nostalgia. Why did he share these stories with me? He must have known I would not understand them. I would frown and frown at his perplexing letters, flattered by his adult attention, my head throbbing not with the dawn of understanding but a foggy migraine.

Now, stumbling to keep up with his long strides as we made our way through that monstrosity of an airport, I felt stiff. There was a clumsiness to our bodies. He kept yanking my small hand encased in his large, sweaty palm, lurching me forward, straining to look behind us, ahead of us, all around us, his eyes flitting from side to side. Finally, he hailed a cab.

"How was your flight?" he said, easing me into the backseat.

"It was nice," I said, my voice hiccupping as the cab lurched forward.

"You didn't get lost?" He looked out the window, scouting the crowds etched in oblique shadows by the dawn light.

"Hmm-hmm."

"Tired?" He looked over his shoulder out the window at the back.

"Hmm-hmm."

We were quiet for a while as the cab nosed out of JFK. We spent a good thirty minutes in that chaotic airport jam, my father tense beside me, squinting out the windows. Then the cab eased onto the freeway and his body loosened, and the air lightened between us.

"Your mother has been calling and calling," he said, ruffling my braids. "She thought they would forget you in London."

I chuckled.

"I heard you took second place this year at school."

My body stiffened. I had never taken second place before. I was my father's daughter and my father's daughter always took first place. He had always been a man who soared, my father, an African fish eagle gliding above the soils of southwestern Zimbabwe, red and wet after the rains, surveying below the smaller birds and the frogs and the crickets chirping and croaking. Mama never tired of going on about his galactic brilliance, how it had stood him apart from the boys who vied for her affections. She had seen from a kilometer away that he was a young man headed somewhere and she'd intended to go with him. When he'd glided away from that rural backdrop in Plumtree all the way to a research school out in the Midwest known as The Program, it had been with the understanding that she'd glide with him. But he went away, and went away, and went away, and when he eventually came back, all he talked about was this astrophysics thing he had studied at The Program and the equations he had pioneered to search our galaxy for planets orbiting stars outside our solar system. And though Mama tried to listen and laugh a coquettish laugh and ask polite questions, it was clear he had become something strange and opaque and—here she hesitated—*awe-full* that dazzled the mind but hurt the heart to see.

"You take after him," she would say, a resolute frown creasing her forehead.

And though, now that I think of it, she may not have meant this as a compliment, her words made me beam, and simper, and walk about squint-eyed one summer demanding a telescope and a pair of oval gold-rimmed spectacles for my birthday.

The cab had come to a halt outside the Greystone Apartments. I turned away from my father and made a face as we alighted upon that rimy Manhattan cold. I was trying to think why I'd taken second place in school. We stood side by side on the pavement and watched as the cab sped off. I looked up into his face: a distant light blinking down at me from the ether. I opened my mouth but didn't know what to say. Closed it. Flinched. Looked away.

"Don't worry too much about it," he said, squeezing my hand, like he knew what I was feeling. "You'll do better next time, won't you?"

I nodded. There was hot air blowing in my face. I didn't know where it was coming from. It made me feel hot inside. I blinked back furious tears. My father hunched his shoulders and peered up and down the street, scanning the cars that skidded past in the snow, their tires spinning. Then he wrapped his big, gloved hand on the back of my neck and ushered me through a set of revolving doors into the Greystone building, across a marble foyer and into a stainless-steel elevator, which ferried us all the way to the top floor.

How could I have known it wasn't my father's modest professor salary that paid for those stunning floor-to-ceiling glass penthouse views that hovered us starlike over Manhattan? I did not yet know that excellence comes at a hefty price, that it's not enough to be just clever or gifted or even industrious. The glass walls coaxed in blocks of the furtive December morning sun, splashing it craftily over the awards displayed on the granite mantle, the oakwood side tables, the marble fireplace. Everything sparkled. The sunlight was everywhere, spilling ponderously over the incongruous items that populated the apartment—a lurid, ceramic bowl on the quartz island, brimming with fist-sized mangoes; a glaring red kettle that overpowered the stainless-steel appliances in the kitchen; a purple love seat that clashed with the alabaster couch in the lounge; a rumpled *Super Mario*–themed duvet in the smaller bedroom my father ushered me into.

"It's bigger than your bedroom back home, yes?" he said, beaming.

I winced; comparing his penthouse to Mama's vanilla-colored cottage, with its humble rooms and box windows, felt like a slight. I tried not to think of Mama, tried not to think of how my father had left us. He led me from room to room, showing off his binoculars and his telescope and his fancy science stuff. But when he tried to catch my gaze, thrusting an astrophotography camera in my face, I turned away from him and tucked my face into my chest.

It was the space suit encased in a glass box behind the large mahogany desk in his home office and the huge framed picture on the wall that brought me back to him. The space suit was made from shiny white material, like nylon. It had a transparent globular visor for the head and a pair of grey boots fastened to the trouser legs. A pair of white gloves with thick black fingers protruded from the sleeves. A bright blue valve shimmered on the suit's broad thick chest. Beneath this was a navy-blue patch with a red-and-yellow star. I squinted at the sky-blue lettering on the white badge fastened to the left breast of the space suit.

"F. SIZIBA 2004," I mouthed. I turned to my father. "That's you!"

"Yes, that's the Sokol-KV2," he said, beaming. "The Russian space suit."

I turned to the framed picture on the wall behind the space suit. There was my father, floating in space. I reeled into the mahogany desk behind me.

"Are you all right?" said my father, placing his hands on my shoulders.

No, I was not all right. I squinted at the photo and tilted my head and tried to catch my breath. A few indeterminate noises escaped my lips. He was in some sort of spaceship or space gadget or something like that, decked in the space suit. The bulbous visor made his head look frighteningly large, like something was wrong with it. It filled me with fright. It didn't help that he seemed to be floating, suspended in the air with his legs off the ground. But he was smiling and waving at the camera.

I struggled with my face. Something awful attempted to fix itself on there, and I tried to resist it. Through a round window behind him in the photo you could see a grid of solar panels and beyond this, our planet Earth. How strange and fragile it looked; a blue spherical dome swathed in whorly clouds suspended in an infinite darkness. A burst of rays sparkled overhead, bathing the solar panels in shimmery golden light and the Earth beyond in sparkling shades of azure. I could make out brown landmasses protruding like scars amid that brilliant blue and its white fluff.

I must have emitted a squeal or a sigh, for my father walked over to the picture and caressed it. "Magnificent, isn't it?" he said, putting on his lecturing voice. "Tommy was so jealous when he heard the millionaire Dennis Tito had gone up to the International Space Station. I knew he'd do something crazy, like offer the Russians a bunch of money to take him up there, too. He asked if I wanted to go with him. I couldn't believe it! But that's Tommy for you, a serial exhibitionist.

"I mean, of course I wanted to go. But you start to think of all the things that could go wrong up there. You really start to contend with the possibility of your death. During those months training for the trip at the Star City complex in Moscow, I couldn't stop thinking of all the ways I could go. I mean, space is really hostile. Don't believe all those sublime pictures you see on TV. I kept imagining something going wrong, some breach of the space station that would eject us into the vacuum of space —our bodies would fry and the air would get sucked out of our lungs!

"And then I went up there and all I could think of was our home, right there before my very eyes. Its thin biosphere was a translucent blue. And I felt, this is *our* planet. I felt it viscerally. This is our planet and I'm seeing it with my own two eyes, and you know what? There are no countries! I couldn't see any borders. I half expected to see country flags rising from the oceans like geological formations. But all I could see were landmasses surrounded by all that blue. And you know another thing? The rivers didn't wind sinuously across the land like a writhing snake, like Father Pius taught us! The water actually spreads its tentacles across the continents like the branches of a tree! I traced those tendrils of water with my eyes. I watched the sun rise and set sixteen times each day. It was an utterly radical experience."

I, too, wanted to have a radical experience. "When are we going to see the Statue of Liberty?" I said.

"I have been thinking about what it means to exist in the world and yet be unthinkable," said my father. "You and I, we were unthinkable, once. We are unthinkable even now, sometimes."

I nodded politely. I didn't know what he was going on about. He was at it again, telling cryptic stories I was too young, or perhaps daft, to understand. I followed him into the kitchen. Right there on the kitchen counter sitting next to a pile of books was . . . a pan. Yes, a frying pan, glistening with oil residue in the buttery morning light. Next to it stood a half-open carton of eggs and a bottle of olive oil. My eyes lit up. I begged him, my daddy, to let me cook for him, to let me do something for him,

I may have been eleven, but I knew how to cook. *Puleease,* I made eggs all the time whenever I got home from school before Mama got there.

He wrinkled his nose and smiled that smile adults smile when they are teetering between saying yes and no, when that inner child they once were is calling out to them to loosen up and not be so adult about everything. I saw my chance and went for the jugular—*please, please, please*—head tilted to the side—*pleasepleasepleaaaaaase*—hands brought up demurely in mock prayer—*prettypuuuleeeeaaaaase.* It was the batting of the eyelashes, like the rosy-cheeked, damsel-diva Darla in *Little Rascals,* that did it.

He caved, slumping his shoulders, his smile wide as he placed the pan on the gas stove and poured the oil and fiddled with the knobs. A bluish flame flickered to life, licking the base of the pan. He hovered over the stove and made a show of checking the heat, making a teasing face as I tap-tapped the shell with a fork, once, twice, gently, a little harder, until it cracked open and the contents splattered shrilly in the hot oil.

The yolk merged with the white and the eggs came out burnt, with a crispy brown coating at the bottom. My father ate them still, straight from the pan, curling the eggs over a fork and sliding them into his mouth. He chewed contemplatively, his lips vaselined by the oil. He saw that I was watching him, that I was holding my breath. He frowned. I frowned. Then his face broke open, and he gave me a thumbs up. Making a chirping little noise, I leaned over and planted a kiss on the back of his hand, brushing my wet lips against the wispy hair on his knuckles.

"Have some," he offered, pronging the eggs from the pan and bringing the fork to my lips. "I bet you're hungry after your long flight."

I leaned forward and slurped the burnt eggs into my mouth.

Just then, the front door swung open and in strutted a tall woman with the most beautiful mane of hair I'd ever seen. A lanky boy huffed in behind her.

"Hi," he said, raising his hand in a little wave.

I paid him no mind. I was busy staring at the woman's hair, admiring its black sheen, the way it sat silky against her milky brown skin. She dropped the plastic bags she was carrying, shrugged out of her magenta winter coat and removed her woolen hat, setting her mane free. Only then did I see her edges, where tufts of kinky, plaited hair sprouted beneath the silky mane. It wasn't her own hair, then, but a weave. I gasped, feeling bruised, and cheated, somehow.

"Mon Dieu!" she said, flinging her silky weave out of her face, her syrupy eyes on my father. "What a fucking morning!"

She strode across the room to my father. They were almost the same height. She was a giraffe. She leaned into him, elongating her neck until their lips touched.

I watched them, the wonder of only a moment before—the eggs, the childish kiss, the marvelous spontaneity of it all—dissipating, and he was, again, my father who lived overseas.

"**B**aby, meet Candice and Péralte," said my father.

The woman named Candice pulled away from my father and turned to me. I dropped my eyes and tugged at my braids, suddenly conscious of my chubby face and my round belly protruding beneath my brand-new yellow turtleneck. I stole a glance at the boy named Péralte. He had plopped himself on my father's couch and was busy punching the keys of my father's laptop.

"Hey," he said without looking up.

I scowled at his big head, shaped like a bus.

"It's so nice to finally meet you," said Candice. She came around the kitchen counter and folded her thin arms around me, bringing her oval face close to my round one, so that our cheeks touched. Then she unsmacked our cheeks and grinned. I stretched my lips at her.

Her arms remained draped around me. I placed a hand on her bony shoulder. Her ears were large and yet strangely endearing on her small head, making the arrangement of her upturned eyes and her Nubian nose and her bow-shaped lips less conventionally pretty and yet somehow more striking.

"Your dad's told me so much about you," she said, showing me her teeth, which looked like everyday teeth, yellowish beneath the translucent enamel. I felt my shoulders relax. "How do you say your name again? *A-tha*—"

"Athandwa Rosa Siziba," I said, and my father and Candice laughed. I laughed, too, though I didn't know what we were laughing at.

"How was your flight?" said Candice. I blinked at her, mute. She dropped her hands from my shoulders. Turning to my father, she said, "You won't believe the email I got from Todd."

I watched as she shuffled back to the cupboards and began taking pots and pans out. She laid them out on the granite counter and stood eyeing them, her lower lip tucked between her teeth.

"How are you feeling?" she said. "You must be tired." I didn't realize she was talking to me until she turned to me, eyebrows raised. I gazed at her, blushing, and gave an obligatory nod.

"Péralte, come put away the groceries," she yelled.

The boy groaned.

"So Todd sends me this email—" she paused, eyeing the half-eaten eggs in the frying pan on the stove. "You made the stale eggs? I told you I'd get us some fresh ones." She cast her light brown eyes on my father, her thick eyebrows bunching up. "You burned them."

"It's my daughter," said my father, winking at me. "She made me breakfast."

The mischief on his face was so unexpected that I froze, not sure what to do. I tried winking back at him, but it was a moment too late; he had already turned back to Candice. Something warm spread in my chest. I stared at my hands.

"The poor girl hasn't been here five minutes and already you're making her slave away for you, Frank," said Candice with a little shake of her head.

She picked up the pan of eggs and shuffled to the corner.

"Don't worry, sweetie," she said, showing her teeth again. "I'll make you something proper. You poor thing. You must be hungry. Are you hungry?"

She depressed the lever and emptied my eggs into the bin. I flinched, as though reeling from one of Mama's stunning claps. I glared at the bin and then at Candice. But she had already turned her back to me and was slicing onions on a cutting board.

"Péralte!" she yelled.

"Leave him alone," said my father. "I'll do the unpacking."

"How many things do I ask him to do in this house?" said Candice. "Let him do it." But my father was already unpacking the groceries, lining them up on the kitchen counter.

"I can help you unpack," I said, straightening up.

Candice said, "How sweet of you," though she didn't invite me to come and help her.

I scowled. If I had teeth that yellow, I wouldn't smile so much.

"Where does this go?" said my father, holding up a packet of beans.

"He knows," said Candice. "Péralte! If I have to call you again, I'm going to come and switch that thing off."

The boy grumbled and got onto his feet. He shuffled to the kitchen and began putting away the groceries my father had lined up on the counter.

"Sorry, fanami," said my father, rubbing his knuckles on the boy's head. "I tried." The boy grinned ruefully. Turning to Candice, my father said, "What happened with Todd?"

"He refuses to approve my Indigenous Astronomy course. He says it's got nothing to do with science. Can you believe it?"

My father walked over to Candice and stood behind her, placing his hands on her hips. "I am sorry, s'thandwa."

I would catch Mama sitting by herself sometimes, staring at pictures of my father in her photo album, reminiscing about how he used to call her *s'thandwa*, his love, a girlish laugh fluttering from her lips as though she were sixteen again and my father a boy of eighteen, courting her under the nocturnal luminescence of Madingeni, "the Dating Star" Venus, a trusted light for rural lovers who could only meet under the cover of darkness.

"He called it my *Indigenous stuff*." Candice was cutting the green peppers now, no longer making tiny squares but hacked-up chunks. She paused. "Fuck. I forgot to buy the fish and the Scotch bonnet peppers."

I gaped at her. She'd said *fuck*. I fought the urge to go over and press her lips together.

"Why do you let him get to you?" said my father, gently slipping the knife out of Candice's grip. He took over the chopping of the green peppers. "You know he's a fossil. Mute your work email. It's the holidays."

"I wouldn't expect you to understand," said Candice, pursing her plump, pretty lips. "Everyone at the university adores you, especially after that space tourism stunt you and Thomas pulled last year. You're like one of those horrid celebrity academics now."

My father placed his hands on her shoulders. "You know that's not true."

Candice shrugged his hands off. "Don't patronize me, Frank." She retrieved two blackened plantains and pressed her fingers into their bruised bodies. Then she cut them in half and dropped them into a pot of boiling water.

"Mom, I've packed away all the stuff," said the boy. "Can I go now?"

His mother shot him a look. He sighed and pulled out a large bowl from one of the cupboards. He began cracking eggs into the bowl, tapping them against the steel rim and splitting them open with his hands.

"Would you like some water?" said Candice, peering over her shoulder at me. And then, turning to Péralte, "Give her some water. Or juice. Yes, I think a glass of juice is fine."

The boy dragged his feet to the fridge and opened it, leaving gooey prints on the handle.

"I just want you to breathe for a minute," said my father, trying to hug Candice from behind. She shrugged him off.

The boy came and placed a glass of orange juice before me. He offered a tiny smile. I glowered at him.

"You don't need to work all the time."

Candice snorted. "That's rich, coming from you." Turning to me, she said, her voice rising an octave, "Do you like plantains?" Without waiting for a reply, she turned back to the stove.

"You know how important my paper on Bantu geometries is," said my father. "I just need a few more days."

"And *my* work isn't important?"

She began sautéing the onions and green peppers and tomatoes in a large sauce pan. "It won't taste the same without the Scotch bonnet peppers," she muttered. She turned to my father. "Do you think you could run to the store and get us some? And some stockfish while you're at it?"

My father sighed. "I think whatever you're cooking smells good."

Candice let out a long and deep breath, dropping her chest. Her small, plump breasts jiggled, like a pair of mangoes ready to be plucked. I ran my hand over my chest and pinched the child fat around my nipples. Blushing, I hunched my back.

The boy began whisking the eggs in the large bowl. "Uncle Frank," he said, "I got an A in my science project. Thanks again!"

*Uncle Fwank*. He had called my father *Uncle* Frank. Something cool and soothing settled like balm over my chest.

"Awesome!" said my father, inflecting his voice, so that it came out as a strange, exaggerated American twang. He gave the boy a high five. "That's supercalifragilililili—"

"Supercalifragilisticexpialidocious," said the boy, chuckling.

I blinked and stared at my hands.

"Thank you," said Candice, her voice soft, almost a whisper, "for being so patient with him."

My father kissed her on the cheek. "I'm dedicating my paper on Bantu geometries to you, you know."

"You don't have to do that," she said, but I could tell from the way she smiled, dimpling her cheeks, that she was pleased.

It was Mama who had encouraged my father to pursue his dreams, first when they were high school sweethearts at Empandeni Mission School, and later when she was at Bulawayo College and my father was attending university in the capital city Harare. Had he forgotten? He never spoke about her with me. I was afraid to ask. But I think I was waiting for something to happen, inside him, inside me, between him and Mama, perhaps. I must have been waiting, without realizing it, without really knowing it, for an epiphany. I was weighed down by a constant, heavy feeling, like the pressure you feel in your chest from holding your breath.

Sitting by the counter in that kitchen, watching my father and Candice, I thought of Mama in one of her sheeny dresses out on the verandah of our little cottage with her friends, twirling a glass of Amarula in her dainty hand as she recounted, for the umpteenth time, the story of how she had found the astronomy scholarship to The Program and encouraged my father to apply, going so far as to print the forms and take the bus all the way to Harare where he was attending university to deliver them to him. There was pride in her voice.

One of her friends once said she had helped him get away, then, by showing him that scholarship. The amusement on his face at this drunken piece of wit made Mama's face get all wet and ripply.

"I wanted him to soar," she said finally, and though I could hear the sincerity in her voice, I also glimpsed in her face something less altruistic.

She looked embarrassed that day, and I was glad her friend was remorseful. In fact, that was the last time she recounted that story. My father did get the scholarship and left for The Program in 1994, the year I was born. And maybe he didn't intend to change, maybe he really intended to come back to us like he'd said he would. But Mama said being in America changed him. She could tell something irresistible had seduced him. Maybe he did try to fight it. But who can stop a pupa from molting into a butterfly? I think I already grasped this intuitively even then, sitting in that kitchen watching Candice and my father, this thing about change, but it did not make it hurt any less.

Candice took the bowl of eggs from Péralte and poured them into the frying pan. She began turning them over with a fork. Péralte rummaged through the cupboards, removing plates, cups, forks, and spoons.

"Here's a yummy Haitian breakfast for you!" said Candice.

She dished out the scrambled eggs and the boiled plantains, garnishing the plates with sprigs of parsley, like she fancied herself a chef. She slid a plate across the kitchen island toward me. It was different from the other three, green and not white.

I scowled. "I'm not hungry," I said.

A spicy, delicious aroma wafted from the fluffy eggs. I eyed them sullenly. A lump rose in my throat.

"But I made all this for you," said Candice.

"I want the eggs we made with my daddy," I said, glancing at the bin.

"You'll love Candice's cooking," said my father. "Why don't you give it a try? She makes the best eggs."

I glared at Candice. Something seared my chest, making it hard to breathe. The next moment, I had picked up the plate. I gripped it. I gazed down at the creamy eggs swimming in the fried onions and large green peppers and a film of oil. Then I lifted the plate high up above my head and brought it down, slamming it to the floor. It made a terrifying, shattering noise, the eggs and plantains and shards of ceramic exploding across the marble floor in magnificent, entropic constellations. I stood there, surveying the mess I had made, thrilled and terrified, panting from the exertion of it. The lump in my throat cracked open and spread like creamy yolk down my esophagus to my belly.

"What's the matter with you?" said my father.

I blinked at him, my eyes a pair of stars, bright and shimmery.

"Uncle Frank, what's happening?" said Péralte in a small voice, peering at me with those chocolate eyes of his. His big head was balanced precariously on his scrawny neck, as though at any moment it would fall off, his glistening face a cacao so rich it made me want to go over and lick him.

"What's gotten into you?" my father said again.

He ushered me away from Candice, away from Péralte, away from all that mess, down the corridor to the small bedroom. There we sat side by side on the bed, our buttocks squishing Super Mario's rumpled, mustachioed face.

"Are you all right?" said my father.

"I don't know," I said.

I had never broken a plate like that before, with deliberate insolence. I would never have dared do such a thing back home. Mama would have lashed my buttocks with her crocodile belt. But I'd seen American children throwing tantrums on TV, and I had been awed by their childlike cunning, amused by the way they brought their parents to tears. Staring at that plate of fluffy eggs and Candice's smug coppery face, knowing it was Mama and me, and not her and Péralte, who should have been here with my father, I had felt a Darla-like rage bubbling in me and erupted just like Darla surely would have.

"Who is the Candice woman?" I said. I didn't face my father as I said this, even as I felt his gaze on me.

"Well," he said, "she's my friend."

"Is she your girlfriend?"

He paused. "Yes."

I nodded and licked my lips. I felt the depression made by his bum on the bed, felt the warmth beneath us, the strange, solid sensation of his body beside mine. He had never been so alive to me before, not even in my fertile imagination month after month and year after year as I read his letters and penned him mine, not even when we spoke on the phone. I was thrilled and disappointed by the reality of him.

"Are you going to marry her?" I said after a while.

My father paused again. "Well, we've been together for two years and she recently moved in with me. So, I think so."

I wanted to ask, *But what about Mama?* But I didn't. Instead, I slid beneath the *Super Mario* quilt and pretended to go to sleep.

Later that evening, I overheard Candice's sharp, staccato hisses and the soft, depressed murmurs of my father's voice coming from the corridor. Mama would never have talked to my father like that. I snickered, something warm and smug settling in the pit of my stomach. Next to me, Péralte sniffled.

began to pinch Péralte that first night when we slept together in the smaller bedroom and I realized I was in his bed. I took in the red-and-blue *Super Mario* duvet, the muddy pair of soccer shoes lying in the corner, the glittery purple kids' telescope standing by the floor-to-ceiling windows and pursed my lips.

I turned over on the bed and watched him. He was sprawled like a little count, his limp body rising and falling with his snores. I reached over and pinched him, twisting the flesh on the back of his hand. He flinched, his tranquil face scrunching up like someone had shoved a lemon between his lips. But he didn't wake. I pinched him again. He writhed and muttered something in his sleep. I did it again, and then again, chuckling hotly in the star-studded city darkness, until I finally tumbled into a fitful sleep.

The next morning, he complained about mosquitoes, showing his mother the rude purple marks on his arms. She inspected them with an exasperating tenderness and said, gently, as though imparting a terrible truth to a gullible child, that there were no mosquitoes in New York during the winter.

"You're so dumb," I said when we were alone. I shoved him and sniggered.

He regarded me with his large eyes.

"Did you hear what I said?"

He just smiled.

I shoved him. "Stop smiling."

"Why?" he said and continued smiling that stupid smile of his.

I didn't know what to say to this. I mumbled something about needing to pee and pretended to go to the bathroom. That night, as he slept, blaring through his nose like a clogged engine, I pinched him again. I pinched him the night after that, and the night after that, too, wrenching the flesh on his arms and legs, clamping the soft skin on his exposed waist. He would groan and swat at some fiend attacking him in his dreams, but he wouldn't wake.

He complained about the mosquitoes again, insisting he'd seen one in his room, one of those splotchy ones with the red bellies, the ones native to the Caribbean, and Africa.

"The *Anopheles* mosquito?" said his mother. "How the hell would an *Anopheles* mosquito have gotten here?"

He glanced at me and then the ground. I glared at him.

"How come she doesn't have any bites, then?" said his mother.

She eventually got him mosquito repellant. Still, the mysterious winter mosquitoes of New York persisted, their bloodsucking stylets fixated on their singular target, bruising purple lumps on his glistening cacao skin.

✳

THOUGH I FLUTTERED about my father's legs like an eaglet during those frosty early days of December, I may as well have been an irritating mosquito whining in his ear.

He spent his days in his home office, perusing neither the leather-bound volumes encased in the bookshelves behind him nor the intimidating tomes piled on his desk. Instead, he sauntered up and down the length of his office, one hand behind his back, the other gesticulating in the air, speaking in soft, hesitant tones. Occasionally, he would pause to scribble on a notepad.

Behind him, the sheeny material of the Russian space suit shimmered, making it come alive—a spy alien slumped in clandestine repose, beaming my daddy's thoughts to a nefarious intelligence in outer space. I sat on the floor, quiet as a house rat. My eyes flitted from the alien hiding in the space suit to the photo of my father in space. I watched him through slits, out of the corner of my eye. He ambled back and forth, back and forth, going on about how humans were made of stardust and so was the land, and did that make the land a living entity or a mere object to be parceled out?

"It's . . . soil?" I said, squinting up at him.

He regarded me for a moment. His eyes were glossy behind his glasses. "Go and play outside," he said, finally.

"It's snowing," I replied.

"Go and play with Péralte. Go watch TV. Ask your mother for some hot chocolate."

Something seared my throat. "I'll ask her to mail a cup to America on the plane," I said, meeting his gaze with equanimity.

A shadow darted across his face.

"When are we going to see the Statue of Liberty?" I demanded.

"I just . . . Daddy's working."

He would never have spoken to Péralte like that, in that high-pitched, infantilizing tone. Péralte was eleven, the same age as me. Had my father always wanted a son? Was that why he had left us, Mama and me, and was now raising another woman's child?

A wave sloshed about in my stomach, making me woozy. "I want to go and see the Statue of Liberty!"

"All right, all right," said my father, slumping his shoulders.

But he turned back around and bent over his notepad, muttering how a mountain was more sacred than a church and how he wanted to be buried next to his umbilical cord in his father's ancestral home and all sorts of other things I couldn't make head or tails of.

I sulked. I whined. I even tried my Darla impersonation, eventually shrinking under his patronizing glare.

He and Candice got into a fight over his millionaire friend Thomas Long, the one who had gotten him a seat to space and turned him into a horrid celebrity academic. It was on one of the rare afternoons when he wasn't locked up in his study and we were all seated together in the lounge, he and Candice loved up on the purple loveseat, Péralte and I languishing on the adjacent alabaster couch. My father said he doubted the washed-out fossils on the science board would read his research on Bantu geometries. He was going to share it with Tommy, instead. The mood in the room shifted, becoming thick and heavy, as though the air were condensing. Candice called Tommy a vampire, the kind of white man she had grown up seeing in Haiti, who loved to play Native, siphoning off Indigenous cultures to rejuvenate himself. Hadn't he invited them to that Boston Tea Party thing of his? That annual re-enactment of the American Revolution, where he and his buddies painted their faces and wore feather headdresses and played Indian?

"He treats you like a safari," she said.

My father laughed, and Candice scowled. The word *vampire* made me shiver. Would this Tommy person slide his stainless-steel fangs into my jugular vein and drain me of my native essence? Would this give him superpowers?

I was able to make out that my father, Candice, and Tommy knew each other from The Program, where they had been students together. Tommy had studied computer science there and spent some years working for the Department of Defense as a software engineer before venturing into the private sector. He was helping my father set up research centers and space symposiums across Africa and the Caribbean. He was a man with fingers in many pots, what Candice called "an unscrupulous spirit," and owned a million-dollar e-commerce company called Artemis.

"You mean he's entrepreneurial," my father said with another chuckle. "Artemis started off selling books, for goodness' sake."

"You know it's not about the books or whatever else he's peddling on there. There's something . . . hungry about that man. An insatiable greed. Give it a few years, you'll see. And I wish you wouldn't do that."

"Do what?" said my father.

"Laugh like that when I say something you don't agree with. It's belittling."

He chuckled. She glared at him.

"You're so secretive about the work you do with him," she said.

My father leaned forward, pouting his lips in a kiss, but Candice ducked, pressing her palm against his mouth. "What exactly do you do with him?"

My father sighed. "Science, Candice, science. I am trying to bring our people into the future. I refuse to be a relic of history. That was the greatest injury the British did to us, writing us out of history like that, making up this stagnant customary law nonsense and making out of us something eternally primitive, a people of the past."

"But must you work with that man?"

"That man is the only one who takes me seriously."

Candice accused my father of being a science slut. I gasped. I wanted to go over and smack her lips.

"Why can't you work with me to drag our people out of the gutter?" said my father. He looked genuinely puzzled. "Haven't we been through enough?"

"Oh, so now you're doing this for our people?"

"Of course. It's always been about our people. At least I'm demanding a future for them. What have you done?"

"Oh, so my work at the university doesn't matter? It's my fault Todd is the piece of shit that he is?"

"It makes you feel superior, doesn't it, having Todd to blame for how things are, rather than digging in the mess with someone like Tommy?"

They kept going back and forth like that, spitting "our people, our people" in each other's faces, now on their feet, facing one another. I wondered what people they were talking about. I watched them, unsettled by their passion, the way it heaved Candice's bosom and darkened my father's face. It seemed too hot, a thing that threatened to inflame them both.

The next moment, they were kissing. I could not imagine Mama kissing my father like that. I could not imagine her proffering her tongue, the way Candice was doing, flickering its pink moistness out of her mouth and into his. She had no shame, busy taking liberties with my daddy's lips like that.

I watched them, a confusing agitation in my stomach.

My father wrapped his arm around Candice's slender waist, his other hand playing with her long, coppery fingers. He whispered something in her ear.

"How cliché," she said, tittering.

"I'm serious," he said. "The day I discovered that you and I both used to look up at the Digging Stars as children and dream of journeying to the heavens was the day the universe revealed itself to me."

"You're so bad at poetry!" said Candice, chuckling.

He said something to her in a strange language, his words jazzy and bass-like. "Is that better?"

She threw back her head and laughed, her neck arching, her weave fluttering away from her face so that I could see her neck muscles tighten and the collarbone strain against her skin.

It seemed utterly magical that my father's tongue could whip out such strange syllables that, when strung together, sounded, giddily, like gibberish, like love gibberish. Here was Candice pealing a glorious laughter, here she was slapping my father on his chest and saying, "Arête ça, toi!"

He was laughing, and she was laughing, and I found myself laughing, too. Péralte joined in our laughter. I stopped laughing and glared at him. He quietened down, blinking at me with his huge chocolate eyes.

Candice and my father staggered across the cedar floors of the lounge and down the corridor, still talking to one another in that combative way of theirs. A door slammed, muffling their voices.

"Don't worry," said Péralte. "Uncle Frank and Mum always get like this."

*Don' wowry*, I twanged silently.

He had managed to get hold of my father's laptop and was balancing it on his lap.

"What are you doing?" I said, staring at the frenetic movement of his hands across the keyboard.

"Playing this really cool game," he replied, his face creased in concentration. "It's, like, super old, so the graphics aren't all that great, but it's, like, really cool! It's set in the Caribbean! Can you believe it? Somewhere in the Antilles. It's called *Freedom: Les Guerriers de l'Ombre*."

I made a face. "Le what?"

"It means "the Shadow Warriors" in French. I also have the English version, *Freedom: Rebels in the Darkness*. You can play if you want. It's really good."

My scowl bloomed into a pout. "Don't you have *Super Mario*?"

He looked crestfallen. "This is even better than *Super Mario*! I promise you! It's like thousands and thousands of years ago, right, like, in the eighteenth century or some', and you're this slave dude on a plantation burning shit down and tryna convince the other slaves to fight to be free! You have to choose an avatar, Makandal or Sechou, or the girls, Solitude or Délia . . ."

I had never heard of girls leading a fight in a video game before. Péralte seemed to notice my interest, for he said, "Yeah, two girls! And they're African! Isn't that cool? Mum says it's about how our people fought against slavery in the Caribbean. I gotta be Makandal. Dude's from Haiti. Mum says that's where we're from. Wanna play?"

I shrugged. No, I didn't want to play. I didn't want him and his mother there. They were taking up all the air.

"You can be the rebel Solitude," said Péralte, fluttering his big eyes at me. "She's from Guadeloupe. Or you can be Délia if you like. I dig her cause she's a maroon, like Makandal. She's really good at getting the slaves to fight."

"But didn't the slaves live in America?" I said.

"Yeah," said Péralte, "they were all over the Americas."

"That's right. Not the Caribbean, dummy."

"The Caribbean is in the Americas."

"The Caribbean is *not* in America!"

"Then where is it?"

". . . You're stupid."

"Don't you know it was the slaves who fought for Haiti? We were the first slaves to lead a rebellion and free ourselves and form a country."

I blushed and averted my gaze. My eyes fell on the laptop on his lap. I lunged forward and snatched it.

"Don't play with my daddy's things," I said, clutching it to my chest. "They belong to me, not you. Got it?"

He winced. I watched as he got up and went to sit by the window with his iPod, his headphones snug over his ears. He bob-bobbed his head and watched the late-afternoon sun hovering over the Manhattan skyline, staining the icy horizon in splashes of orange and pink.

I glared at him, but he refused to look my way. When I tired of glaring, I turned on my father's laptop and tried playing *Les Guerriers de l'Ombre*, punching random buttons and squinting at the French subtitles and squealing at the pixelated brown faces that appeared on the screen.

✶

I NEVER FORGAVE my father for fobbing me off on Candice while he worked on his Bantu geometries.

She had somehow gotten it into her head that shopping was what girls liked to do, and she winked clandestinely as she dropped a clink of coins in my lap. I refused to wink back, making it a point to roll my eyes. But I slipped the coins into my little turquoise purse.

There was one particular coin that caught my attention, a copper one-dollar piece that glinted in the light. I palmed and unpalmed it, marveling at its gold tones, at the Indian woman gazing across her shoulder out of history and straight at me, her beholder, a knowing smile on her lips. A sleeping baby was tied to her back. The word *LIBERTY* glistened over her head, like a crown or a wreath. At the back of the coin was an eagle with its wings flared out. It looked like an African fish eagle. I ran my thumb over it, savoring its roughness, its majestic wingspan, something warm and heady spreading across my chest. I decided not to spend it. I would give it to my father.

Candice took me window shopping on Madison Avenue, the way middle-class, aspirational people do. She would drag me into a Chanel or a Prada or a Saint Laurent and try on heaps of clothes. Afterward, we would leave a mess in the brightly lit changing rooms for the shop assistants to clean up, crinkling our noses like a pair of heiresses.

Whenever Candice found something she thought becoming on me, she would laugh and cup her cheeks and say how we were like mother and daughter.

*In your dreams*, I thought, an intense heat welling up in me.

Still, I was drawn to her. But only a little bit. Only a little bit. It was the stories about her childhood in Haiti that got me, like how she would drop random objects from the balcony of her family's villa in Pétion-Ville.

"Why?" I asked.

"To test their weight," she said, raising a smug, bushy eyebrow.

What a thing to do! She must have been a stupid child. When I didn't say anything, only continued gazing at her, she sighed and picked a hat off a bald-headed mannequin in a corduroy two-piece suit. We were at Chanel New York, ambling past glass-entombed leather handbags haloed in ambient lighting and jewelry pieces glinting off the branches of these cute little bonsai trees. A salesgirl in a black skirt and a matching polo neck-tracked us.

Candice said, quietly, turning the Chanel hat over and then slapping it on my head, how she had dropped her father's gramophone from the second floor of their villa one afternoon many days after he'd left in his army fatigues at the behest of President Duvalier Junior and never came back.

"The sound of it crashing into the verandah below was so soothing," she said.

"But it must have made a terrible sound," I said.

"It did," she replied.

I tried to think of something to say. "Did you try and look for your father?"

She gazed up at the Christmas lights winking down at us from the store ceiling. "Look for him where? A man who runs off somewhere, you can look for. A man who disappears as though he never existed can never be found. I damn nearly lost my mind."

She called the stars her ancestors and said something about them being androgynous or Indigenous or something like that. She went on for a long time about how they had saved her. It sounded nonsensical and poetic and beautiful. I think, like me, she believed that by reaching for the stars, she might grasp their magic, and in grasping their magic, rediscover her father.

"I had serious dreams, real dreams," she said, "of working high up in the International Space Station."

I tried to imagine these serious dreams, real *real* dreams and not the unreal dreams I had that were of things that could never happen.

"You've been to space like my daddy?" I said, eyes wide. I had never met a woman astronaut before. "You've been to the stars?"

Candice laughed, a cackling, mirthless laugh. "Perhaps if I was US American I could have been a Mae Jemison or a Stephanie Wilson or a Joan Higginbotham. Or at least if I were a man, even an African man, like your father, I may have stood a chance. Or maybe it's my own fault, having had a child so early in my career." Her mouth fell, etching a sad, downward line. "Maybe I could still do it, one day, if Haiti or one of the countries in the Caribbean or Africa manage to get a space station up there."

"So you're not a real astronaut? You only teach at the university with my daddy?"

Candice frowned, regarding me with her coppery eyes. Then she snatched the Chanel hat she had angled on my head. "It does not suit you," she said, slapping it onto a bonsai tree, making the jewelry jiggle. The salesgirl rushed toward us.

In the evenings, after our days together, I would stand in front of the mirror in the small bedroom I shared with Péralte and pretend to puff delicate whorls of smoke, shouting, "It does not suit you!" and "What are you looking at?" at anyone who dared give me more than a passing glance, trilling incandescently at my reflection.

*Does not*!

*Suit you*!

*What are you*?

*Looking at*?

✳

ONE NIGHT, just as I was clenching a tender piece of flesh above Péralte's throat between my thumb and forefinger, his eyes popped open. He stared at me, the whites of his eyes little reproachful half-moons. I let go of his flesh and shut my eyes, pretending to sleep. I dared not open them again. I could feel the prick of his gaze.

That morning, he didn't show his mother his bruises, but he kept staring at me, a stupid smile on his face. I resented that smile, its pity, its piercing comprehension.

I didn't pinch him again after that night, though I watched him as he slept, his body rising and falling to the rhythm of his whistling snores, dreaming of smothering him with a pillow.

My father finally took me to see the Statue of Liberty.

I had been in New York for nearly two weeks. We boarded a ferry in the late afternoon from Battery Park in Manhattan.

"Look, Daddy, Lady Liberty!" I cried, thrusting a finger as Liberty Island came into view.

There she stood atop a star-shaped base, getting larger and more magnificent the closer our ferry chugged toward her. She loomed before us like Jesus on the cross in her turquoise robes and her spiky crown, her torch raised to the skies in perpetual martyrdom. She looked, poised like that in her green, oxidized sacrifice, like a super star, a bright Sirius come down from the sky. On the other side of her, the Manhattan city-scape mapped itself onto the dimming sky like *Tetris* blocks.

I tried to elbow my way through the crowd as we docked, but my father held me back by the hood of my jacket, and I had to wait meekly and walk single file off the ferry. We piled onto the pier and shuffled through the dock shed and down the stone path that led past a café with gold stars painted on its glass doors, to where Lady Liberty stood on her pedestal facing the water. The walk seemed to last a long time. But finally, we were there, standing before her in a sea of tourists. We stood side by side in our puffy bomber jackets, cheeks shredded by the cold, faces raised to the sky in the hope of getting a lick from that late-afternoon winter sun shining grimly without a splash of warmth. My father kept looking furtively around us, glaring at passersby and clutching his briefcase whenever anyone seemed to get too close. Then, noticing my raised head, he slumped his shoulders and began lecturing me about the Statue of Liberty.

He had come and stood at this very spot every day for his first week in New York, he said, trembling as though a superpower were coursing through his veins. The notion of a republic that had sloughed off the stuffy garments of British aristocracy to take on egalitarian, democratic principles had thrilled him. He had been enthralled by the belief that, here, a man could make and remake himself, an untethered vessel, a constant work in progress, ever yearning toward yet more ambitious horizons. Freedom and conquest; he had not understood at first how those two synonyms for the American Dream were intertwined. Rather, he had gazed at the rippling waters of the Hudson River, filled with gumption. There had been something transcendental in the feeling of it.

My heart fluttered at the word *superpower*.

"See how symmetrical she is," said my father, "the way she looms on the horizon above the water. Note the power of the gaze."

I nodded foggily.

"It's not just about capturing an image, but about directing the gaze. That is the real power."

It was the animation on his face that I remember achingly, as he raised a gloved hand to Lady Liberty, forgetting for a moment that I was his little audience, until his eyes fell to catch me staring not at the statue but at a couple smooching unashamedly in the distance, to our right. I looked up to see a flicker behind his specs, brief and flitting, of annoyance, and then his gaze softened and he began to stutter, struggling to share with me his passion for the colossal statue in a language I could understand.

I wish I could have understood him; I wish I had, at least, made an effort! But I was eleven, I was pouting, I yawned openly, not bothering to try and keep my eyes open. I was getting bored, I was fidgety, I was tired of all this trudging up and down the New York thoroughfares. I wasn't used to the snow.

My father pointed at the sky somewhere above Lady Liberty. It was only 6:00 p.m., and yet the winter sky was now sheathed in a velvety blue-blackness. The New York night lights glittered in the distance, covering the sky in a pale haze.

"You can't really see them because of the light pollution," he said, "but the Digging Stars are somewhere over there. The Greeks named them the Pleiades—the children of Pleione, goddess-nymph of the ocean."

He explained how some of the stars in the Greek constellations had Arabic names, like the fiery orange-red star known by its Arabic name Betelgeuse that marked the shoulder of the giant Greek hunter Orion.

"There was a time when the skies belonged to all of humankind," he said. "You could find vast networks of knowledge between Islamic and Greek astronomy, and between the Islamic and Chinese astronomers, too." His eyes went all dreamy. "What wonderful promiscuity!"

"Promiscuity!" I mouthed, giggling.

My father sighed and gripped his left arm. "Father Pius wouldn't hear talk of the Digging Stars. 'Pleiades!' he would shout. 'It's Pleiades!' " He winced. "For a long time, I hated the Greeks."

I tried to rub his left arm. He flinched and pushed my hand away.

"We must learn the lessons of history," he said, tucking his arm behind his back. He inclined his head toward Lady Liberty. "We don't study history enough. Zimbabwe is already learning the lessons of turning its back on history. Look how divided the country is, how it's going down the drain."

"We are not going down any drain," I declared, trembling, thinking of Mama back home standing in those never-ending food and money queues. They had burgeoned all over the country after the government sanctioned the War Veterans to invade the white-owned farms and claim back the land. I looked up at my father and thought of how he had left us. "We are better than any place," I said, thrusting my lips at him, "better even than this America of yours."

He regarded me for a moment, his face ruffled with amusement.

"Is that what they teach you at school?" he said, finally.

I nodded, beaming.

He shook his head, a little sorrowfully. "And how are you liking school? Do you like going to school in Zimbabwe?"

"Mrs. Mlilo hit me," I said.

"What?" his face shadowed.

"I didn't do anything," I added quickly.

"It does not matter what you did or didn't do, corporal punishment is an outdated form of discipline!"

"She hit me on my cheek," I said, rubbing my cheek as though it still stung.

"The whip has no place in the free world!"

I gazed at my father, eyes wide, thrilled by this display of outrage. "Mama refuses to get me a PlayStation. I want to play video games, like Péralte."

"Those teachers act like they are running their own little plantation!"

"Yes," I said.

"The postcolonial nation is becoming a disgrace, an utter disgrace, I tell you!"

"A disgrace," said I, my head going bop-bop with newfound wisdom.

I watched my father as he gesticulated, twitching his limbs like the street dancers we had encountered in the subway, going on about all the reasons why Mrs. Mlilo shouldn't have hit me, which I no longer understood. I watched his pockmarked face intently as he spoke, enamored by the basso cantante timbre of his voice, the pronounced stroke of his lips enlarging and collapsing on pink-tongued, cavernous syllables, globs of white collecting at the corners of his mouth.

"How would you like to come and live with me in New York?" he said, finally.

I gazed up at him, his woody, pecan face ruffled in a pensive furrow. I saw that he was serious. Really serious.

"You mean with you? Here? In America?"

"New York is not the whole of the USA and the USA is not the whole of the Americas. You are going to have to learn to be precise in your language. It's a very important skill, especially here, especially for you. But yes, here with me."

I clasped his hand. Together we stood side by side, blinking at Lady Liberty, taking in the balmy words on the plaque at her feet:

"GIVE ME YOUR TIRED, YOUR POOR,
YOUR HUDDLED MASSES YEARNING TO BE FREE,

THE WRETCHED REFUSE OF YOUR TEEMING SHORE,

SEND THESE, THE HOMELESS, TEMPEST-TOST TO ME,

I LIFT MY LAMP BESIDE THE GOLDEN DOOR!"

✳

"STRIKING, ISN'T SHE?"

"C!" cried my father. "What are you doing here?"

We had been standing there, contemplating Lady Liberty, awed by her colossality, when Mr. C appeared out of nowhere. He stood next to us, a sturdy tower of a man in tight fitting blue jeans and a khaki-colored sweater beneath an indigo winter overcoat. His face was raised to the statue, bringing his wide jaw into profile. It was only when he cast his umber eyes on my father that I saw how large his nose was. It was fleshy, with a short dorsum and wide, prominent alae—handsome in that ugly, appealing way men sometimes are.

"Congratulations on making it to space, old friend," he said and smiled, the space between his eyebrows crinkling. "You beat all of us."

"Thank you," muttered my father.

"Why didn't you tell me?"

My father shrugged and licked his lips.

Mr. C's eyes glittered. "And who is this?" he said.

I had been hunched over beside my father, happily unnoticed when Mr. C's gaze settled on me, his lips spreading in a full-toothed smile. I fluttered my eyes at him, sucking on a breath of winter air. I winced as it knifed my throat. A stale, metallic smell wafted from the bay water, aggravating my nose.

"She's the spit-image of you!" said Mr. C. And to me: "I was there when you were born." He looked down at his gloved hands, which were raised to his chest, palms up, as though cradling a baby.

I gazed up at him, eyes wide. I hadn't ever heard of him. I felt my father's body stiffen, as though bracing himself, and I stiffened, too.

My father asked Mr. C if he was following him.

Mr. C laughed, and my father's left cheek spasmed. Mr. C placed a hand on my little shoulder and fastened his gaze on Lady Liberty. His shaved head shined like a jewel.

"What did you teach the child about her, Frank? Libertas, goddess of freedom. Mighty Columbia of the USA. Virgin Mary of the Protestant persuasion. Protectress of the world's wretched! You do know the original personification of America in Europe was an Indian princess? They dressed her up in a feather headdress and a plumed skirt of feathers. But then, after the American Revolution, the founders switched to the Greco-Roman style. Apparently, the Indian princess was disparaging to Americans. Which ones, I wonder?"

My father sighed. "The Indian princess was never about America, C. She was a European projection, filled with all sorts of prejudices. Must I now school you in history?"

"You will really pretend not to understand my point?"

"You always were a weak thinker. Always settling for easy distortions."

Mr. C lifted his hand from my shoulder, taking away its warm, solid assurance. A flock of ducks took sudden flight, their wet, silvery heads oily in the evening light, their mottled dark feathers flapping around Lady Liberty in frantic, ungraceful movements.

"Look!" I cried, flapping my hands, the balls of my feet levitating.

My father pushed his spectacles up his nose, his eyes following the formation of ducks gliding over the bay, their wings suspended as though they were dead things merely floating. Suddenly, they each dipped a wing, flocking to the right, this time in one graceful movement, as though one body.

"How did they do that!" I cried.

"What do you want, C?" said my father.

"I just want to talk," said Mr. C, inclining his neck to rub the back of his head. A rash glistened on his chin.

My father sighed. "I'm with my daughter," he said.

"Just one drink," said Mr. C, looking down at me with a smile. "A cup of coffee. I'm sure my little niece would love some hot chocolate."

I made a chuckling little noise, tucking my chin into my chest.

Mr. C pointed vaguely to the left. My father sighed and clasped my hand and began walking back the way we had come. Mr. C fell in step on the other side of him. I peered over my shoulder and waved goodbye to Lady Liberty. She now donned luminous robes, illumed by orange light spilling from her polygonal base. A flame blazed from the green torch in her outstretched hand.

We made our way down the stone path, in the direction of the pier. But we didn't return to the ferry. Instead, we plodded up some stone steps to our right and to the café. Mr. C swung open the glass doors and ushered us in with a sweep of his arm, a wide grin on his face, making him look a little more handsome.

We walked up to the counter. My father shrugged when Mr. C asked if he still took his coffee with milk. The food came—two coffees, one milky, one black, and a hot chocolate and a burger for me—and we carried it on a tray to one of the round tables. My father plopped onto his chair and cupped his coffee and stared through the glass walls of the café. I followed his gaze to the water. A pearly full moon hung low, its light burnishing the night sky into the same deep blue as the rippling bay water.

I slurped my hot chocolate, which was sweet and lukewarm, and then bit into my burger, smearing tomato sauce and mustard across my cheeks.

Mr. C watched me and said, "Do you remember our university days, Frank? I miss us."

My father eyed Mr. C.

"Remember our first day in Space Science class?" Mr. C went on. "I knew we would get along the moment you eyed those white boys and opened your big mouth and wondered out loud why we were the only Africans in the class and whether we were still in Rhodesia."

"Heyi, those boys thrashed me afterwards!" said my father, rubbing his chest.

He seemed to relax, his body slumping, no longer taut, and I felt my shoulders loosen, too.

"What about those smelly cigars you got from that boy who claimed he had brought them from America!" said my father. "We almost died!"

Mr. C made a choking motion. "I was trying to help you complete your look! You were the one walking around in Jimi Hendrix bell-bottoms and an Afro shaped like a big globe on your head!"

I giggled. I could not imagine my father with a globe-shaped Afro.

"Yah, those were the days," said my father, laughing, wiping tears from his eyes.

They reminisced about the '90s, what my father called "the happy decade," ten years into Zimbabwe's independence. NASA in the USA had launched the Hubble Space Telescope to study the universe and had begun a collaborative space program with Russia. At home, whispers of an ancient observatory in the Great Zimbabwe ruins, a sort of Stonehenge, almost like the Nabta Playa in Egypt, were making the rounds, firing up my father and Mr. C.

"We really could have built a strong astronomy program at the university, you know," said Mr. C. "We had it in us."

"I miss the days," sighed my father, "when a man in a place like home could dream big dreams and not feel outrageous."

"We can still do it now, you know," said Mr. C. "We just need you to come back."

My father snorted. A misty breath hissed from his lips. "Finally, we get to the real reason you are here," he said wryly.

Mr. C's body tensed. He leaned forward, his eyes becoming large, the sclerae bright, his umber irises glinting. "Listen, Frank, if you could just share some of your research—"

"So your general friends can sell it to Russia? Or is it the Chinese these days?"

Mr. C was quiet for a moment. He wiped his mouth and looked down at me. I smiled, and he frowned and said, "What do you want?"

I smiled uncertainly. "A PlayStation?"

But he didn't smile back, he scowled and wiped his mouth again. I stiffened, mesmerized by his large nose and the moist nose hair trembling within.

"Are you here as my friend?" said my father. "Or as our government's errand boy? Wait. Don't even answer that."

I realized, then, that Mr. C hadn't been talking to me but to my father, and I felt relieved. I picked up my burger and pretended to munch on it. My father took a gulp from his coffee and shoved his chair back. It made a loud, grating noise.

"Listen to me!" said Mr. C. He was no longer mirthful now, his eyes smooth, shiny pebbles.

My father leaned forward, bringing his face close to Mr. C's, an embarrassing intimacy, and I averted my gaze. "Do you remember what you said to me when I told you what happened to my parents in the '80s in Matabeleland?"

Mr. C leaned back in his seat. He looked tired. He pinched the space between his eyes. "Frank."

"You wouldn't even get me their records from your government friends," hissed my father. "All I wanted was to know where they had died during the massacres, so I could perform the ancestral rites for them. And you laughed! And changed the subject!" My father's face darkened.

His eyes were bright and pearly in the pool of his glasses. I dared not breathe, dared not move. Something menacing had descended upon us, on that table, making the room cold, making me hot, distorting my father's beautiful face.

Mr. C scowled. "Listen, if you could just hear me out—"

"It's time for you to leave," said my father.

Mr. C leaned forward and grabbed my father's arm. "You're playing a dangerous game, Frank," he said, his voice no longer warm. The rash on his chin glistened.

"Is that a threat?" said my father.

"We know about your work for the Americans."

"I need you to go. *Now*."

People had turned to stare at us. I looked up at my father and then at Mr. C, and then down at my hands.

Mr. C stood up. I watched him out of the corner of my eye. He was slowly backing away, his hands raised in a conciliatory gesture. "It was good to see you, old friend." He cast his umber eyes on me. "You look just like your baba," he said. "I bet you're smart like him, too. I bet you'll make better choices." His pinched mouth bloomed into a pout. "Watch your back, Frank."

With that, he turned and walked away, out of the café and down the stone pathway, in the direction of the ferry terminal, upsetting a flock of buffleheads busy pecking the icy ground, begging for morsels—as if for a little bit of understanding—from the winter tourists, and was gone.

✳

MY FATHER ASKED me not to tell Candice about Mr. C.

I nodded, my heart skipping at the thrill of this secret we now shared, unsullied by Candice or Péralte. We were supposed to visit the Statue of Liberty Museum after visiting Lady Liberty. But my father said he wasn't feeling well and that we were going home instead. He looked dreadful, and I tried not to cry as we trudged down to the pier and hopped on a ferry.

Back in Manhattan, he walked rapidly, his eyes flitting behind his spectacles. "I begged C," he said, his mouth twitching. "Did I not beg him? I said, 'C, help me find umama lobaba. We have to stop this madness of who belongs where and who doesn't.' I asked him, was Shona a tribe before the British? Was Ndebele? Are we just going to accept how the British bastardized us?"

*Bastardized*, I mouthed, and hiccupped.

"Where were his Marxist beliefs then?" hissed my father. "Where did he leave his sense of decency?"

I squinted at the hazy velvety sky, trying to think where Mr. C had left his decency.

"We're colonial inventions," said my father, his voice low and staticky, bunged up in a way I had never heard before.

"Yes," I replied, marveling that someone other than God had invented us.

"Can we ever be who we once were?"

"Uh . . . ye—no?"

"And who were we, even, before the British bastardized us?" He sighed. "It's these wretched colonial borders that messed us up. What's a colonial border, anyway?"

"It's a fence?" I replied.

"A fence!" he said. "Whose fence? That is the question."

"The government's?"

He sighed and quickened his pace. I stumbled to keep up with him. I kept looking around us, just like he was, lifting my head to gaze at the flags fluttering atop the New York City Hall in Lower Manhattan— there was a flag with red, white, and blue colors; then a blue, white, and orange flag with the blue seal of an Indian in a feathered headdress on one side and a man in piped pants and a wide-brimmed hat who looked like a boy scout on the other, an eagle with its wings spread out perched above them; and then, lastly, a flag that looked identical to the second one, with the stately eagle embroidered on its nylon cloth, only instead of "SIGILLUM CIVITATIS NOVI EBORACI," its seal read, "BOROUGH OF MANHATTAN."

"Look, Daddy, a fish eagle!" I cried, pointing at the first and then the second identical flag.

My father laughed. "That's an American eagle."

I marveled at this, taking in the wingspan of his shoulders. I had not imagined there could be other kinds of eagles, other kinds of majesties. I was glad I'd made him laugh. But his face crinkled again, and a moment later he was far away. I followed suit, squinting into the distance like he was, twisting my neck this way and that.

"There's Mr. C!" I cried, thrusting a chubby finger at a man in an indigo winter coat across the street.

"What? Where?" said my father, stopping short.

But the man was too stocky to be Mr. C. My father hissed at me, yanking me along by the hand. By the time we got home, my face was creased.

"What's the matter?" said Candice when she saw me.

"We saw Mr. C," I burst out and burst into tears.

My father sighed. Candice wanted to know where we had seen

Mr. C. Why had he met up with us? Why was my father talking to him? Had my father been meeting up with him, all this time? At first, my father spoke in mollifying tones, trying to explain how Mr. C had just appeared out of nowhere. But Candice kept shouting, asking the same questions over and over. My father said, finally, his voice gravelly, that Mr. C was his friend, they went way back, and he could talk to him whenever he wanted.

Candice laughed long and deridingly hard, an unpleasant cackle I hadn't heard from her before. "A friend? That man is not your friend."

My father said he didn't want to talk about it anymore, and that was that.

My father finally shared his paper on Bantu geometries one morning during breakfast. I studied the pages in his hands, slighted by their lightness. I had expected them to be more substantial. He had worked on them and worked on them throughout my stay, the foolish man, shooing me out of his office as though I were an *Anopheles* mosquito.

He gazed at us across the kitchen island, his face illumed by a slab of sun spilling through the floor-to-ceiling windows and across the cedar floors behind him. He grinned and looked down at the pages in his hand, and then cleared his throat and read:

BANTU GEOMETRIES: AGAINST EUCLIDEAN AUSTERITY

OR

THE WORLD IS A POEM: I CAN'T THINK IN STRAIGHT LINES!

"Wow," said Candice. "You were right—the science board was never going to publish *that*."

"Wow," I said, not to be outdone by Candice. Next to me, Péralte grunted and continued thumbing his game console.

My father began his paper by sharing the memory of communing with the Digging Stars as a child, tracking their trajectory across the sky with the help of the lone marula tree on the flat Savannah horizon. He never tired of observing the cosmic dance between the Digging Stars and the umThala, the stars shadowing the crescent arc of the sugar crusted galaxy like children trailing their mother.

Those nights spent stargazing were a lesson in patience, in the art of attunement. He felt a deep, satisfactory accomplishment in learning to read the smallest deviation in the sky's movements, noting the fine-tuned, corresponding screech of the cicadas or the anomalous flurry of the bats. He knew when it was time to prepare the fields for the planting season just by looking up at the night sky and listening during the day to the stringent tweets of the Kalahari robin and by sniffing the ambrosial scent of the red marula flowers. What was time but a river sparkling across a lapis lazuli sky, sucking you into its bottomless currents, so that you felt at once infinite and infinitesimal?

To know a constellation, then, was to face not only one's immensity and one's insignificance, it was to know the vista that participated in its membering. It was to befriend the creatures that swirled in its cosmic dance. It was to know its story. This knowing had been so intuitive to my father that he had taken it for granted as a child until he got the scholarship to the Catholic mission school and it was beaten out of him, with books and Euclid's straight lines and Father Pius's sjambok.

He was enthralled by the empiricism of the ancient Greek astronomers. Time no longer ebbed and flowed like a river but became discrete and linear. He found he could chart his day without paying heed to the stars' or the moon's voyage across the skies or the seasonal migration of the birds. Occasionally, while deep in the throes of some linear math problem of Euclidean geometry, he would be startled by the piquant smell of gardenias invading his nostrils, or the rust-colored hills thrusting their nipples into the sky's blue mouth in the distance. And then the moment would dissipate, and the world would become a thing again merely filled with other things.

"Would Neil Armstrong have walked on the moon without Hipparchus?" Father Pius would say, bopping his balding ecclesiastical head. "Would there be Newton without Ptolemy?"

"Didn't the Greeks also learn from the peoples they conquered?" ventured my father. "The Egyptian and Mesopotamian astronomers?"

"Those infidels didn't help the Greeks with anything," declared Father Pius.

"But they even adopted some of their gods," insisted my father, and then, in a lower voice, "unlike the British." Catching Father Pius's glare, he added quickly, "And the Islamic astronomers also collaborated with the Greeks. I've been thinking about the Digging Stars—"

"Humility," said Father Pius, wielding his sjambok. "This is the unwavering foundation not only of science, which has given us many great and astonishing wonders, but a life pleasing to God."

Something roiled in my chest. I couldn't get angry at Father Pius for the sjambok because he was a father. But what about Euclid, who had upset my father with his straight lines? Whose friend Descartes later used them to snuff out the magic of the stars, turning them into dots that he Carted off in an Asian plane? And what about that other man with the curly wig that made him look like a dame, Newton, whose Newtonian cosmos reduced the world to static objects, transforming stars and mountains and rivers from living entities into things to be possessed, a doctrine those overzealous Europeans evangelized across the world?

It wasn't until Tommy offered the Russians a bunch of money to take them up to the International Space Station like they had Dennis Tito and my father saw our planet from outer space that he came full circle. Seeing the Earth as one interconnected tectonic whole, with no borders, he had felt the way he imagined Galileo must have felt when he laid eyes on Jupiter's moons for the first time. Gazing at the tendrils of river water branching across the Earth's surface in complex, fractal patterns much like a tree and not in the smooth, untroubled shapes of convention, which we mistook for the real thing, it had dawned on him how science could tip over from the light-filled halls of inquiry to the stifling chambers of worship. It, too, could be wielded like superstition.

"Oh, my goodness," said Candice and cupped her cheeks.

I didn't care who all these men in my father's treatise were or why the postulations of their large bus-shaped heads should matter. They had taken my father away from me. Instead of spending time together, he had spent my visit arguing with them, pacing up and down in his office and staring into space and muttering to himself like a lunatic. I squinted at him, the familiar stirrings of a migraine pulsating in my temples.

"I'm proud of you," said Candice, leaning across the kitchen island and kissing him on the lips.

"I'm proud of you," I mimicked, crawling across the quartz island to give my daddy a kiss.

Candice and my father laughed.

"What's funny?" I said.

This seemed to make them laugh even harder. Péralte joined in their laughter.

"What's so funny?" I said again.

I slid off the bar stool and ran down the corridor to the bathroom, where I turned the lock and sat on the toilet seat, my face in my hands.

✳

I TOLD MAMA about Candice.

I knew I shouldn't have, but I did. When I told her about Daddy's friend who spoke French, was teaching me this funny language called Creole, and had the shameful habit of smooching Daddy in public, she became uncharacteristically quiet.

"Hullo?" I said. "Mummy? Are you still there? Hullo?"

Her voice came over the phone, low and guttural, in a way I had never heard before. "What kind of name is Candice?" she said. "How very silly!"

I didn't tell her Candice was anything but a silly woman; she had two degrees in astronomy and taught at the same university as my father. Instead, I tittered conspiratorially, my heart performing little acrobatics in my chest.

Mama ordered me to put my father on the phone. At first, he spoke in drawn out, even tones, but gradually, his voice rose, and he began to pace up and down the sitting room, the cordless receiver clutched to his ear, gesticulating with his hands as though he were speaking to someone standing in front of him.

"I mean, I'm trying to do what's best for you by getting you over here," he said as he cut the call. "Does she want you to get stuck over there, with all the mess that's happening?"

I simpered, not knowing what to say. I thought of how the government was forcibly taking away the white-owned farms, and how food was disappearing from the shelves and money disappearing in the banks. I didn't want Mama to stay behind and get stuck in the mess. Maybe she could come and live with us in America? But then there was Candice. And Péralte. I tucked my lower lip between my teeth.

"I'm also a parent," said my father. "I have my rights, too!"

I eyed him out of the corner of my eye.

In the months leading up to my New York trip, Mama had accused my father repeatedly of using material enticements and "the glitter of overseas" to try and take me away. He had left her to raise me alone while he left for America to advance his own life, she had said, sobbing into the phone, cupping the receiver to her mouth as though to get all of the anguish through to the other side. All he had done was send check after check, as though checks could parent a child, and now, just because *he* felt like playing baba, suddenly everyone had to be all right with it. Mama had worried so much in those months leading up to the trip, convinced my father was tricking her into sending me over so he could then refuse to give me back. She almost hadn't let me go on the trip at all.

But my father had intended for the visit to New York to be a test run, to see if I wanted to live with him, if I could fit into his life in America. At the end of four weeks, he put me on a plane back to Zimbabwe, just as he had agreed with Mama, with the promise that he would come home in August the following year to give Mama a talking to and bring me back with him for good.

✳

WHEN HE DIED that following August, I thought maybe if I hadn't told Mama about Candice, making Mama even more skeptical than she already was about my going to live with him, then he wouldn't have had to make that trip home to convince Mama that moving to America was the best thing for me, for all of us, and then he wouldn't have had the accident.

He flew in to Harare from New York, where he hired a car to drive to Bulawayo four hours away. I spoke to him after he landed, panting as I twirled round and round in Mama's sitting room until I became entangled in the telephone cord. He was about to drive to us, he said on the phone, his voice misty with fatigue. He would see us in a few hours!

"Okay, Daddy! See you later! Mcwaah."

He died on the 94-kilometer peg along the Bulawayo-Gweru road. That's what his death certificate says. It says, under *Cause of death* that he died of *Head Injuries*. That's what it says, but the truth of the matter—whether I overheard this from Mama or some other person or whether someone actually told me I can no longer recall—is that his car was forced off the road by a truck. There were even whispers that it hadn't been an accident. The driver was overtaking my father's car when he swerved back into the left lane too soon, so that one of the carriages of his truck—I imagine it was one of those Optimus Prime Peterbilt 379 models with the big heads that haul behind them one and sometimes even two partitions, like the carriages of a train—rammed into the smaller vehicle, elbowing my father off the road. The driver was never apprehended.

I visited the 94-kilometer peg along the Bulawayo-Gweru road only once, when I was eighteen, and I was repulsed by the emptiness of that road, its unremarkableness. I imagine the truck driver glimpsed my father's car through his rearview mirror, careening as he elbowed him off the road, his tires mewling, the protest of rubber against tarmac stinking up the air. There were no witnesses on that dry stretch of tarmac, only the parched savannah grass and refractions of light playing mirage with the heat in the distance. I imagine the truck driver quickly released his brakes, angled his truck back onto the road, and sped off.

I hope, at least, that someone called an ambulance.

I hope my father died a quick death.

We did not hear of his death until hours later.

I was watching a rerun of the sitcom *Family Matters*, chuckling at poor, bespectacled Steve Urkel making yet another fool of himself in front of sweet, perm-curled Laura Winslow, when two men rumbled into our yard. At first, I paid them no mind. I wondered dreamily if I would soon be going to school with the Laura Winslows of this world.

It was Mama's keening that beckoned me to the window. I pressed my face against the pane, panting, making it misty. The men were standing next to a Mazda 323—was it red?—busy biting and licking their lips. Mama's face undid itself and redid itself and fell apart all over again.

"Mummy?" I called out.

"Go and play with the twins next door," Mama ordered.

"Mama? What's wrong?"

"I said go next door! Ask Mrs. Zulu to give you ice cream."

How greedily we sucked on those lollies, the twins and I. They filled our mouths with giggles and icy sweetness, painting our tongues orange and green and red, and dribbling generously down our chins.

"I am going to America to live with my daddy," I told the twins.

"You are lying," they cried.

"Am not!"

"Are too!"

"Am not! He's coming to get me today, you'll see. And you'll wish you were nice to me, because then I won't send you things from America."

"OK, sorry! Sorry, sorry!"

"Here, have my lolly."

"No, have mine!"

I ate the twins' lollies one by one, sucking on them until there was nothing left, while they watched, eyes wide, their hands clasped demurely in front of their frocks. Afterward, we kneeled on Mrs. Zulu's padded stool in front of her mirror and tried on her assortment of perfumes and stuck out our tongues as far as they could go, marveling at the colors, "rainbow tongues" we called them, squinting our eyes and stretching our lips, like party women.

It was Khulu, my mother's father, who came to pick me up the following day and took me with him to his house in Queenspark East, where I usually spent the weekends, sitting beneath the lemon tree at the back of the garden beside him, my khulu, my math and English books spread across my lap. And though my eyes flitted about for my father as we alighted from the khombi in Queenspark East, I didn't ask after him. I had been asking for him since the evening before and, failing to get an answer, had resigned myself to awaiting his call, my lips pursed in petulance.

The jacarandas seemed unusually purple that day, their leaves curled into fists, the petals bruising under my feet. My mouth was chattering faster than my brain could keep up with. I was just going on and on and on, because that's what I do when I'm nervous, and the worry lines on Khulu's forehead, the set line of his lips, made me nervous. My breath reached my ears in sharp rasps.

"What's that?" I asked, pointing to the piece of black cloth pinned to Khulu's Scotch jacket with woolly, blue and gray crisscrossing threads, one of his numerous district administrator of education jackets.

After a while he said, "It's a sign."

"A sign? A sign of what?"

"A sign we wear when somebody close to us dies."

"Who died, Khulu?"

He didn't reply.

"Khulu, who died?"

When he didn't answer, I shrugged. He squeezed my hand. I tried to squeeze his big hand back, stumbling to keep in step with his rapid strides. Presently, we came upon his house, sitting well back from the gate, my gogo's garden of gloriosas flanking the gravel driveway, the patch of grass to our left a shaggily decent height, the same color as the spring-green walls of the house, its viridian asbestos roof glistening with a fresh coat of paint. *Colonial style* was what my teacher called the houses of Queenspark East, with their generous rooms and equally generous gardens.

It was eerily quiet that day, Khulu's house, or perhaps this is how I like to remember it, so befitting in retrospect, the usual laughing and shouting, thudding and dithering failing to reach my ears—for he had twelve children all in all, my khulu, some, like Mama, grown, others, like my aunt Sihle, the last born, only three years older than I, and a handful of grandchildren and grandnieces and grandnephews, so there was never a dull moment in that house.

But we didn't bump into a soul as we went in through the back, past Gogo's kitchen with the ancient blue fridge that belched and farted incessantly, although meat was boiling on the stove, a beef-smelling steam rising from the huge black pot, a squad of flies hovering nearby.

He took me straight to his room, my khulu, where he made me remove my Bata sandals and sat me on the edge of his bed, my feet pressed against the cool, shimmering maroon floor. He dragged a chair from his desk, where his district administrator things sat, arranged neatly in sheaves of papers and piles of books, his reading glasses resting on their leather case, a tin of Vicks VapoRub next to it, its minty scent filling the room. There he sat, opposite me, my khulu, his eyes angled not at me but the polished floor—where if you looked hard enough, you could see your reflection—suddenly a crumpled old man.

"Ubabakho kasekho. Kube le accident . . ."

Your father has passed away. There has been an accident.

It was as though he was not speaking to me. He said I should not cry; how it was not good to cry and cry, and if I cried, I would end up crying myself sick.

I dragged myself out of Khulu's room to the bedroom next door where we girls slept. It was midmorning, and yet I remember this moment as dusk.

*My daddy. Is dead.*

*So that means. I shall never see him again.*

*But we're going to America. I spoke to him. Yesterday. Did I not speak to him?*

My father was the world.

He could not die.

The world could not die.

I lay in that dusk, on one of the double beds that stood on opposite ends of the girls' room in Khulu's house, a giddiness in my stomach. The sunlight—it was August, so it must have been quite fierce—punctured Gogo's lace curtain and struck the maroon cement floor between the beds in tinder-colored bricks. And yet, that sensation of nightfall never left me. It laved me. Everything was palled in enigma: the coral-colored walls studded as they were with sheeny posters of Destiny's Child and TLC and Boys II Men; the sagging wardrobe with its polished skin of frothy cappuccino and coffee black molting to reveal beneath the delicate, bruised flesh of matte pine; the purple duvet on the empty bed across from me, whose smells of child sweat and vomit and urine and Gogo's Surf powder now seemed perplexing.

I went to sleep, even though I did not go to sleep. I simply lay my cheek against a pillow. It was soft, the pillow, my cheek; my cheek sunk into the pillow, the pillow sunk against my cheek. I shifted, turning from my stomach to lie on my side, my knees folded almost up to my chest, my hands palmed together beneath my cheek, languishing in that mid-morning, that gloam.

*My daddy. Is dead.*

*I shall never see him again.*

*There is no America.*

# Part II

returned to America twelve years later.

I was twenty four.

I had dreamed, for a long time, of returning. Zimbabwe had continued to spiral, just as my father had predicted. The year he died, I watched a rerun of the farm evictions on national television and imagined the conversations we would have had.

*What is this thing we're fighting over? This land? What is it?*

*It's . . . soil?*

*Is it private property? Or a living entity?*

*How can land be a living thing?*

*You and I and the mountain all come from the same basic chemistry.*

*What about you now? What are you? Are you a spirit? Where are you? Where do people go after they die?*

*Remember what I taught you: Learn to question your habits of thought.*

I wrote him letters, just as we had done when he was still alive. I told him about my life, about my ambitions, about Mama's desolation over his passing, the way she spent hours staring at pictures of him in her photo album.

For a long time after he died, I would squat in the grass next to the postbox and watch the postman riding his silver bicycle in the distance, pretending to wait for a letter from overseas. There was a thrill in the anticipation, even as it was accompanied by a dull throb in my chest. I would squat for a long time afterward and pretend one of the phone or electricity bills had my father's name on it, and imagine the star-spangled fables my father, alive and well in America, had written me.

And then, one summer afternoon in January, when the blackjacks were in bloom, their barbed awns catching on one's clothes, the postman came cycling down the dusty path that led to Mama's vanilla cottage with a ribboned box balanced between the handlebars. He came to a stop by the postbox, where I squatted, plucking the blackjacks from my frock. Wiping sweat off his brow, he said, "Whew! A big box from overseas! Your da-dee must love you very much, heh?"

He handed me the box. I accepted it with both hands, turning it over to see the name and stamp on the back. It had come all the way from New York, and it was addressed to *me*. For a wild moment, I thought it must be from my father, proof, somehow, that he was still alive.

"Yes," I said. "Aren't I the luckiest girl in the world?"

The postman chuckled. "Yes, you are, girlie! I wish I had a da-dee like yours."

I ripped the box open, not bothering to wave back at the postman as he rang his bell and cycled off. Inside was a leather-bound book titled *Stars of the Sub-Sahara*. Accompanying the book was a card. *Happy Birthday*, it read.

*You are finally thirteen! Your father and I put together these stories of the southern night sky in university. We were going to inspire young minds and change the world! I could ask your father anything about the stars, or books, or ideas. But he never discussed his feelings. I did not know he was going to be a father until the night you were to be born, when he asked me to drive him to Bulawayo. I was there when you were born! I held you in these hands of mine. You were a big baby. Frank looked down into your little face as though he was holding the whole world. I hope this little book fills your world, grass-hopper! Love, Uncle C.*

I remained squatting in the grass by the postbox for a long time, clutching the card and the book. I could feel my face becoming wet. I wanted so much to be happy at Mr. C's kindness. And yet, a part of me felt bruised, making my chest sore, making it hard to breathe.

From then on, every year, on my birthday, I would receive a gift accompanied by some remembered snippet about my father, sometimes from the capital city, Harare, where Mr. C lived, at other times from some exotic place half a world away, where he must have traveled for work. A part of me resented his thoughtfulness. But I did come to look forward to his gifts, becoming anxious as my birthday drew nearer, at times so sick my tummy churned, throwing up whatever food I had taken down.

In letters I wrote to my father, I told him about the presents Mr. C sent: a dull, black meteorite with rough edges that fit in the palm of my hand; a Lego International Space Station set; and a book of cosmology equations that was too advanced for my age. I told him how he contin-ued to live on through Mr. C's mouth. I told him just how far Zimba-bwe had regressed, much worse than he had predicted, turning us into a people we no longer recognized. I told him how we endured—with the foolish good humor of something you think is temporary but realize with growing horror may last the rest of your life, become the whole of your life—years of crippling food shortages and fuel shortages and money shortages and a shortage of air, metaphorically speaking, like the future was slowly being squeezed out of us.

I told him about my stargazing escapades, narrating in detail the evenings spent in Mama's yard with his bulky Celestron Ultima 2000 telescope and the book he and Mr. C had written. I used their specialized star charts to star hop and pinpoint objects in the sky, marveling at how the stars were identified not by their conventional Latin and Greek names, but as they were known by the Bantu, as my father had known them as a child.

I would settle the telescope on a patch of grass in Mama's backyard and, using a torch light, squint at the star charts and attempt to map the stars in the sky using the telescope finder. There I would stay for hours, sucked into the charcoal-gray night. At first, I couldn't pinpoint anything, only blobs that looked the same. During these moments, I felt so far away from him, my father. Little by little, though, the secrets of the stars began to reveal themselves to me. It was like learning a new language. Where previously I had only seen murky blobs, I now greeted each star like a friend, swinging the eight-inch circumference of the Celestron in careful, circular motions, calling each celestial object by name.

The first time I saw iNdonsakusa, Jupiter, it was a gray blurry sphere hanging low in the early evening August sky. It looked squashed, as though someone were sitting on it. I tracked it for several nights, staying out later and later until I was able to observe it high up in the sky, when its light traveled a shorter path through our atmosphere to reach us, making it easier to see. There it was, a huge, marble-like planet, so crisp I stretched out my hand as though to touch it. Alternating bands of whitish zones and rust-colored belts ran across its surface. You could tell from their cloudy texture that the zones were much cooler than the belts, whose fiery color gave off a hot, effervescent feeling.

I dreamt of iNdonsakusa. In my dream, I was up there with my father. We approached her as though from a spaceship, descending through her gaseous atmosphere, which was incredibly hot and made mostly of hydrogen and a little helium. The heat was unbearable, and yet we bore it. I looked up at my father and smiled. He gave me a thumbs up.

All around us was a translucent fog. Nebulous cumulonimbi floated before us, emitting a bioluminescent glow, like an alternating swarm of fiery fireflies and a smack of blue-glowing jellyfish. The air became cooler and cooler the deeper we descended, falling to sudden, drastic temperatures. It was like going from Death Valley straight to Antarctica. The fog became wetter and wetter, morphing into the continuous, misty spray one is subjected to when standing on a bridge before a deafening waterfall, like our own Mosi-oa-Tunya in Zimbabwe, one of the Seven Wonders of the World. There was a rainbow in the distance, only instead of the colors red, orange, yellow, green, blue, indigo, and violet, we saw an alternating swirl of whitish blue and rusty red.

The liquid came upon us suddenly. One moment we were floating in iNdonsakusa's atmosphere, and the next we were sinking through her surface, which wasn't rocky and solid like our planet Earth, but was slippery and gaseous. The gases beneath her surface had cooled and become a bath not of water but hydrogen, which liquefies at extremely cold temperatures. We should have died here from the cold, but we did not. We had transcended to a realm beyond death.

Suddenly, we were no longer bodies but pools of liquefied hydrogen, no longer rigid but formless. I saw my father as a floating pool of hydrogen, and he was beautiful. I reached out to him, stretching my amorphous form so I could flow toward him and our currents could become one. But before I could reach him, I was paralyzed by a great and terrible pressure. It squeezed me from all sides. So powerful was it, so awful, that I felt I would burst. We had now sunk to iNdonsakusa's very core, which raged like a thousand volcanoes.

There was a terrifying *pop pop* sound, like the ear's eustachian tubes unblocking themselves. Electrons, unable to withstand the great pressure of iNdonsakusa's core, popped out of our hydrogen atoms, destabilizing us and turning us from a cool liquid to a hot, metallic hydrogen. We began to crackle, like sparks flying from a polyester shirt against dry skin. An electrical current charged through us, from one electron-deprived atom to the other, gathering power and momentum. We could feel our collective current vibrating throughout the whole of iNdonsakusa, which is larger than a thousand Earths. We shook the whole of her, shuddering her from side to side like a massive dynamo. Our atoms flowed into one another, so that I was my father and my father was me.

Rudely, abruptly, I woke up.

Each night I willed myself to dream that dream again. I stayed out later and later, communing with iNdonsakusa. She was a pleasure to behold during those nights when the electricity went, submerging the neighborhood in pitch blackness. Those morbid nights of load-shedding were excellent for stargazing, unveiling a stygian sky that, devoid of light pollution, startled in its starry extravagance. I swung my telescope from iNdonsakusa in search of the Flock of Birds, the stars that can be seen chasing other stars in the sky. I zoomed in on one of the birds, the bright red star Pollux, and imagined the recently discovered exoplanet, Pollux b, orbiting it. It was just a year after my father's death. I wished he had been alive to enjoy the discovery of this monstrous marvel with me. She was twice the size of iNdonsakusa—as large as two thousand earths!—and likely gaseous, too.

"See, you have a cousin planet," I whispered in the darkness, swinging my telescope back to iNdonsakusa. "Maybe we do, too, somewhere out there."

In that jetty, bejeweled darkness, I could drown out Mama's incessant, increasingly nonsensical chatter, those lurid fantasies she liked to dream out loud about the future, becoming outlandish the more we stood frying in the sun in those suffocating food and fuel and money queues, straining our necks to glimpse the Rolls Royces and the Ferraris that vroomed past, the government officials and their children squealing as they lurched into crater-sized pot holes, flinging their laughter out the windows like insults.

"We, too, will get there, one day," Mama would say, watching them, at once buoyant and wistful.

I would turn away, my eyes searching for somewhere to go, not knowing how to hold this shame Mama carried at finding ourselves suddenly poor, blinking into the bright, hazy sun and the glistening faces around us as though she didn't know how she had gotten there.

I sought refuge in iNdonsakusa. She and I were both progenies of the stars, and yet she was so exotic, so terrifying, even a little alien. There was something enchanting about her otherworldliness, as though she might help me escape my life. I would stare at her and dream of the mysterious wonders of our galaxy with its hundreds of billions of stars and the hundreds of billions of galaxies that made up the universe. What other worlds roiled out there, as yet unknown to us? What might they teach us about the cosmos, about our own planet, about ourselves?

I brought my A4 sketch book and my purse of pencils out with me one night. INdonsakusa was high up in the sky, crisp and clear. She filled the whole of the Celestron Ultima's lens. I began by tracing her wide, slightly elongated spherical body. Then, using the delicate lightness of a 6H pencil, I sketched her North and South Equatorial Belts, which ran across her portly becomingness as a series of thick, rust-colored bands separated by the milky strip of the Equatorial Zone.

I traced the Great Red Spot that blazed on the lower right edge of the South Equatorial Belt. It looked like the bloodshot eye of a grumpy giant. It glared down at me. I gazed up humbly at it, attempting to tamp down its malevolence with my pencil.

Next, I moved my pencil in rhythmic susurrations, tracing the rusty clouds that swirled across the equatorial belts. They looked, etched on iNdonsakusa's marmoreal surface, like Khoisan rock art. It took me several nights to get these swirls and the smaller, paler eyes dotting iNdonsakusa's equatorial belts down. For one, the planet rotated rapidly, as though expressing the fury of her raging, liquid metallic interior. This made it hard to capture the detail of her magnificent troposphere. For another, I was overwhelmed by her complexity, which became apparent in my clumsy attempts to draw her. It was like gradually learning a face, which looks, at first, familiar, but whose careful study of each component renders the whole strange, and ambiguous, and therefore all the more intimate.

I sketched the festoons garlanding her belts. They started as light bumps at the edge of each belt before swirling across the entire band in recurring loops. Next, I worked on the Equatorial Zone that separated the two belts, twirling the festoons from the edges of the North Equatorial Belt into the Equatorial Zone's lighter, puffier-looking clouds.

Here, I switched to a 2B pencil. I moved my hand back and forth in rapid movements across the rust-colored belts to give them a bolder value. I darkened the concentrated spots of condensation on the planet's surface. The festoons in my sketch seemed a crude copy of the image beaming at me from the telescope. They were darker and starker in my sketch; too dark, too stark, possessing none of the originals' dreamy swirliness.

Adding details to the giant red eye was a terrifying experience. I stared into its glare and trembled. I could feel myself being sucked into its fiery current and tossed about from side to side. The eye was an anticyclone that had been raging on iNdonsakusa for centuries, spinning without any solid ground on which to land or any solid object to slow down its trajectory. It was a pirouette without an audience. I was now its audience. I held its glare, committing the red streaks to memory; the rust-colored ball in its middle like a giant pupil; the festoons swirling in its bloodied sclera like a knot of veins. My hand danced mimetically across the page, committing to paper the roiling fire that also roiled deep within me.

Afterward, I slumped over the Celestron Ultima, spent.

I had gained a world, but something still felt irretrievably lost.

Loss not as an event, but a process.

Twice I would lose my innocence about the world. The first time would be when I finally encountered Euclid in my high school mathematics class. I was fourteen. He appeared as a three-dimensional plane on Mrs. Bailey's blackboard running along three axes—the $x$-axis, the $y$-axis, and the $z$-axis.

"Imagine you are standing on this plane," said Mrs. Bailey. "And you can move in a straight line along any of these axes from point A to point B to point C. This is how we experience space. Welcome to Euclidean geometry."

"Euclid!" I cried, straightening up in my seat. "I can't think in straight lines."

"What?" said Mrs. Bailey.

"The world is a poem."

". . . A poem? Oh no, this is not a poem, Athando, we're in the maths period. Though you *could* call Euclid a poet." Mrs. Bailey beamed.

"Euclid got it all twisted, Mrs. Bailey," I said. "Space isn't straight. It's curved."

"When we want to disagree with a fellow thinker, Athando, we don't call them 'twisted.' Rather, we engage respectfully with their ideas—"

"It's not even space," I said, smirking. "It's *spacetime*. If Euclid was so smart, why didn't he figure it out?"

"That's enough, Athando—"

"*Athandwa.*"

The class tittered.

"I want to butcher Euclid the way you butcher my name, Mrs. Bailey."

The titters erupted into full-blown chortles.

"Athan-dwa," said Mrs. Bailey, her face pinkening. "Yes, space is not linear. It's curved. And it's true that how we move through space impacts how we experience time. But we're getting ahead of ourselves. For the purposes of this class, we're going to treat time as uniform. Is that clear? Because that's how we intuitively experience the world."

"Intuitive to whom?" I said.

"Enough, Athando," said Mrs. Bailey, her pink face reddening. "Let's open our maths books to chapter four. Who would like to read the introduction to Euclidean geometry?"

"We should learn Bantu geometry," I said.

"There's no such thing," said Mrs. Bailey.

"Yes, there is," I said.

"If you don't stop, I'm going to send you to the principal's office. Open your maths book to chapter four. *Now*, Athando."

Later, as I sat in the lobby outside the principal's office—marched there by Mrs. Bailey, as though I couldn't very well walk by myself, as though I might flee the consequences of my delinquency—I thought of how Father Pius had beaten Euclid's straight lines into my father with a sjambok and I felt angry all over again.

The second time I would lose my innocence would be the year

I turned twenty. I was dating Rufus Rogers when the government evicted his family from their farm. I remembered the Rogerses' farm from the one trip my father had taken with me to his tribal home when I was seven, during his only visit home from the United States. The farm sprawled across a grassy, fenced plot of land with a rusty sign on the gate that read ROGERS' FARM—PRIVATE PROPERTY, right next to the colorful huts that made up the rural home where my father had grown up. My father had pointed it out, explaining how before Cecil John Rhodes came prospecting for gold—which he never found—with his British South Africa Company and forced the Bantu onto nonarable land in the reserves, our people, the Bantu, had lived a pastoral existence all across this land, on the Rogerses' farm and the other farms in the area. His face creased as he spoke, becoming leathery and hard and shiny. I had wanted to reach out, then, and touch him. But I didn't; I just looked out at the Rogerses' farm with its segregated rows of maize and pumpkin and bean stalks, overwhelmed by my father's nostalgia, by this mysterious grief he carried for a past he had not lived.

Later, as the government took Rufus's family farm away, I thought about this history that entwined us both. His mother, Mrs. Rogers, was shown weeping on BBC as the people from the government swarmed the farm like locusts, her arms stretched toward a striking baobab tree on the horizon. Her grief was palpable, almost overwhelming the scene, eclipsing that tree and the landscape, eclipsing me as I watched from the sofa in Mama's living room, Rufus seated next to me. The clip played over and over on BBC and was later picked up by CNN. Mrs. Rogers, in her outsized grief, became through repetition a word, the word for any person who had ever been torn from their home and the things that gave them meaning and without which they lost their sense of being.

Watching Mrs. Rogers's puffed-up face fill the TV screen, pink with grief, I clasped Rufus's hand and wiped the tears from his plump, reddened cheeks. He showed me photos on his phone of cattle kicking up clouds of dust in the hazy twilight of a spring evening, and leafy maize stalks shimmering seductively in a shower of summer rain, and the majestic baobab crowning the savannah horizon with its tremendous trunk, its sprawling branches tinged by a sepia autumnal haze. I felt there was something profound he was trying to show me in those photos, something that was now irretrievably lost. He was the first boy I ever loved. He had a beautiful smile that lit up his impish jade eyes.

When I revealed to him my own troubles, a mysterious dread I had come to know as The Terrors, Rufus got scared. I confessed how Mama had taken me to see a nyanga, a traditional healer, to try and cure me. Rufus said he didn't want any part of my African voodoo or whatever the hell was wrong with me, and he dumped me, just like that. Maybe he was genuinely scared. I was too. The Terrors had been assaulting me for years, but I had never let anyone get close to me like that, the way I had Rufus, never allowed them to see me in that stupefied state we slip into when grappling with the terrors of being human.

Later, after the Rogerses were evicted, a government minister and his family moved into the farm, sweeping up two other farms in the area in the process. I watched the scandal playing out on BBC, feeling a guilty sense of retribution, as though Rufus's rejection of me and the national theft now playing out were somehow correlated.

I scribbled my father a lengthy letter about the heartache of first love, as though the act of writing could dull the ache in my chest. I wished, for once, that he could reply. My letters to him were long and rambling, written in cursive, by hand. It was these letters, full of my stargazing escapades and my crude sketches of celestial objects and my juvenile excursions into astronomy, that I would use to apply to The Program. I figured if my father had gone there, then it must be an excellent place. The Program was built in the 1960s, at the height of the Space Race. It has since expanded into other branches of art, science, and culture—astronomy, botany, biodiversity. It's a highly selective place.

I claimed in my personal statement to be interested in contributing to an ethnographic study of the stars, though God knows that hadn't ever been on my mind when I was writing those letters. But The Program loved this ethnographic ambition, and I was awarded a Thomas Long Fellowship to go there.

t had always seemed inevitable that I would return.

I had been desperate to escape those never-ending queues, alarmed by the ease with which I adapted to it all. Sometimes, I would try to think back to those afternoons as a child spent grocery shopping with Mama, ambling past brimming supermarket shelves, picking through the plump, shiny fruits and the fresh, glistening vegetables in the market. The memories felt like something I had made up.

I hated this, the treachery of memory, the humiliations of poverty, the sneaking suspicion that this was all my life would amount to, days and years spent in riotous queues brawling with neighbors and friends over a loaf of bread or a sack of mealie-meal, punctuated by the increasingly chilly understanding that those who didn't know how to control their thoughts or their vocal chords would be disappeared, just like that, as though they had never existed.

I had worked myself to the proverbial bone to make it back to America, raking in titles and accolades like a serial hobbyist in my last year of private school. I presided over as many as five meetings a week, deploying mouthfuls of banter and ladylike laughter as Toastmasters' president; outmaneuvering opponents with wily strokes of verbiage as president of the Debating Club; scribbling letters in iambic pentameter to the United Nations on behalf of the refugees of Afghanistan as vice president of Amnesty International; leading increasingly blasphemous Bible discussions as the president of Scripture Union (until I was sent to the principal's office and ousted by my board for calling the chimpanzees our cousins); and policing skirt hems and sock lengths with autocratic zeal as a senior prefect, all the while studying mathematics, physics, and chemistry. And French. My navy high school blazer had dripped with gold and silver medals filigreed with all manner of coats of arms and organizational insignia. I wore that dripping jacket every single day of my final year of high school, careful not to rip my stockings or smudge my leather shoes as I elbowed my way through the boorish crowds rioting in the city center.

And then, as an undergrad, I had been one of the youngest people invited to represent my country at the World Youth Summit in Zurich, where I worked wood-paneled rooms replete with portraits of dead counts and window views of travelogue-style vistas, disarming presidents with my supersonic wit, sharing innovative solutions to social problems affecting the youth with secretariats and ministers, and drawing up Sustainable Development Goals with the world's monarchs, including one of the princes of Saudi Arabia, who let me take a selfie with him and later tried to grope me in one of the bathrooms.

These were the teleological blocks that I'd hoped would lead me back to America. My return felt preordained, as though I were leaving behind an impostor existence. I had always felt the shadow of another life behind my own, the life I could have lived had my father not died and had I gone to live with him. I landed near the little Midwestern college town where The Program was tucked away in the unbelievable humidity of late August. The tiny local airport held none of the glamour of New York's JFK. The heat was damp and fervid, the ground outside the cluster of buildings glimmering like a mirage.

Seated in the back of the yellow cab on the drive from the airport, I was struck by the monotony of the sprawling maize fields—*cornfields*—rolling toward the horizon in tightly packed rows of green, their reedy sun-washed bodies sashaying to some tranquil wind-sonata. They proliferated on either side of the highway, variegated occasionally by a farmhouse or some other nondescript building in the distance. I sat with my hands pressed to my sides, my bare legs smarting against the funereal black leather seat, watching the stalks of maize—*corn*—speed past, their limp tassels bowed as they stood in prayerful congregation around my hearse with its merry colors of a bumblebee, ushering it in sunny procession down the freeway.

Later, my flatmate, Shaniqua, would tell me how the Midwest had once been a kaleidoscopic sprawl of prairie grasslands and marshes and bison and more species of birds than she could count, with a medley of Native, French, British, and mixed-race families formed by the modern encounter, whose communities flourished around the fur trade and whose networks stretched from the Gulf of Mexico to what was now Canada.

"That monochrome landscape you experienced today," she said, curling her lips, "is not the triumph of modernity but the banality of ruin."

I mouthed this, *the banality of ruin*, charmed by its poetry.

I found Shaniqua sitting outside the apartment on Fairchild Street, perched atop the porch steps, doodling invisible patterns on the ground with her finger. When the cab pulled up, she looked up, her face bursting into sparkles.

"How you doing?" she said, like that, like she was singing, getting up and coming down the steps, brushing the dirt off her floral dress, which stopped just below her hips, allowing her striking, sturdy legs to flourish. Her kinky, chocolatey curls complemented her skin, which was warm, like an overripe mango.

"You must be tired," she said. "Welcome! I haven't had a roommate from Africa before."

I wanted to tell her that it was something special to be standing there with her drawl pealing in my ears like she'd just stepped through the TV in Mama's living room back home.

"How do you do?" I said instead, extending a shy hand.

Shaniqua's tawny eyes glittered. "You sound British!" she said, clasping my hand. "Come, come on in. I expect you must be tired after that long trip. Where you coming from, again?"

"Zimbabwe," I said.

"Right, right."

Still holding my hand, which made me feel at once reticent and relaxed, Shaniqua led me up gloomy stairs to our two-bedroom apartment on the second floor. She was also enrolled in The Program and had been one of the few people to reply to my online posting on Craigslist for a flat to share, and she was the only one who hadn't rescinded when I had told her I was coming all the way from Zimbabwe. Now, entering our space, I was excited to be sharing a flat with her and to have a place I could call my own, a signature marking of adulthood.

The most striking feature of our two-bedroom affair was the little buddhas and buddhesses that proliferated everywhere, gold and bronze casts, wooden and porcelain sculptures, poised in various, sometimes ghastly states of animation suffusing every nook and cranny with an aura of wisdom, including the toilet, where a brass Yokozuna squatted contemplatively on the tank above his own little potty, in the midst of a great upheaval.

My eyes darted from the Yokozuna to Shaniqua and back. I nodded politely and said, "Nice."

I thought Shaniqua must be into some deep religious stuff to be hoarding all these buddhas and buddhesses like this. Ever since the lessons in my physics class in undergrad about how the human body is composed of elements that were formed in the stars, I fancied myself an agnostic, harboring a healthy skepticism about whether there really was a God. Still, I wanted to hold on to the glimmer of hope that my father still existed as a floating ball of energy somewhere, perhaps beyond the spectrum visible to the human eye, beyond the wisdom of human understanding. Each star's death swept all the elements that had been generated inside it out across space to form the next generation of stars, which also eventually died and sent out their elements, and so on and so forth, combining in different ways to create something out of nothing, like magic, birthing species of gas and minerals and asteroids and planets and then water and celluloids and plants and, finally, humans. Surely when people died, their stardust combined to make other wondrous, luminous beings. Otherwise, what was the point of the human experiment, of humanity's special purchase to consciousness, tragic little celestials that we were, if all that luminosity we carried inside ourselves shriveled up along with our bodies?

Shaniqua showed me to my room. It was bare except for a futon— "Mine," she said, pointing to it, "but you can use it until you get a bed"—and a lone chest of drawers on which sat a laughing buddha. She hovered by the doorway, watching as I dragged my suitcases and unzipped them and unsheathed my father's Celestron Ultima 2000 telescope. When I looked up at her, she grinned and said again how she had never had a roommate from Africa before.

"Thank you," I said, because I didn't know what else to say. I stood there, eyeing her, a towel and soap in my hand. And then, "I would like to shower, please."

"'*Please*,'" Shaniqua mimicked, backing down the corridor, giving this surprising burst of laughter. "You sound British!"

"Thank you," I said again, making her laugh even harder.

I washed off the grime of twenty-seven hours and two connecting flights and then lay in my room on Shaniqua's futon, facing the laughing buddha perched atop the chest of drawers. I intended to sleep. But instead, I stared at the buddha's mirthful, cherubic face ringed by rolls of bronze flesh.

I began to hiccup.

What had I done, packing two suitcases and leaving home without a backward glance? It had felt romantic at the time. Mama had been stressed by my decision to leave. But I had been feeling precarious, on the brink of something dreadful, and I had needed to leave.

"You're running away," Mama had said with a wry smile.

"Don't be absurd," I had replied.

I addressed Mama like this when she was inebriated and too lazy to sober me up with a slap, speaking to her the way the rude American children I had seen on TV spoke to their parents. I had always been envious of their surly entitlement, their unwavering confidence in belonging to the world.

"You're leaving me."

"I'm going to grad school."

"Oh, Jesu. It's happening all over again."

I sighed. "Mother."

"You're just like him. Do you know what a little fox he was? More in love with ideas than with people. What kind of person is that?"

"I'll be back."

"That sonofabitch."

She spoke like this when she had had a glass or two of wine, using American swear words from the movies I made us watch together. I

gazed at the floor and muttered something under my breath. I was trying hard not to resent her. All she ever said about my father was how
he had fucked her over. He had promised to come back for her and then
kept her waiting all those years. She had become miserly about her most
generous memories of him, as though sharing them would deplete them
or diminish them, diminish her, somehow.

"See how hard it is here," she said. "What will I do, all by myself?"

Surely, she could find some nice, middle-aged man to love her?

"I'll send you lots of money," I said. "In US dollars. Wouldn't you
like that?"

I had left without a backward glance, so eager to be out in the world.
But now, I felt drenched, feeling none of the catharsis I had expected
to feel upon setting foot on American soil. The heaving, when it came,
was unexpected, unhinging my shoulders and spewing out of me in
dramatic sobs. I cupped my mouth and tried to force the sobs back in.
The thud of Shaniqua's feet reached me, but I was too consumed, or
embarrassed, to look up. I pretended not to hear her.

"You poor child!" she said.

I felt her soft hands around me. I let my face sink into her bouncy,
lavender-scented bosom. When I finally stopped sobbing enough to
raise my streaked face, she cupped my cheeks, her hands soft and deli-
ciously warm, radiating the scent of shea butter. I felt shy, unable to
look her in the eye. As though she could sense my uncertainty, she said,
"Come now," and that lilting, sing-song drawl in her voice, at once
strange and familiar, like it was coming straight from the TV, like *I* was
inside the TV, part of a predetermined script, the end fated before it had
even begun, was a thrill, a comfort.

It was in this way, sobbing in my new flatmate's arms like a child,
soppy memories of Mama and blurry memories of my father filling my
head, that I went to sleep on my first day back in America.

✴

THE FOLLOWING MORNING, I woke up to find Shaniqua hulking over me.

I let out a scream, but what came out was more of a terrified, ineffectual squeak. Shaniqua looked, standing over me in a billowing black kimono, like Jack the Ripper out of the thriller movie *The Lodger*.

"Sorry," she said, stretching her hands in apology. "I just came in here looking for one of my dresses. I used to keep some stuff in this room before you came, and you looked so peaceful sleeping and . . . I haven't ever had a roommate from Africa before."

I still didn't know what to say to this, so I pulled the top sheet up to my chin and flashed Shaniqua an awkward smile. The night had been repulsively hot, even with the little wall air-con sputtering throughout. I had slept only in my panties. I was lying there half naked, my breasts spilling all over the place. I wondered how long Shaniqua had been standing there watching me, whether she had had a good look, the way people take the liberty of doing when someone is asleep.

"Tell me about Africa," said Shaniqua, taking a seat by my feet, at the edge of the futon.

I was pressed for the loo, but I didn't know how to tell her to leave so I could get up and put on something decent, and I was too self-conscious about my love handles and my shuddering thighs and my spilling breasts to just get up and walk to the toilet with her, a stranger, watching me. So, I crossed my legs beneath the sheets and tensed my pelvic muscles.

"Well," I said, feeling suddenly bashful, what with the earnest way she was regarding me. "Africa is really big. I myself don't know the whole of it so well."

"No, I don't mean *that*," said Shaniqua. Her eyes went all dreamy. "Like—tell me about Nefertiti."

"Nefer-who?"

"Girl, bye!"

She began quizzing me about Nefertiti, like I knew who the hell Nefertiti was, like she lived right next door to us or something. And then she started going on about somebody called Ranavalona, queen of Madagascar, and then Aminatu, Hausa warrior queen of Zazzau. She beamed at me, like she was waiting for me to add something to her impressive biographical epitaphs. I blinked at her. When she continued regarding me with her sparkling, tawny eyes, I cleared my throat and said I knew Beyoncé. Had she heard of Destiny's Child? And TLC, did she know TLC?

Shaniqua cast her eyes on me, giving her head a tragic little shake. "Are you sure you're from Africa? How come you don't know none of this stuff?"

"I'm sorry, but I really need the loo," I said, finally. I couldn't keep it in any longer.

"The what?"

"The *toilet*. I'm pressed for the toilet."

"Oh, don't you know where it is? Down the hall to your left."

"I know. I need you to get out so I can get up."

Shaniqua paused, this inscrutable, amused look on her face. "Girl, honestly. Don't you have sisters? What are you hiding underneath there that I don't have or haven't seen before? This girl . . ."

Shaking her head, muttering under her breath, she got up and shuffled out. I listened for her footsteps until I was sure she had stepped into her own room. Then I grabbed my nightie, which lay crumpled on the floor, slipped it on and made a dash for the loo.

During those first days waiting for classes at The Program to start, I imprinted on Shaniqua like a duckling. She was the big sister I had never had and whose presence in my girlhood might have tamped down the fancifulness of an only child. She was thirty-three, a decade older than I, though she didn't behave like any of the thirty-something-year-olds I knew, who were terribly boring and frumpy, looking like they were confused about what age they were, about what they were supposed to be doing with their lives, not yet quite old but no longer young.

I followed Shaniqua wherever she went—to the grocery places like John's and Hy-Vee and an open-air place called the farmer's market, where she greeted the vendors by name and took her sweet time picking through the fruits and veggies, inspecting the tomatoes, which were plump and shiny and red; bagging some zucchini and these bright, gnarled carrots; weighing an eggplant the size of a man's penis in her hand; and selecting this exotic cabbage with crisp emerald leaves she later told me was bok choy. She even got us some freshly baked bread and some pecan-crusted apple pie.

The bread smelled so sweet and fresh and aromatic. I pressed it to my cheek and savored its warmth. I fought the urge to grab as much of it as I could and make a run for it. It would be there the next day, I muttered to myself over and over, clenching and unclenching my fists.

"Will you take me to Walmart?" I said to Shaniqua, swallowing a thick pond of saliva that had pooled in my mouth.

"Why the hell would you wanna go there?" she said, wrinkling her nose.

I squinted at her. Surely she knew Walmart with its dizzying ten flavors of everything? I wanted to feel dizzy. But Shaniqua was having none of that. This was where I should come and buy my food, she said, sweeping her arm across the open-air market before us with its fresh, dewy bounty. She would even take me to the Red Earth Gardens, an organic farm run by the Meskwaki Nation out in Tama, about an hour's drive away. They had the best veggies and the freshest herbs and the juiciest fruit. But not Walmart. Did I even know where the food from Walmart came from? Did I know what was in it? Did I know which sweatshops in Thailand or India those two-dollar blouses had come from? I nodded dutifully, frowning when she frowned, though I knew I'd slink off to Walmart the first chance I got. I intended to snap selfies of myself standing before all those dizzying shelves and send them to the people back home. *Look, bitches, I made it!*

But I gave my head a duteous shake as Shaniqua ranted, going on about universal product code and global supply chains and coerced labor and whatnot, grunting and murmuring "unbelievable" as she went on and on, a heavy and unpleasant feeling settling in my chest. I wasn't interested in whatever it was she was going on about. What did the people of Thailand or India have to do with me? I had come to America that I might be reckless in my joy.

Shaniqua asked me to go mushroom picking with her. She needed the mushrooms for her biophysics experiments. Like me, she was on a Thomas Long Fellowship at The Program. She was studying melanin.

"Melanin?" I said. "As in the thing that gives us color? That makes our skin black?"

"Yeah," said Shaniqua. "And your skin is not black, it's brown. You are Black."

"But why?"

"Why are you Black?"

"Why are you studying melanin?"

"Why not? What could be more liberating than understanding the physics of our skin color? Did you know our skin absorbs color? Our melanated skin is the color in the visible light spectrum that isn't absorbed by our skin. We're like walking little rainbows. Super cool biomolecule, don't you think? We even got neuromelanin in our brains."

"I've got melanin in my *brain*?"

"Your brain couldn't function without it, sweetie."

"So, everyone has this melanin in their brain? Even white people?"

"Girrrrl. We're all melanated hos, the whole damn species."

I chuckled. I liked the idea of being a melanated ho, of melanated ho-ism binding us humans together. We set off for the maple forest in a rickety truck Shaniqua had borrowed from one of her vendor friends at the farmer's market. It was the last week of August and the summer air was thick and damp, unlike the dry summers back home, making it hard to breathe. It felt like someone had placed their hand over my nose and mouth. I worried constantly that I'd run out of air. Shaniqua drove with the windows of the truck down, creating a welcome, artificial breeze.

I was struck by the alternating maple stands and denuded plots we passed along the way. Stumps of lumbered trees dotted the landscape, the only evidence of their once-towering existence. Some of the cuttings were fresh, the stumps still oozing sap. The lobed leaves of the tall maple trees turned the landscape into striking bands of green hardwood plots and brown barren lots that had been abandoned by loggers.

The maple stand Shaniqua parked next to was nothing more than a group of stumps on one of the barren lots. Shaniqua picked her way through the wreckage, her eyes flitting over the tree stumps and the snapped branches and the gouged-out soil. I followed behind, picking my way through pioneer thickets of elderberry that crawled across the lot, hogging all the land and the sunlight and crowding out other species.

Shaniqua crouched beside a brittle-looking maple stump. I crouched beside her. I wondered why she had brought us to this bruised landscape. All around us was ruin. How could anything flourish here? What could make a life here? And yet, something did. Shaniqua fingered a cluster of curly, ear-shaped mushrooms sprouting from the base of the tree stump. They gave off a faint, woody odor. I sniffed them and sighed.

"See?" she said, fingering the lobe of one mushroom. "This dark brown pigment is melanin. Just like our skin."

She murmured something in a language I couldn't understand.

"What are you saying?" I said.

"I'm greeting them," she replied. "And thanking them."

She caressed each curly mushroom, murmuring her thanks in the peculiar language. Then she held each fungal ear by its concha and plucked it from the maple stump and dropped it into a Ziploc bag. She handed me my own Ziploc bag to fill with mushrooms, directing me to pick an orange, flute-shaped species with veinlike threads under its belly.

"You're picking chanterelles," she said. "I'll fry them in butter tonight. You won't be able to get enough of them. Don't mix them with the wood ear mushrooms in my bag, though. They're yummy, too, but they're for my experiments."

"Can we eat them afterwards?" I said, eyeing the curly-eared mushrooms she was stuffing in her Ziploc bag. It would be a shame to let food go to waste. How horrified people back home would be to learn we had picked mushrooms only so Shaniqua could cut them up, glare at them under a microscope, and then throw them away.

"There're concepts in Choctaw you won't find in English," said Shaniqua, as though she hadn't heard me about wanting to eat her experimental mushrooms. "Like how to acknowledge our kinship with the plants and the trees, with these fungi here."

I eyed the mushrooms and their strange, tumorlike shapes. "So you talk to it as though it's a person?" I said, wrinkling my nose.

"A *nonhuman being*," said Shaniqua. "Do you only speak English? Don't y'all have a local language back in Zimbabwe? How do your people understand the world?"

I made a face. My isiNdebele was passable, but we had always been instructed in English at school and spoken English in public and browbeaten our parents with our pristine English at home.

"Plants and trees have a language of their own," said Shaniqua. "The fungi here help the maples share nutrients through their underground network, which is what's prolly still keeping these stumps alive. Their kin are tryna heal them."

I thought fondly of the etiquette lessons we'd been made to attend at Girls' College when I was thirteen and in my first year of high school. I had learned how to pipe English through my nose, much to Mama's pride and the awe of anyone who heard me piping like a piper on those streets. English was the language of shock and awe, and shocking and awing was what I was all about. Sometimes, I even shocked and awed myself.

"I hear folk talkin' all the time about how the world is so hyper-connected now," continued Shaniqua. "And I be like, pshhh! How you gon' be talkin' about being hyperconnected when you don't know half, a third, even *ten percent* of your kin? Our basic DNA is the same as the basic DNA of this mushroom. Did you know that? Like, if you put those strings of code side by side, you couldn't tell which was which."

My eyes widened.

"Listen, listen. How do you capture the fact that the atoms in one teeny weeny molecule of DNA are as numerous as the stars in our galaxy? How do you hold that in your being? You got a tiny galaxy inside you. There're galaxies inside this mushroom, inside this tree stump. That's a web of galaxies everywhere. That's a trillion little universes."

I wondered if Shaniqua was high. She was talking "high talk." I, too, felt high on the elixir of her words. I gazed at the leafy maples and the spike-needled pines and the shaggy basswoods sloping down a hill in the distance, awed by their rejuvenating green tones and the pleasant shock to the senses of vanilla-scented sap.

I was so enamored of Shaniqua for introducing me to the minuscule world of mushrooms and the galaxies flourishing in their fungal bodies, for now not only was I a speck in a galaxy in a universe full of hundreds of billions of galaxies, I, myself, contained galaxies. I was a giant fractal.

Later that afternoon, when I found Shaniqua in the bathroom with her head angled awkwardly into the sink, trying to wash her hair, I jumped in and took over. It was the least I could do. It was marvelous how her Afro thrived. It rose from her head in a fine thicket, dense and soft to the touch, like wool.

I plunged my fingers into her lustrous kink, working shampoo into it in slow, circular motions. Next, I rinsed her hair and doused it in leave-in conditioner, while it was still wet. And then we sat in the sitting room, I on a chair and Shaniqua on the floor with her head on my lap, by the window that took up the whole of the western facing wall, enjoying the late afternoon sunlight. I blow dried her hair and oiled it with coconut oil, and then worked it with an Afro comb, the pick-shape and thick teeth perfect for disentangling her thick strands.

She didn't ask me to, but afterward, I began to work her hair into a plait. I used a fine-toothed comb to part the luscious Afro, partitioning it into even portions by drawing straight lines down the length of her head with the tail of the comb. And then I began plaiting it, working methodically from one end of her head to the other, weaving worlds into each other. My hands moved in quick, fluid motions, my wrists jerking in rhythmic movements, my fingers dipping in and out of her thicket like I was playing an instrument.

Sitting all comfortable like that with her head on my lap, Shaniqua began sharing bits of herself, her voice taking on a pleasant, rumbling timbre.

"I take after Pa," she said. "My hair. I didn't get all of his mocha skin, but I sure got his head of nappy hair. His hair grew wild, child. Whoosh! That's how my hair grow, too. Pa loved my hair. He used to do it himself. He'd pick at it with his greasy mechanic fingers, just dreaming up whatever hairdo came to his mind. He said it was like operating on a motorcycle, you had to be delicate with it and you had to make sure you had all the little nuts and bolts and you had to let it tell you what it needed.

"He just took off just like that, one day. Upped and left us. Took nothing except his motorcycle. Indian Chief, that's what it was called. Not his name for it, but the motorcycle brand. It was made by Indian Motorcycle, the company where Pa worked all his life. There was nothing he loved more than that motorcycle.

"Sometimes, he'd tuck me between the seat and the handles and take me on a drive. It was thrilling, having the wind whip my face and tug at my pig tails, tucked between Pa's huge arms like that, his minty after-shave in my nostrils, his voice crooning that Charlie Patton blues song about goin' home. Maybe he imagined we were riding back to Africa! It was the closest I ever got to him. But the whole thing made Ma furious.

"'If you wanna die on that stupid bike, go right ahead, but you're not taking my baby with you,' she'd say.

"So, Pa'd hole himself in his garage and tinker with his motorcycle. He spent his weekends on it, oiling it and polishing it.

"'When you last touch me like that?' Ma'd say.

"Pa'd go on caressing it like he hadn't heard her, running his hands over that Navajo blue, playing with the tassels dangling from the black leather seat, varnishing the silver Indian head in the feather headdress on the fender, buffing the 'Indian' logo scrawled in cursive across the tank.

"'See, you and yours are famous,' Pa'd joke with Ma.

"Ma'd laugh this little laugh and say how everybody owned the Indian except the Indian. Look how even Pa's negro ass worked all day assembling Indian Chief motorcycles for his Caucasian bosses. She'd say it like that, *Caucasian*, all bookish and shit. Never, *the white man*.

"I saw Pa wince, once.

"I think Ma was angry with Pa for other things, angry for having loved him, angry about the sweet nothings oozing from that strawberry tongue of his, making promises he couldn't keep, like how he'd take us away to some place better after the Choctaw folk refused to let Ma enroll me after I was born. They said it was because I didn't make the blood quantum. Ma was already at the limit, one half Indian, and she'd chosen to marry Pa, and so!

"Pa said Ma's people wouldn't enroll me 'cause I was Black. He said if I'd been born looking less like him and more like Ma, her people might've let me in. Ma snapped that it was because of federal law, it had nothing to do with the traditions of the nation, Pa knew federal law was shrinking the Native nations, so what the hell was his problem? And what did it matter anyway, wasn't he taking us someplace else? But Pa never did take Ma and me away from Mississippi, like he'd said he would. He and Ma settled just outside Pearl River, where Ma could be near her people. I think Ma was happy to be near her people, though she never did forgive Pa for that, for the humiliation of being so close and yet now so far."

"Wait, so you're like, *Indian?*" I said.

Shaniqua nodded. "I'm Choctaw from Ma's side of the family, and I got Ojibwe from Pa's side, though the census folk snuffed out that part of his lineage a long time ago. My Choctaw name is Osyka. It means 'Soaring Eagle.'"

"Soaring Eagle! My name means 'Loved' in isiNdebele."

"Loved! I like that. Now, we gotta work on getting you a little more loved-up, girl. You been bopping around like a headless chicken ever since you got here."

I chuckled. "I only ever saw Indians in the Westerns on TV," I said, after a while. "We'd play cowboys and Indians with my cousins, and everyone always wanted to be the cowboys."

"You also played that game?" said Shaniqua. "Back in Zimbabwe?"

"Uh-huh," I said. "That's what we watched on TV, America."

Shaniqua sighed. "Pa was always dreaming about Africa. Maybe that's where he ran off to." After a while, she asked, quite suddenly, "Did you grow up with your pa?"

I paused. "He lived in New York."

I told her how I had visited him as a child. I went on and on as though I were back there, transfixed by my father's animated face as we stood—me, him, Candice, and Péralte—expelling frosty breaths atop the Empire State Building; or, another time, the four of us still, watching the East River flow porpoise-colored beneath us as we stood on the Brooklyn Bridge, dragging sheets of ice in its currents; or the time when it was just the two of us, my father and I, puffed up in our bomber jackets before the Statue of Liberty like a pair of exotic, migratory birds. Somewhere in the background, Mr. C's Cheshire face loomed large.

Shaniqua became uncharacteristically quiet.

"What is it?" I said.

"Nothing."

"Tell me."

"It's just . . . you talk about your pa like he's Superman, or something. Like he was perfect."

"But he was."

Shaniqua snickered. "These men be some real trash daddies."

I felt a heat welling up in me. I wanted to slap Shaniqua. To slam her against a wall. To punch her into it. To punch her through it. To jump onto her back and curl my legs around her waist and tear into her neck.

"My daddy loved me."

Shaniqua opened her mouth, but then seemed to change her mind. Shrugging, she stared at me through her hand mirror. I couldn't read her expression, but it made me feel itchy, and shy.

I pulled on her hair as I plaited the rest of the cornrows.

"Ow," she cried over and over, raising her hand to stay mine. "Ouch!"

"Oops," I said, pulling and pulling. "Sorry."

The rest of the cornrows came out crooked, like the cornfields of the proverbial village drunk who staggers from homestead to homestead begging for something to soothe his parched throat before the sun has even struck noon.

Professor Elbaz's shadow gleamed on the polished surface of the oakwood table, pantomiming his movements. I watched first the table, following the murky sweep of his light-beige shadow as it flicked a wrist, and then raised my eyes just above his head.

There were eight of us Programmers seated around the heavy, oval studio table in one of the rooms on the first floor of The Program building. We were each from a selected concentration, astrophysics and quantum mechanics and ethno-astronomy and biophysics and space technology and computer programming and musicology and one of the lesser arts, fiction or poetry, I couldn't remember which. Professor Elbaz, convener of our special, eclectic class, sat at the head of the table.

He was telling us about his role as director of The Program, though he didn't mention his groundbreaking work on exoplanets—he'd just discovered a young, Earthlike planet orbiting a supergiant star in our galaxy, and his face was everywhere: in the scientific journals and in the magazines and on the front page of the *New York Times*, where he narrated his beginnings as an astronomer crouching beneath the fibrous Joshua tree in his parents' backyard in Mesa, Arizona, at age eleven, gazing at the stars through a cardboard telescope he had made.

*Looking up there filled me with awe and wonder but also a profound loneliness*, he said. *I felt so small. "Are we all there is?" I wondered. Well, we no longer have to look up at the skies and be confounded by the mysteries of the universe—we can now point at a star and know other planets outside our solar system exist! Ours is one planet among many. We're a cosmic community. And we're just at the tip of the iceberg. It's only a matter of time before we discover alien life, perhaps even a life form like ours.*

He didn't look at all like a celebrity academic in his creased powder-blue shirt, with his balding round head and his shadow beard. He didn't speak like one, either, his tenor voice hushed, his hands making fluid motions in the air, like he was painting a diagram.

I'd read, in the *New York Times*, that he'd named the exoplanet he'd discovered Zara, after his daughter.

I stared at his pearly teeth. They dipped into handsome, wine-red gums. I tried to imagine his daughter. When I looked up into his eyes, I saw that he was watching me. Shaniqua nudged me, and I turned away, blushing, and fixed my eyes on the wall opposite.

A print of a drawing titled *Allegory of America* hung on the wall. It was of the Florentine explorer and astronomer, Amerigo Vespucci, and his discovery of America. In it, he stood with a brass astrolabe in one hand and a banner of the Southern Cross constellation in the other. In the far distance, to his right, fluttered a ship. Before him, a bare-breasted woman in a feather headdress and a matching skirt sat on a hammock. Her right hand rested on the net for support, while her left was raised toward Amerigo. The inscription *A M E R I C A* curved toward her from behind a tree, written back to front.

I supposed the print drawing was meant to inspire us, to symbolize the discoveries we could make and the greatness we could aspire to with the innovations of astronomy. Perhaps we, too, could discover our own New Worlds.

I glanced at a box of donuts sitting on a small, round table in the corner by the large window overlooking a sloping lawn, which was shaded by a giant, ropy tree. I licked my lips and swallowed, swallowed and licked my lips.

As though he could read my mind, Professor Elbaz said, "Please, those are for you. Seminar starts in twenty minutes."

For a moment, no one stood up. Then a thick boy in baggy jeans and a form-fitting, checkered shirt buttoned all the way up to his Adam's apple got up and made a beeline for the donut table. I leapt after him. I stood next to him, pretending to contemplate the donuts, waiting for a civilized amount of time to pass before selecting one. I wanted nothing more than to grab them and stuff them all in my mouth.

My heart sank when the boy's long, greedy fingers curled around the biggest donut, the chocolate one with a hole in the middle. I watched as he brought the delectable delight to his lips, sinking his teeth into its chocolatey softness. Flakes flicked to the ground, begging to be licked.

The boy turned and held out his free hand, blinking at me through a pair of oversized, prescription aviator glasses. I glared at him and opened my mouth, ready to exchange some nasty words. Instead, I began to stutter, taking in his shimmering cacao skin, his fleshy lips a titillating pecan tint where they met.

"Péralte? Is that you?"

"What!" he said, spreading his thickset arms. "What?! Come here, you!"

I took in the pimpled expanse of his face, the shadow of a mustache shading his upper lip, his heaving chest straining against his shirt.

"You've grown so big," I said.

He threw back his huge head and laughed. I lowered my eyes. People had turned to stare. But he didn't seem to mind. He stepped forward and threw his arms around me.

"To think we used to share a bed!" he said, chuckling.

I blushed, remembering how I had pinched him night after night, aiming for his arms and his waist and the soft, tender flesh above his throat. The night he caught me, he'd stared and stared at me in the darkness, his breath stale and warm on my face, his eyes boring lunar holes through me. I had almost wished, the following morning, that he'd ratted me out to his mother. I had hated the weight of this secret between us, this sense that I owed him for his silence, which had felt like kindness but also like condescension, somehow.

"What are you doing here?" I said, averting my gaze.

"What are *you* doing here?" he said, chuckling. "I just returned two weeks ago from Haiti. It was my first time there! Can you believe it? Probably would've spent the rest of the year there if Moms hadn't intercepted my acceptance letter from The Program. We got in, baby!" He grinned.

I scowled at the mention of his mother. I had sent her rambling emails in my teens fantasizing about how she could help me escape my life, and she'd never replied.

"You OK?" he said.

I wasn't about to tell him about my unrequited letters to his mother, and so I blurted the first thing that came to mind. "How was Haiti?"

"It was a lot," he said, his wide brow creasing. "Like, some real nasty shit went down when I was home."

"You consider Haiti your home?" I said.

"'Course it's home, what d'you mean, do I consider Haiti home?"

"But you're American," I said.

"What the fuck does that mean?"

"You twang a lot, like you're trying to force air out of your nose, and don't sound like the Haitians, who talk like they're spitting something out of their mouths."

I'd seen Haitians on TV, and they definitely didn't sound like Péralte.

"What the fuck is your problem?" he said.

"No, I—"

"Careful not to drop that jaw, sis."

With that, he turned and shuffled away. I watched him, his buttocks bouncing in his baggy jeans as he walked. My eyes darted about, the heat rising to my face. I pretended to study the donuts on the round table, assessing their circumference, the sheen of their coating, the fluffiness of their rotund bodies. I picked up a caramel coated one and tried to stuff it in my mouth.

"Well, that was something."

I turned to find a lanky boy with a shag of blond hair standing behind me. His eyes were an impossible shade of jade, shimmering like a pair of Lanx Borealis, the only greenish star in the sky visible to the naked eye.

"I'm Richard," said the boy. "Though I'm no Dick." He grinned, revealing a pair of chipped front teeth. Then, as though somebody had let slip a gaffe, he cupped his mouth. When I didn't say anything, he added, curling his lips over his chipped incisors, "My friends call me Rick."

I shook his hand. "Athandwa," I said.

"What's that, miss?" Even after a few tries, he couldn't get it right. "You're the first person from Africa I've met," he said, grinning.

I raised an eyebrow. "I'm from New York."

He laughed, his shoulders heaving.

"You think it's funny that I'm from New York?"

His laughter gurgled, drying up in his throat.

I sighed. I was already tired, in my short two weeks back in America, of having to answer the same damn questions everywhere I went, like how come I spoke good English? The first time this happened I was at Boulder Bank trying to open an American bank account. The teller kept saying she couldn't hear what I was saying. I'd wanted to tell her that she was swallowing her *T*s, but how come I could hear her perfectly well?

Instead, I said, "I'm sorry," and then, speaking slowly, "Open. Account. *Please*."

"Oh! I'll be happy to help ya! Just gimme a sec!" She turned around and disappeared behind one of the glass cubicles at the back.

I resolved to try and speak slowly, so the people of America could hear me, letting the words drool from my mouth as though I were only just now learning how to speak. I thought, something hot rising from my neck and up to my face, how my teenage etiquette lessons weren't helping me now, in America.

Our head girl, Grace Hendricks, had stood straight-backed in front of our etiquette class, her navy blazer made as though to match her eyes, her blonde hair pinned severely into place, with nary a strand astray, and commanded us in the ways of womanhood.

How to walk: *Walk with your back straight, tummy tucked in. Don't slouch—nobody likes a sloucher—you'll end up with a hunch back. Walk with pride—come on! —walk like a Girls' College girl.*

I'd walked that walk nearly every weekday for six arduous years, marching across the city center to catch the school bus on the other side of town, pausing before food and mealie-meal and fuel queues, like a lady, and mumbling, "Excuse me? Sorry? Pardon me, sir? Please, may I pass? Excuse me?" to the brawling crowds, who neither excused me nor let me pass, forcing me instead to elbow my way through and battering me about in the process. I admit, I gave as good as I got.

How to drink tea: *Always pour milk before the tea, either/or when it's coffee. Sit with your legs crossed or pressed firmly together. Hold the saucer at chest level, bringing the cup daintily to your lips. Don't make that uncultured slurping sound.*

I had made it a point, at funerals and weddings and other such family gatherings, to sit demurely in the corner, among the adults, holding my saucer to my breast, or otherwise one of those flat, plastic plates popular in less fortunate homes—for I could not very well drink tea without a saucer of some kind, though I often had to do without milk, which was in short supply and had become a luxury. I would incline my head every so often and take a sip from my teacup, frowning pointedly whenever an aunt or some visitor or, much to my chagrin, Mama herself, slurped their tea, making that embarrassing sucking sound. My cousins, who were constellated nearby, would watch me, snickering and giggling. I ignored them with the hubris of one destined for greater things.

How to laugh: *Don't throw your limbs all over the place and yawn your mouth so wide everyone can count your teeth. Why, a lady doesn't behave that way! Bring your hand to your lips and laugh politely—a soft 'hahaha,' and not a rowdy 'HAHAHAHA.'*

"Laugh with me!" Grace Hendricks had declared, like a cheerleader, marching back and forth, her hands clasped behind her back with what then seemed a lofty sagacity. "Come, try it out!"

"Hahaha! Hahaha! Ha. Ha. Ha . . ."

"Make it sofff-ter, come on, a little soffff-ter, like this, hahaha, you hear that? Keep it polite. Let's try it again, hahaha . . ."

"Hahaha . . . Haaaa. Haaaa. Haaaa. Ha."

"Much better. Let's do it one more time . . ."

"Hahaha . . . haahahaaa. . . ."

"One more time!"

"Hahaha! . . . Hahaha. . . . Haaaaa haaaaa haaaa . . ."

I'd worked hard to get the softness of that laughter right, to mold my mouth into just the right oval shape. All those hours spent etiquetting, straight-backed until my back hurt, smiling through it all, piping English through my nose, and now the Midwesterners of America, who swallowed their *T*s and drawled their *R*s, were telling me *they* couldn't hear what *I* was saying. It was an abomination upon my tongue, and upon the skills of my etiquette mentor, Grace, and upon the English language in general. Why, our ancestors, the British, would be absolutely mortified.

When the teller reappeared from one of the cubicles at the back with a form, she'd said, "Your English is so good!"

"What?"

"Your English! It's so good!"

"Thank you," I said. "So is yours."

She began to snort uncontrollably.

"Are you OK?" I asked.

She paused. "Oh, you were serious? I thought . . ."

"Yes. Your English is very good. You must just stop swallowing your *T*s."

She'd begun laughing again, all giggly, like she had the hiccups. I hadn't known what to do with this, so I'd thanked her again. Later, when I told Shaniqua what the bank teller had said about my English, she scowled and called the teller "a dumb ho." It was the kind of sassy thing an older sister would say. It pleased me to know Shaniqua had my back.

The second question that irritated me no end, was where was I from? The speaker would pause when I said I was from New York, and then ask where I'd come from before that. I'd scowl and shrug and ask why the hell it mattered, rolling my eyes at having to state the obvious: "America is a nation of immigrants." And, to prove this point: "Where is your family from, originally?"

"Ireland."

Or,

"I'm a third generation American; my grandfather emigrated from Germany."

Or,

"Immigrants? Settlers is more like it. What d'you mean where the fuck am I from? I'm from here, *yes*, right here, wherever the hell you're standing. I was here when the bison were humping on the prairie. This damn glass and steel is the soil of where I'm from. What the fuck kind of question is that, where am I from? Where're *you* from?"

Or,

"Why are you asking where I'm from? Are you with immigration services? Is it ICE? Are you ICE?"

. . .

I would delicately steer the conversation back to the matter of my origins, reiterating, "My father lived in New York. I'm a New Yorker, like I told you."

The more belligerent species of American would accuse me, indignant with patriotic fervor, of dealing in non sequiturs.

"Where are you from?" I asked Rick now.

"Gainesville," he said. "Down in Missouri. Well, my pops' great-great-grandpops lived in Boston for a few years after he came over from Scotland on one of the ships. But other than that, we're prairie bred."

"So, you're from Scotland."

"No, we're American," he said, frowning. "From right here."

"Are you Native American?"

"I'm *American*, like I already told you."

"Then—" Sigh. "Never mind."

"My pops' great-great-grandpops helped throw the chests of tea off them British ships into the Boston Harbor way back when the British were tryna force their colonial tax down our throats," Rick said, speaking slowly, like I was hard of hearing.

I didn't know what to say to this, so I said, "The British colonized us, too."

"The bastards," said Rick, chuckling. Then, leaning toward me and inclining his head, he whispered, "I guess we're the misfits here, huh?"

I was about to ask what his problem was, why he and I, and not anyone else in particular, should be misfits at The Program, when Professor Elbaz cleared his throat. There was a collective hush as we took our seats.

"I want to assure you that you're meant to be here, all of you," began Professor Elbaz, his tenor voice trembling. I wondered if he, like us, was nervous, but of course this was silly: we were the novices and he was the master; he had even shaken Obama's hand, and we were here to learn from him, perhaps with the hope of one day also shaking a presidential hand.

"Some of you may be suffering from impostor syndrome," said Professor Elbaz. "I want you to rest assured that you've been carefully selected. The Program has a zero point five percent acceptance rate. We believe one hundred percent in your talent . . ."

Zero point five percent acceptance rate! I looked around the table, my heart hammering my chest. I wondered if some of the others were suffering from impostor syndrome, like the professor had said. Rick was fluttering his eyes about as though he did not know where he was or how he had gotten there. And Péralte looked too cocky for his own good, glancing at me every so often as though I'd insulted his mother. I scowled at him. I, certainly, did not suffer from impostor syndrome. This exclusive club was all I had dreamed of, ever since my father died; this dream deferred (Would it dry up like a raisin in the sun? Or fester like a sore—and then run?).

"Our ragtag seminar is going to parse out the intricacies of world-making," said Professor Elbaz, his voice an enigmatic whisper. "What does it mean, *to make a world*? We're not just scientists and artists and thinkers. We're *influencers*. The culture-makers of tomorrow." He slapped the oval table, his sausage fingers splayed like a surgeon's.

"Professor," I said, raising a tentative hand. "How about we go around and introduce ourselves? So we get to know everybody?"

I thought it a good sign, to show verve. I was firing a warning shot at my peers. *Get ready, bitches.*

"Dean," said Professor Elbaz.

I hesitated. "Professor Elbaz—"

"My name is Dean."

". . . Din."

Titters rose and crested in my wake.

"*Dean*. Say it with me—*Deeean*."

"Sorry," I mumbled. "Professor El—Dean."

"There you go!"

I dropped my eyes.

"I'll go first," said Rick, flashing his chipped front teeth. He was studying astrophysics, he said. His mission was to understand the sublime building blocks of nature at the quantum level. He was going to solve Einstein's theory of everything. The class broke out in excited chatter. Rick grinned and cupped his mouth.

He'd always seen numbers in his head, he said, from the time he was a boy, even when they'd gone out into the forest with his brother Willie. Willie had shown him how to stand still and watch for the four-foot beavers along Lick Creek. He taught him how to watch and how to wait. The only thing that moved as his brother tracked the beavers was the rifle in his hand, gliding through the air with stealthy intuition. And then a gunshot would crack the still, vanilla-scented air, lurching

Rick's heart, crawling ants up and down his legs, scrambling the tidy numbers in his head. And so he took to painting, instead. He hadn't thought he'd be any good at it, but it calmed him, gave the world a different kind of orderliness, and he found he could dab the four-foot furries onto paper until the splotches were the likeness of the real thing.

Rick's Lanx Borealis eyes shimmered. He placed his hands palm up on the table. They were big and tan and leathery, not at all how I imagined a painter's hands would be.

Willie was good with his hands, Rick said. And though he'd called Rick a sissy for the hunting, he'd made the paintbrushes Rick used, when he wasn't making car pipes at General Motors. Well, first he was at General Motors, and then he helped bottle drinks at Coca-Cola, and then he helped grow sugar beets at Amalgamated, and now he just stayed at home.

"First in my family to go to college," said Rick, pressing a hand to his chest.

I thought this would make him proud, but he grimaced and looked away.

"I love painting 'cause it helps me with my math," he said, his face radiant again. "Something about putting a world together on a canvas and trying to make sense of it through numbers. And it's all come together." He grinned. "I'm working on some paintings for this big science project at Infinity! Got a call from Tommy Long himself. I'd say more, but they made me sign some papers." He smiled as though ruefully with his lips pressed together, but you could tell he was anything but.

I couldn't pretend not to be jealous. I would have died and bore the pain of resurrection ten times for the chance to work with Thomas Long, especially at his new aerospace company, Infinity Inc.

Tommy Long had seen Rick's paintings in his alma mater magazine, said Rick, grinning like a Cheshire cat. He liked their *nostalgic futurism*, he'd said. They harkened to the forgotten splendor of the Midwest, taking the viewer back to a pristine wilderness.

"Pristine wilderness?" said Mausi.

"Didn't they teach you about that at Harvard?" said Rick, sneering. Suddenly the air was still, and consequential.

I gazed at Mausi, filled with sudden admiration. I didn't know she'd gone to Harvard. She had come to The Program from the Hopi Reservation in northern Arizona and was also studying quantum physics, using the latest advancements in Hopi astronomy and Indigenous science to build on Einstein's quantum theory. I was eager to learn about her work in Hopi astronomy. I was hoping it might help me decipher my father's work on Bantu geometries.

"*We* were your pristine wilderness," she went on, seemingly unfazed, blinking at Rick, whose rigid, homiletical face had turned pink. "We paid the price."

"I thought it was the slaves from Africa?" said Bhaskor. He had come to The Program from New Delhi, and the words *slave* and *Africa* rolled off his tongue with a thick, particular emphasis, ending in a high pitch.

The class looked from Péralte to Shaniqua to me. I blinked at them and then at the oakwood table. I didn't know any slaves, and I didn't think anyone in my family had been a slave.

"What the fuck y'all looking at?" said Péralte, his wide brow glistening.

"I dunno why y'all got eyes on me," said Shaniqua. "I'm Choctaw."

"Did you just say you're Native American?" said Lisa, tucking a blonde strand of hair behind her ear. She had come down from San Francisco on the West Coast. If I squinted hard enough, I could see brunette roots sprouting from her scalp.

"Afro-Choctaw," said Shaniqua. "You got a problem with that?"

A clumsy silence ensued. I looked around, from Lisa, to Rick, to

Bhaskor, who wore a baffled, lopsided smile, to Chun, who had their thin, almost translucent eyebrows raised—they had come down from NYC, where they had graduated summa cum laude from Columbia.

Mausi's candor hovered in the room, large and incongruous. Something struggled on her face. It made her lips twitch, and I felt my lips twitch. Her left cheek spasmed. My hands tingled.

"We're onto something here," said Professor Elbaz—Dean—clasping his hands beneath his chin. "What does it take, to build new worlds?"

The silence stretched before us. I didn't know what to do, if maybe I should get up and excuse myself and go to the bathroom or something. Then Péralte opened his mouth and began talking loudly about his project, and I found I could breathe again.

He introduced his project with the same entitlement he'd exhibited by the donut table while munching on the flaky, rotund chocolate donut I'd been eyeing. I became incensed at the thought of the chocolate donut. I knew it was irrational, but I couldn't help it. The donut ballooned in my mind, becoming this gigantic, insurmountable thing that somehow belonged to me and of which I'd been unjustly deprived.

I stared at Péralte. He was going on about designing some software for astronomers. All I saw when I looked at his glistening cacao face was the sugar-dusted chocolate donut. He said something about artificial intelligence and computer graphics and 4D galaxy simulations. I stared at his moving lips and saw the donut's hollow center.

"Any astronomer will be able to plug theoretical data into the program and get a simulation of the galaxy they're studying," he said. "It will, like, give them instant info about the properties of the hundred-billion-plus galaxies observable in the universe."

"A hundred billion plus?" I said, like I was hearing this for the first time. I felt compelled to say something, anything. I wanted to bite off a chunk of his sugar-dusted chocolaty face.

"Yup, and counting," said Péralte, looking pleased, as though he were the one who had discovered the galaxies.

I wanted to dive into his donut hole of a mouth.

"It's pretty amazing." He sighed. "And we're the intelligence that gets to apprehend it all. It's super cool stuff. I'm also hoping to use the program for my gaming and video-game design stuff." He grinned sheepishly.

"You design video games?" said Shaniqua. "That's so cool!"

"My step-dad and I used to play," said Péralte. "He was pretty good. I taught him a few things about gaming, and he taught me some pretty cool stuff about the universe."

He threw back his head and laughed, his voice a melancholic basso cantante timbre. It engulfed me, sweet and mellifluous. I thought about the things my father could have taught me about the universe, the things he should have taught me but had taught Péralte instead, these teachings that now made him throw back that huge head of his and yawn his mouth so wide and laugh so heartily.

Suddenly, I was no longer in the studio room seated around the oval table but in the middle of the maize fields behind Mama's vanilla-colored cottage. I was a child, and Mama was bellowing my name. Her yell was a Pavlovian bell; I abandoned whatever activity I was ensconced in—the solitary, fanciful games of an only child, such as training my beloved ants for their Olympic Games—and set off for the cottage. I ran past the peacocks marching back and forth in the backyard, their parakeet- and basil-colored plumage on display, the sapphire ovals at the tips of their feathers shimmering, so sublime, like the eyes of God.

Into Mama's cozy, box-shaped cottage I hurtled, mercifully cushioned by her gingerbread sofas clothed in their maroon crocheted covers, my feet leaving dusty imprints on the polished cement floor, which gleamed so brilliantly you could make out the outline of your shadow mimicking your movements in doppelgänger fashion. I grabbed the receiver from Mama's hand, ignoring her cries at the sight of my powdery prints that had carried onto her meticulously scrubbed maroon carpet, and yelped into the phone. There it was, the bass-like tenor of my father's voice, trundling across the airwaves all the way from America. There I stood, suffused with visions of him there with me, at home in Zimbabwe.

Here was Péralte's canorous basso cantante voice floating across the room. No, that basso cantante timbre belonged to my father. It was my father calling me.

I knew, with a sinking feeling, that The Terrors had returned.

was twelve when The Terrors began.

They started as a surge of heat rippling through my body one rainy December day. I was standing in Mama's tiny kitchen, stirring a pot of frothy porridge on the four-plate stove, the tap leaking into a bowl in the sink to my left, the fridge humming incessantly behind me.

The heat clutched my chest, making the steely sky peeping through the high, rectangular window above the stove smart and hurt my eyes. I gasped. My hands dislodged at the wrists and hung suspended in the air. I lurched forward, overcome by nausea, almost lobbing my face into the pot. But nothing gushed from my mouth, only the involuntary, retching simulation of vomiting, and the terrible feeling of sickness that accompanies it.

I called out to Mama, my voice a whine. She rushed to the kitchen and placed a soapy hand on my arm—she must have been doing the laundry that day. The weight of her hand seemed to bring me back to myself. I allowed her to lead me down the short, cement corridor of our gingerbread house to my room, where I lay on the bed and buried my face in the StaSoft-scented duvet, the only fabric softener Mama ever used.

The Terrors would attack on a seemingly random day, a tingling coursing through my limbs, making me shiver, followed by a feeling of . . . *dread*. This is the only word I can think of that comes close to capturing that sensation, so terrible was it, there are no words adequate enough to describe it. I would black out, coming to, to find I had somehow moved from the toilet seat, where I had suddenly slumped over while peeing, to the bed where Mama stood over me, my ankle throbbing.

My high-pitched whimpers became a familiar feature in the house, a siren that would send Mama bolting to my side. Though The Terrors were so awful, I came to enjoy the attention she lavished on me as a result.

At first, Mama's eyes sparkled at this new, mysterious challenge posed by The Terrors, injecting her with a new energy. She took me to CIMAS Medical Center. I was thirteen. The doctor was a short pimple of a man with stained teeth and a startling, jolly laugh. He shined an oblong white instrument shaped like a toothbrush into my ear and tapped my knees with a strange little hammer and prodded the space between my budding breasts with a black-roped proboscis, chuckling like there was something amusing to be found there. Finally, he declared, beaming his brown teeth at us, that he was unable to find anything physically wrong with me. Irked, Mama took me to another doctor, and then another and another, but they, too, couldn't find anything wrong, linking The Terrors to the travails of puberty or hormonal imbalances caused by my menstrual cycle, or something I might have been allergic to.

Not long after, The Terrors, which had brought Mama and I closer together, began to mutate, and like a bad omen things really went south in the country, the shortages escalating, becoming so severe as to morph into a permanent feature of our lives, just as my father had predicted.

The Terrors metamorphosed, as though some insatiable virus that, having conquered a territory of the body, moves on to new ventures. They caused my body to do all sorts of strange things that, when not outright terrifying, were just plain embarrassing. My days became filled with the dread of anticipation. Out of the blue, I would be taken over by a feeling of nausea, an unpleasant, metallic taste tingling on my tongue. If I were eating, I would be compelled to spit out whatever was in my mouth, or else I would start spitting globs of saliva at whoever was near me, unable to control any of it.

Sometimes, I would sprint down the street while walking, without cause, as though perhaps trying to quell the heat swelling in my chest. I would sit abruptly on the ground and begin bawling, outright wailing and sobbing, my face cupped in my hands, unable to stop.

One day, while standing in the longest bread queue known to man outside Meikles Supermarket in town, my legs gave way. I began to convulse, my limbs twitching involuntarily. I was sixteen. The sight of a dozen strange faces huddled above me, crumpled with concern and a voyeuristic curiosity, filled me with fear. They continued to stare, some fanning me with their hands and items of clothing. Someone shoved a piece of bread between my lips, so I wouldn't bite my tongue, they said.

No one bothered to call an ambulance—it wouldn't have come, there was no fuel in the garages. And besides, I did not want to go to one of those terrible government hospitals and have to crowd with the city's poor, stacked in the halls and out on the pavement, making suffering so normal as to evoke no state of urgency from the nurses, who walked about with hardened eyes. The government hospitals were overwhelmed, and people died from common ailments they should not have otherwise died from.

It was during those days when the hospitals had gotten bad, really bad, the nurses always on strike, the wards always short of basic meds and supplies. Only the private hospitals could be trusted to provide proper care, and because the country was imploding, with inflation at some crazy quintillion percentage no one had ever heard of in the history of the world, so that a new million or billion or trillion dollar bill had to be introduced to the national currency nearly every week, these private hospitals refused to accept medical aid, demanding payment in cash before they would admit you, and usually in rands or US dollars, at that.

I became increasingly afraid of The Terrors, afraid for myself but also for Mama, who was a civil servant and got paid in the local, useless currency, and couldn't afford a hospital stay should I need to be admitted. My father had been dead for four years. We were having problems with his estate, thanks to a fall out between Mama and the estate lawyer. The lawyer stopped replying to Mama's letters, saying there was no money, hyperinflation had gobbled it up and the imploding economy had eroded our stocks and investments. He had complained about the cost of my private education and how Mama kept asking for more and more money for my upkeep. But Mama was relentless, insisting this was what my father would have wanted, for me to be cared for, for me to get the best education money could buy. And though this, trying to live as though my father were still alive and could exercise his will, was absurd, if not a little tragic, Mama's efforts to try and fill this hole that could never be filled made me love her all the more.

There had been so much money, she said to the lawyer. How could it all be gone? The lawyer must have stolen it. The lawyer threatened to sue, and mama threatened to sue. The lawyer sent a letter from his lawyers, and Mama sent a letter from her lawyers. And so, this was going on, we were in a sort of limbo, and The Terrors were terrorizing me, and I worried constantly that I would have to go to hospital.

I grew suspicious of my body and its endless machinations. I was at that age when one is laden with self-consciousness, when one's body seems to be nothing but an oddball of chubby limbs still clinging obstinately to child-fat and also strange new passions, and every gesture or call of attention feels like an awkward misstep. And now, here was my own body failing me, announcing some defect on the part of its owner and calling attention to itself where I would have liked to hide.

Khulu, my grandfather, suggested we go and see a nyanga. He and Mama got into a fierce argument about it, Mama accusing Khulu of trying to invite evil spirits into her home with his pagan traditions. Eventually, Mama capitulated. That was when I knew things were bad, really bad, because there was nothing Mama loved more at that time than her beloved church.

Whereas you could walk straight-backed into a doctor's offices with the stamp of civilization on your back, a visit to your local nyanga was the kind of heathen thing you wouldn't exactly share with your church group over tea. I was sworn to secrecy about it, to tell neither my friends nor my cousins nor any one of our nosy, gossiping relatives, and especially not the church ladies.

You had to know which nyanga was really a traditional healer and which one was a witch or a wizard, in the business of concocting curses and the like, and which one was a downright charlatan, with no ability to even turn your irritating neighbor into a lowly rat. Khulu said though he couldn't vouch for everything that would come out of this particular nyanga's mouth, his herbs and medicines were known to work wonders, curing even the most confounding ailments. And so, we visited his room-sized shrine at the back of his township house in Mzilikazi.

The room was round with a conical asbestos roof. It was at the back, taking up all the space in the yard. Incense rose from a firepit in the center, making the interior at once foggy and spectral. Mama, Khulu, and I knelt before the nyanga, our heads bowed. I kept darting my eyes at him. He was lathered in oils from his neck right down to his paunch, his spindly legs protruding from a skirt made of cow skin. I was thoroughly frightened by the animal hides hanging on the walls and the wooden dolls lined up on the floor.

The nyanga grabbed my hand and turned it palm up. He traced my lifeline with his finger, running it across the width of my palm, muttering under his breath. It tickled. I couldn't help it and burst out laughing. The nyanga glowered at me, the leopard-skin coronet atop his dreadlocked head shuddering. I gazed into his glinting penny eyes and tried to keep the contents of my face in their proper, solemn order.

He retrieved his medicine bag and held it up to my mouth. I gazed at it, my nose twitching from the mélange of herbs wafting from the stained, brown muslin cloth. The nyanga instructed me to blow into the bag. I obeyed, blowing and blowing until I began to cough. The nyanga instructed me to stop. He began to shake the medicine bag, chanting an incantation I couldn't make out. He chanted for a long time, until my legs began to burn from kneeling.

Suddenly, he upended the medicine bag, flinging its contents across the shimmering, charcoal cement floor. Bones, stones, feathers, and other objects I couldn't make out scattered, forming peculiar constellations. The nyanga peered at them, prodding them with his stick. He sat still for a long time, his eyes flitting from one celestial object to another in his little cosmos. Finally, he regarded me.

Was there a boy? he said.

I stiffened, thinking of Rufus and the Rogerses' farm.

There was a boy, said the nyanga, chuckling.

I could feel Mama's eyes on me. I swore there was no boy. There had never been a boy. There would never be a boy.

The nyanga chuckled.

There was also an aunt, he said.

"An aunt?" said Mama.

Yes. An aunt with the tongue of a snake who had bewitched the family.

I could see Mama making mental calculations, trying to work out which aunt the nyanga may have been talking about. There was one aunt, Aunt Tho, whose slimy tongue had always reminded me of a lizard.

The nyanga handed me an herbal concoction in an old two-liter bottle of Coca-Cola. I was to bathe in it twice a day, first thing in the morning and last thing in the evening right before bed. Khulu thanked him and handed him a crumpled envelope. The nyanga licked his thumb and began counting the crisp, blue hundred-trillion-dollar bills, flicking them between his fingers. Finally, he nodded. Khulu, Mama, and I shuffled out.

Later that day, Mama listed all the relatives we had visited in the past months, grouping them by "deaths, weddings, baby shower" and "miscellaneous." We would need to stop visiting for a while, she said, until she figured out who the nyanga had been talking about. I had never known her to be superstitious. I should have realized, then, the toll The Terrors were taking on her. They had wrecked not just my world, but hers, too. But I was too self-absorbed in the mundane travails that seem colossal in adolescence to think of her. Rather, her superstition embarrassed me.

I lamented how I would no longer get to practice my etiquette lessons. No longer would I enjoy sipping my tea like a lady and side-eyeing my aunts slurping theirs. No longer would I get to turn my nose up at my cousins who, though they smirked and tittered, had started holding their saucers to their chests like I did, inclining their heads and molding their mouths around the rims of their cups and letting the tea seep silently between their lips. With whom would I play these cultured games now?

I poured out my troubles to Rufus. I must have been madly in love or madly in despair, for I had never divulged my shameful condition of The Terrors to anyone. I told Rufus about my visit to the nyanga and how he had been able to divine that there was a boy in my life. That was when he dumped me.

For the rest of that year, The Terrors didn't bother me. For a while, despite Rufus, despite heartbreak, despite the curtailed family visits, it seemed as though I would be all right.

✳

I HAD BEEN so sure The Terrors couldn't follow me across an ocean. But here they were, having scurried into my luggage and followed me to a new world, announcing themselves to people I didn't know. I was so angry at myself, at my body for failing me, at the helplessness I felt at being unable to do anything about it.

For five minutes, ten minutes, I just lay there. Faces had gathered above me, peering down where I'd fallen and now lay, unable to command my limbs to pull my body back up. The faces looked oversize and garish, squeezed together like that, like a bunch of sunflower heads with their petals torn off.

They blurred. One lone face got bigger and bigger, until it was right above me, the magnificent expanse of it filling the whole of my vision. It was Péralte, and he was saying something, but I couldn't make out what. All I could see were his round lips moving in slo-mo, blobs of spit tumbling slowly but determinedly toward me. The bridge of his nose ruffled together, like a pair of pleats. His eyes were magnified by his glasses. I felt them straining to pull me out of my misery. His face moved closer, until it was almost crushing mine. I thought he was going to kiss me. He thrust something to my lips, a cold slip of metal, and a sweet, fizzy liquid sputtered into my mouth. It was Coke. I didn't know what he thought Coke could do for me, but I tried to drink it. I couldn't swallow, and I began to cough, and he tried to lift my head, the sweet boy.

Somebody had called an ambulance. I kept trying to signal that it was OK, all we needed was to give it a few minutes and The Terrors would go away by themselves, just as they had come. I didn't want to go to hospital. I squinted, trying to remember how Zimbabwe had once been the breadbasket of Africa, and I felt very depressed.

The next thing, I was being picked up and placed on a stretcher, and then I was up in the air, bobbing through the crowd and out the door. The dewy, dense September air wrapped itself around me, like a plastic bag. Lights were flashing on the street, firing up the night, like fireworks or parade beacons, swishing red and blue, red and blue. I saw the hulking, black police SUVs parked out on the street, and suddenly the reality of it all hit me, being here on my own, being ferried off to an American hospital with Mama so far away. I began to cry. The blinking cop lights led the procession to the hospital, ahead of us and behind us, clearing the traffic like I was somebody important. The paramedic kept shoving his square-jaw in my face, asking how I was doing, and I was feeling embarrassed of myself and didn't know where to look, so I kept my eyes shut.

At the university hospital, I tried to explain The Terrors to the doctor, but she kept asking me to slow down, to repeat myself, what did I mean, "the terrors"? Could I describe them? When I told her they were like death, she pressed her lips together and scribbled something on her clipboard. I strained to see. *Disoriented. Drugs?* I began to cry. I couldn't help myself. I was exhausted, and frustrated, and I just needed someone to understand me. It seemed to me that even I didn't understand myself. The tears wouldn't stop. They took over, a terror of their own. The doc ordered the nurse to take my blood and run it up to the lab, and to sedate me.

I didn't want to be sedated. I didn't want to be here. I didn't want anything, only to be understood. Only to understand myself. But once the nurse injected the sedative into my drip, I was grateful for it. My body loosened, easing into a foggy, welcome dusk.

couldn't very well call Mama and tell her about The Terrors. She'd get sick with worry, especially since I was far away and she was helpless to do anything about it. She still hadn't forgiven me for leaving, I knew. She might convince me, in my fragile state, to jump onto the next plane home, and then what would become of me?

I'd been feeling like a piece of meat since being admitted to the hospital the evening before, when the nurses had carted me from floor to floor, administering test after test, blood tests and a urine test—for which they'd made me squat over the toilet seat and pee in a stupid little cup—and a mortifying physical exam.

I wished, not for the first time, that I could call Mr. C. But I didn't have his phone number, only a P.O. box address, to which I'd sometimes sent polite thank-you notes for the birthday gifts he sent every year. He never replied, not even when I'd written letting him know I'd gotten into The Program and given him my new address. I'd checked the mailbox every day in the weeks leading up to my trip, but there had been nothing from him. No congratulations for getting into The Program, no acknowledgement of my pending move, nothing. I had stood by the mailbox, swallowing painful breaths, and stared into the distance, across the sprawling savannah grass and the lone mulberry tree standing sentinel, at the houses clustered on the horizon and the swath of pale-blue sky beyond.

I had tried, over the years, to google Mr. C. Nothing ever came up. There was no Facebook account, no LinkedIn, no articles, no pictures, no digital footprint, nothing. He was like a spook.

I'd seen him only once since the ill-fated run-in at the Statue of Liberty; at my father's funeral. I had been standing by the graveside, among the mourners, when this massive man appeared out of nowhere, like an apparition, though he was no apparition at all.

He was towering, he was alpine, he was lofty, he was colossal. He was big—hefty—and big—weighty. His face was wide and solemn and pimpled—and pecan colored, like my father's. He filled the charcoal suit he wore, filled it and filled the world and on that day at my father's funeral he looked down and enveloped my twelve-year-old hand in his adult hand and bent over until his wide face was close to mine, filling the whole of my world, and asked me if I remembered him from New York. It was a while before I recognized Mr. C, that sagging, sorrowful face of his so unlike the charming personality who had ambushed my father and me as we stood contemplating Lady Liberty.

"I'm sorry," he said.

He spoke with a whiff of an accent, something cultured, like our version of the British intonations, with that familiar, clipped stoicism the British like to exude in the face of feeling, recognizable in the men of his age, men like my father who, in their youth, had been experiments in and ambivalent products of a Macaulayan education.

"I'm so sorry . . ."

I looked up at him and was met by his broad nose, so large, that nose, trembling with grief and nose hair, each breath and sigh trembling, trembling through every fiber of that man.

"So so sorry . . ."

He'd kept saying this, that he was sorry. I hadn't known what to do with this, what it was expected I should do with sorry.

No, I couldn't call him, and I couldn't call Mama, either. There was no one to call. I lay my head on the pillow and stared at the breakfast tray by my bedside, brimming with pancakes and juice and a bowl of fruit, and palmed my hands beneath my cheek.

Later that morning, the doctor came with my test results. They had all come back normal, she said. She'd been unable to find anything physically wrong with me, just like I'd known she wouldn't, just as I'd told her, even as she insisted on doing all those tests. She released me, muttering something sinister about my "psychosomatic symptoms."

All I heard was *psycho*. I could feel a terrible headache coming on. I couldn't get out of there fast enough. I was nauseated by it all, the antiseptic smells of the hospital, the drips and the beeping machines, myself.

At home, I lay on Shaniqua's futon in my room surrounded by the comfort of food—an unopened packet of Lays, a plastic bottle of Coca-Cola, and a can of Daufuski oysters I had bought during a clandestine trip to Walmart. I forked the oysters out of the bright red can and into my mouth. I had never had oysters before, and I felt like a fancy bitch, eating the slick, chewy things.

I held the can up to the light as I chewed, appraising the face of the Indian on the cover. He was in profile, as though to show off the large feather headdress draped over his head. The headdress was fastened by what looked like a bejeweled crown, which in turn was held in place by a blue horn. The horn looked disparate, incongruous with the tender mollusks in my mouth. I chewed and studied the can, masticating the oysters with enthusiasm until my jaw ached.

I planned to finish the oysters and then get some sleep. But Péralte came by. Shaniqua showed him to my room. She winked at me, and then frowned at the can of Daufuski oysters in my hand.

I shook the can at her, but she scrunched up her nose. "You know the Native folk of Daufuskie Island, that's where that damn brand gets its name from, didn't even wear them Plains-style headdresses."

She made a face and shuffled out. I placed the can on the floor, beside the futon, and turned to Péralte. I lay sprawled in a block of sunlight slanting through the window. The Saturday sun had a hazy, ephemeral quality, uncannily soft for a humid summer afternoon. Péralte sat on the edge of the futon, his upper body swiveled so he could face me. He clutched a lidded plastic bowl in his lap. My room suddenly seemed so bare with only the futon and the lone chest of drawers, even as the hazy, late-afternoon light softened the harsh bareness of it all. My eyes flitted about, picking out my bra and underwear lying on the floor.

Péralte half-opened the bowl in his hands and stretched it out to me. A nutty, banana aroma filled the room. "I made them myself," he said.

I eyed the muffins and congratulated him on his feat, barely keeping the sarcasm, or was it resentment, out of my voice.

He asked how I was doing. I was feeling embarrassed of myself and didn't know where to look, so I shut my eyes.

"Is there anything I can get you?" he said. When I didn't respond, he whispered, "What happened?"

I pretended not to hear him, hoping he would think I had fallen asleep. But I knew my eyelids were giving me away, fluttering like a bird in fright. I didn't know what to say to him. I didn't want him there. I didn't want anyone there, coming to check up on me. I mumbled for him to leave, please, he had to go. But he just sat there. I opened my eyes and glared at him. He smiled an inscrutable smile and made a cryptic comment about how sometimes, people experience things for which there is no language, and often, the language created to apprehend such inarticulable moments is a fiction in and of itself, shaping worlds and sensibilities out of raw data, at times falling terribly short. He wasn't looking at me as he said this but was gazing at the floor where my dirty undergarments lay strewn.

I inclined my face away from the resplendent light gushing through the window. I told Péralte I didn't want him to visit again. I didn't want him to see me like that, the way I was; I wasn't myself and this was not the impression I wanted him to have of me. He said all right, although he wanted me to know he had formed no impression of me. I felt somehow disappointed to hear this. I wasn't sure what was worse, him having no impression of me or the prospect of him having *some* impression of me, no matter how unflattering.

He was back again the following afternoon. "You're coming over to my place," he said.

"To do what?" Who the hell did he think he was?

"I cooked. Your roommate can come too if she wants. What's her name again? La'Quaysha?"

"*Sha*. Ni-qua."

"Right. Come, get up, put on something, and let's go."

I groaned. "I don't feel like myself," I said.

Péralte shook his head and grabbed my hand, mock-attempting to drag me off the futon. "You'll love my cooking. Besides, you're not well and you're far from home. What would your moms say if she found out you were feeling sick out here all by yourself and no one hadn't bothered to do something nice for you, like make you a home cooked meal? Come on. I'll wait for you in the sitting room. I'll go ask Shantaqua if she wants to come with. I'm giving you five minutes to get ready. OK?" He grinned and winked at me. Then he shuffled out of my room. I could hear him talking to Shaniqua, their muffled voices susurrating into my room.

We set out for Péralte's place, the three of us strolling lethargically in the asphyxiating heat. It was the second week of September, and the summer was still going strong. We ambled down cobbled streets. The charming burnishes on the brick-stone made them look like steaming loaves that had been left in the oven for too long. We walked past wood-paneled, double-story houses with classical white columns and prominent gables, some with steeply sloping roofs and rectangular chimneys, others with intricately patterned eaves and ornate lanterns hanging over the front doors. Some of the houses had white finishes on the windows and quaint, empty wooden swings oscillating on the front porches. They tinged the atmosphere with a suburban nostalgia, as though at any moment a woman with large rollers in her golden hair might come out from one of the houses with the filigreed balustrades, a basket of laundry on her hip, and offer us a pitcher of lemonade.

We passed Infinity Inc., posters with the grinning face of Thomas Long plastered on the trees and electricity poles, their corners limp in the damp heat.

Péralte scowled. "Oh great, the billionaire guy and his space company are in town," he said.

"My cousin worked at one of his Artemis warehouses over the summer last year," said Shaniqua. "He says he couldn't even go to the bathroom without them damn cameras everywhere recording his every move. And they wouldn't pay his medical bills after he hurt his back at work carrying their boxes."

I studied the poster of Thomas Long. He was TV-handsome, with a symmetrical face and striking cheekbones slanting into a strong jaw.

His cobalt eyes complemented his red tie. His blond hair shimmered at us from the poster, as though someone had smeared it with pomade.

"He's pretty," I said.

"Oh, Lord," said Shaniqua, rolling her eyes.

"I wonder what he's doing in town," said Péralte, squinting at the poster. "What the hell is this?"

He ran a finger along a chalky streak running across the poster's pitchy background. Other than Thomas Long's pretty face and the words *Infinity Inc.* at the top in smooth, minimalist Centauri font, there was no context to the poster.

"It looks like an inverted tick," said Shaniqua. "You think it means something?"

"That's Shackleton crater," I said.

"You mean, like, on the moon?" said Péralte.

I nodded. "That's a sliver of sunlight running along the crater's rim."

"Oh wow. So, Infinity Inc. is here for something to do with the moon," said Péralte.

"You think they wanna put a human on there?" said Shaniqua. "Revive NASA's Apollo program 'n' shit?"

"Maybe *he's* the one going to the moon," said Péralte. "I hope they leave him there."

I imagined my father would have gone on this voyage to the moon with Thomas Long, just as he had accompanied him up to the International Space Station all those years ago. Maybe this time, I could have even gone up with them. I simpered.

"He should be president," I said.

Péralte glared at me. "Are you out of your mind?"

He started going on about what kind of place a world built in the image of Thomas Long would be: there'd be more tax cuts for the rich and higher taxes for the rest; a dismantling of worker's unions, like Artemis was already doing, shrinking the income for working class folk so they'd have to compete with one another for fewer and fewer jobs; Thomas Long would monopolize everything, like his company was already doing, buying up distribution companies and gobbling up competitors so everyone, from the government to rival businesses, would have to use his platforms to conduct their businesses; and worst of all, *worst of all*—here Péralte wagged a finger at me as though at a wayward child—the democratic freedoms that had been hard won in the '60s and '70s and were already being eroded, like workers' rights and women's rights and civil rights, would all but disappear; we'd all become wage slaves and work not to realize our own dreams or better our own lives, but to make Thomas Long even richer than he already was, the perfect minions for his dominion.

"Wage *slaves*?" I said, snickering.

"What's wrong with you?" said Péralte. He turned to Shaniqua. "What's wrong with her?"

Shaniqua shook her head. "Pshhh, don't mind her," she said, appraising me like I was a pitiable pet. "She don't even know nothin' 'bout Africa, the history, nothin.' "

They continued talking like I wasn't there. I had half a mind to turn back, but I was really hungry and I couldn't wait to taste the food Péralte had cooked. Just thinking of it made my mouth water.

It was true Shaniqua kept bombarding me with all these mystical questions about Africa. Her tawny eyes would go all sparkly, and out of the blue she'd start quizzing me about Kandake, or Yaa Asantewaa, or Makeda, or Nandi. These last two I knew, at least, Makeda because she was the Queen of Sheba, and who didn't know the Queen of Sheba? And Nandi because she was the mother of Shaka, king of the Zulu, from South Africa, and—here I had paused solemnly, dramatically—the Ndebele, my people, were descendants of the Zulu.

I'd hoped this would impress Shaniqua, but she'd just blinked at me and continued reciting the names of ancient African queens and women warriors I'd never heard of, shaking her head tragically at my blank stare.

Presently, Péralte turned down a stone pathway that led up to a two-story house. It sat at the corner of Dubuque and Bloomington, just two streets down from where Shaniqua and I stayed. A half-tower with large windows and a conical brick-tiled roof rose to our left, append-aged to the rest of the rectangular, wood-paneled house. To our right, a pair of thrushes frolicked in a fluted, copper-colored bird bath partly shaded by a tall, zesty witch hazel shrub. One of the thrushes was dip-ping its pouting beak into the bird bath. Its throat bulged with each gulp. Its companion puffed up its white chest, bringing to prominence black spots that looked like pawpaw seeds etched across its breast. It let out a whistle. I paused to listen to its tweet, overcome by the pleasant timbre, like a high C note on the flute.

"Hurry up," said Péralte, beckoning me. "It's too hot to be outchea."

I shuffled after him and Shaniqua, up a pair of steps, through a swinging screen door and into the apartment on the first floor. He and Shaniqua disappeared into the kitchen. I hovered in the living room and admired a huge, leafy potted plant beside the door to my left, busy pho-tosynthesizing the place, executing its purpose in life, unlike me, who was just standing there like a decoration, yet to discover mine.

The blinds were drawn, draping the interior in gloom. It took me a while to make out the room. A huge flat screen TV loomed over me on the wall to my right. It looked ethereal mounted on there, like some giant extraterrestrial eye. Ambient red lighting glowered behind it, heightening its alien effect, spilling also from the wooden TV stand below, where video game controllers and DVDs and books and a Rubik's Cube poured out. A PlayStation stood in one of the compartments of the TV stand, black and sleek and gorgeous looking. Next to it was a wireless modem.

I stared at the TV, overtaken by a feeling of being inside a spaceship. Multicolored shelves ascended on either side of it, powder-blue and lime and orange and red and green and navy blue. They rose in a stepwise fashion, three on each side. There were PlayStation games lined up on each shelf. The shelves looked like they were made from some sort of glowing neon material. I went over and ran my hand across the red shelf. It was made of glass. Little LED lights glowed inside.

I turned around and circled the room, eyeing the various electronic gadgets lying around, wands and gaming guns and a virtual reality headset, and other stuff I couldn't make out.

It was the space suit in the alcove behind the yellow couch to my left that made me gasp. I stumbled toward it and pressed a palm against the cold, dusty glass casing. I couldn't stop my hand from shaking. I yearned to caress the *F. SIZIBA 2004* badge tucked beneath the dusty visor head, to slip my feet into the trouser legs all the way to the appendaged grey boots. The white-and-black gloves were missing, making the suit look ghastly, as though the hands had been amputated at the wrists. I shuddered and backed away.

The framed photo of my father high up in the International Space Station came into view. It hung in the corner next to the space suit, above a computer desk. My father was smiling, his face glistening beneath the globular visor. I was eleven again, awed and terrified to see him up there. Our teeth had dips and burrows in the same places. We had the same smile, the same button nose, the same lines curving from our eyes to our cheeks. For a wild moment, it was me and not him up there.

I staggered and slumped over the desk. I thought of my father that morning in New York as he presented his paper on Bantu geometries to us, his face haloed by sunlight but also by a luminescence that seemed to emanate from within. Suddenly, I was desperate to go up to space, too, somehow. I needed an epiphany.

"Uncle Frank used to suffer from vertigo, too, just by staring at that photo. He said it felt like he was back in the ISS again."

I spun around. Péralte was standing by the kitchen entrance, robed in a checkered apron, a ladle in hand. He appraised me, smiling.

"You had no *right*," I said, pointing at the photo and then the space suit.

His smile disappeared. "Uncle Frank gave it to Moms," he said, raising his hands in the air. "And she gave it to me when I got into The Program. You know, for inspiration." The ladle wobbled in his raised hand like a clumsy weapon.

"You're lying," I said. My nails were digging into my palms; I hadn't realized I was clenching my fists. "You and your mother are a bunch of liars and a bunch of thieves." I tried to relax my hands.

Péralte wiped his hands on his apron. "I'll talk to Moms," he said, finally. "I . . . I'm sure she'll at least let you have the picture or something. She was really excited to learn you'd also made it into The Program. She said you take after Uncle Frank."

I paused, not knowing what to do. I was pleased to hear what Candice had said about taking after my father, but I couldn't stop trembling.

"Food's ready," mumbled Péralte. He stared at the ladle in his hand.

"Thanks," I said and tried to smile. "I'm really hungry."

Péralte nodded. I tried to look him in the eye, but he wouldn't meet my gaze. He turned and disappeared into the kitchen. I shuffled after him.

I had let my mind go wild with visions of being deprived of the scrumptious smelling food and told to "Get!" but Péralte handed me a plate and pointed out the djon djon, which was a pot of sticky black rice bubbling on the stove, giving off a spicy aroma. He had laid out some pots on the redwood kitchen counter. They were lined up next to a pair of greasy wooden ladles, some half-open spices, a bottle of olive oil and a box of butter with an Indian woman in a feather headdress and a buck-skin cinched around her waist. I peered at the Indian woman. She was kneeling in a meadow, with a blue lake behind her and green cedar trees in the distance. *Land O'Lakes* arched overhead in large, red font. The Indian woman carried what looked like a box of Land O' Lakes butter with the same miniature image of her in her hands.

I pointed at the box of butter. "I keep seeing the same image of Indians everywhere. On everything."

Shaniqua sighed. "Phew, chile. I don't have the energy right now."

Péralte's cooking skills deserved a spot on *MasterChef*. I had thought I could cook, but no; I was trash and had no idea what cooking was. Boy had cooked his heart out: he had made a bright pumpkin soup called joumou, and a dish of pork pieces marinated in Haitian spices called griyo, and pickled cabbage mixed with bonnet peppers, called pikliz, and some sweet-and-sour plantain, jambalaya, mac 'n' cheese, curried corn bread, and apple pie.

I tried to eat it all. But even after stuffing my face, there was still so much food left. Péralte offered us take-home skaftins. Shaniqua said she was too full to ever want to eat again. I eyed the food and then the plastic takeout containers, and then back again. I wanted so much to do the civilized thing and say no. But my greed trumped my shame, and I accepted the djon djon-joumou-griyo-pikliz-sweet-sour plantain-jambalaya-corn bread-apple-pie-filled skaftins Péralte pushed into my hands. I felt ashamed, being so obviously greedy like that.

As we left, I went to the alcove behind the yellow couch and tried to lift the glass box with the space suit. But it was too big, taller than I was, and heavy. I settled for the framed photo of my father high up in the International Space Station.

"I'll be back for the space suit," I said to Péralte.

He lunged forward, then halted. Something on my face must have stopped him. There was a look on his face. It almost made me drop the photo. But I didn't, I clutched it to my chest. I wanted to shout, *You're not even his son*. I wanted to remind him that he'd only lived with my father for a year before he'd died. But then I remembered: I hadn't lived with him at all.

I turned and stumbled out, Shaniqua in tow.

I staggered home with the framed photo under my arm, a bag of Péralte's leftovers in my other hand. In the apartment, I hung the photo opposite the futon. It commanded the room, giving it character, a presence.

"What do you think, little buddha?" I said, eyeing the laughing buddha perched on the chest of drawers.

He chortled approvingly.

"You feel it too, huh," I said, winking.

Waking up to that photo every morning, at times with it haloed by a slab of sunlight, balmed me. It was quite large, 30 by 40 inches, and yet it felt much larger, a world unto itself. I yearned to disappear into it, to become yet another particle in the universe, a frequency of vibrating energy copulating with other energies.

I gazed at it and thought of my father and tried not to think of Péralte.

His cooking gave me a different kind of energy, a tingling euphoria that made me feel alive and present in my body. I did not know food could do that to you, that it could be a different kind of spiritual experience. I wasn't about to swell that big head of his by telling him this, but I planned to make his food last for as long as I could, stretching it over several days. I managed this by taking small, torturous bites and long, thorough chews, savoring the richness of the food, the complexity of the flavors, the sheer quantity of it all. One night, having dreamed I was back home in a rabid food queue fighting a grandma for a bag of mealie-meal, elbowing, kicking, and outright biting her wrinkled hand, I woke

up in a sweat, and rushed to the fridge to make sure the last of my precious skaftins was still there.

It wasn't. There was a gaping hole in the fridge where it had been,
like it had never existed, like our Sunday dinner earlier that week at
Péralte's hadn't happened, as though I'd dreamt the whole thing up,
dreaming up my own existence in this kitchen in this town in this place,
dreaming up all these people, dreaming up everything. Were The Terrors back again, playing their dirty tricks? I began to hyperventilate. I
pinched myself. I jumped up and down, so I could hear the thud of my
feet on the tiled kitchen floor. I opened and shut the fridge, then opened
and shut it again.

Shaniqua yawned into the kitchen the next morning, my empty,
greasy skaftin in hand. She dumped the Tupperware in the sink like
it was nothing, mumbling something about having arrived late in the
night from her biophysics lab suffering from the munchies.

I didn't speak to her for two weeks.

Returning to Dean's class after my episode of The Terrors felt awkward.

I wasn't sure whether to say something about what had happened or whether to say nothing at all. I didn't want the class to make a big deal out of it, but I also wanted to get ahead of the narrative. I was busy debating this, wiping my sweaty palms on my lap, when Chun asked if we'd seen the exposé article in the *New York Times* about Columbia University's ties with slavery.

"Ain't no surprise there," said Shaniqua, sniggering.

"I saw another piece, also in the *New York Times*, about how at one time slaves were *actually* auctioned off at the *actual* president's house, on the *actual* campus, at Princeton," said Lisa.

There was an ongoing spate, said Chun, of institutional exposés. Bhaskor wondered if anything would happen, and when Lisa said "restitution," Shaniqua burst out laughing. We all turned to her, and I smiled and mumbled something about a reckoning with history, relieved that the scandals going on over at Columbia and Princeton had overtaken the scandal of The Terrors.

Dean pulled up a graph on the screen projector and signaled for class to start, and we quietened down. He asked us what the graph was, and though I recognized the line that dipped along the $x$ axis like a giant pothole from my father's papers, I didn't say anything. I had decided to keep a low profile after The Terrors. I worried that The Terrors were a confirmation of something off-kilter in me.

"It's an exoplanet," said Péralte, finally.

Everyone turned to look at him, and I scowled and wished I'd spoken up.

Dean nodded. "I'd like to introduce you to Zara," he said.

There was a collective gasp.

"She's beautiful," murmured Lisa, as though she were gazing at the *Mona Lisa* and not a line on a graph.

"Yes, she is," said Dean. "A product of beautiful, precise data. She's about one and a half times the size of Earth and about half as old," he went on, "so two billion years old. She's a young planet."

I squinted at the light curve and tried to imagine Zara, his daughter. Might she be half his age? Or maybe she was still a little girl, young and supple, brimming with possibility, yet to cultivate her own intelligence.

"We know she's too close to her supergiant star and so everything's probably molten over there. But who knows, things may change in the next several hundred million years. She takes about seven hundred and eighty-three days to orbit her star. So, what kind of world could you imagine blooming there?"

"A super-hot one," said Bhaskor, and the class tittered.

Dean's face twitched. He didn't address Bhaskor's quip but fixed his gaze on the monitor and pressed a button on the little remote control in his hand. Another light curve appeared on the screen.

"What about this graph?" he said. "What would you say about this?"

"It's another exoplanet," I piped up.

"This is Earth," said Dean.

The class broke out in chatter.

"But we're Earth," said Mausi. "How can we be an exoplanet?"

"From an Archimedean point in the Andromeda Galaxy, this is what Earth would look like. Imagine an intelligent life form like ours also searching for a sister planet in the universe. This is what we would look like to them."

"But we don't look like anything at all," said Chun.

"Yes, but that's us," said Dean. "A representation of us, anyhow. It may feel as though we're looking at something else, but we're actually looking at ourselves."

It was strange, looking at ourselves from some objective point in the universe. It had always felt, even if this was not true, that we were at the center of things. We were the intelligence that did the looking. The possibility of being looked at, of being caught in the crosshairs of some super-telescope floating somewhere out there in the Andromeda Galaxy, was disconcerting. Would we want to be found? Would the aliens be nice?

"I mean, it's a nice thought experiment," said Mausi, "but the Archimedean point is itself a fiction. Depending on what the aliens are looking for, and how they're looking for it, they might see us and see something completely different from what we see when we look at ourselves, or them, for that matter."

"Hell yeah!" said Rick with a smirk. "Hello, quantum physics! Like, they could see the world in infrared!"

"They could even see the world in quantum," said Mausi, nodding. "Everything as vibrating packets of energy. Suddenly, everything's alive, and that shit about matter being inert gets blown out the water."

"Welcome to world-building 101," said Dean. He looked pleased. "Let's take a break."

Lisa nudged me. I turned to my left, facing her. "How are you feeling?" she said.

She had spoken loudly, and now everyone had turned to us, looking at me.

"Yes, Rosa, how are you doing?" said Bhaskor.

I blinked, discombobulated. No one at The Program could pronounce my isiNdebele name. Someone had randomly started calling me by my second name, and now everyone called me Rosa. The constant sound of it in the mouths of others made me feel like a different person, a thrilling transgression, like I was putting on an identity.

"I'm fine," I said.

"You're so brave," said Lisa. She reached out and squeezed my hand.

I flinched, trying not to recoil from her words, trying to appreciate her gesture and its effusive warmth. I didn't know what she meant by that, why I had been singled out for this award of bravery. There was something pitying about it. I couldn't stand being pitied. I felt a great pressure in my chest. I rummaged for my phone in my backpack and googled my name to show my classmates. It was always a strange and flattering yet anxiety-inducing experience to see my face popping up on the screen like that. Sometimes, when I was bored, I would google myself and scroll through the results. It had become a habit, the kind of thing I did compulsively without reason. My thumb would tap my phone reflexively, and my heart would soar at the sight of my name, as though these other versions of myself that lived on the internet confirmed something about the world and my place in it.

I clicked on *Images* and scrolled down until I came across a picture of myself in *Africa Magazine*. It was for a story they had done on the trip I'd taken to represent Zimbabwe at the World Youth Summit in Zurich in my second year of undergrad. In it, I had my head angled up at the camera, tilted to one side. My eyes looked unusually big. My forehead protruded beneath my braids, which had been pulled back. My cheeks delineated the edges of my face, curving to a neat pointy chin. My lips were pressed together in that self-conscious, insincere way one does when instructed to smile impromptu for the camera.

"This is me," I said, thrusting the photo in Lisa' face beside me.

She took the phone and studied the picture. "Nice," she said politely and passed it down the oval oakwood table to Bhaskor, who was seated on the other side of her.

"Which movie character were you trying to look like here?" Bhaskor said, chuckling.

Two days before, in our Introduction to Space Physics grad class, I had walked up to Bhaskor and told him he looked like Pi Patel from the movie *Life of Pi*, which I'd watched on the plane coming to America. He'd shaken his head, his thick, glossy hair shuddering in tandem, mumbled, "Oh God," swiveled on his heel, and walked away.

I made it a point to ignore him now and addressed the rest of the table, clearing my throat as the picture continued making its rounds.

"I'd just come back from Switzerland for a youth conference," I offered, something warm rising to my throat. "We'd been having food shortages in Zim and stuff. That was a crazy time! I remember I went to gym a lot that year. Anyway, here I am getting fat again in America!" I let out a full chortle. "Fatter and fatter! In America!" My chest rose, leavened by nostalgia.

My eyes caught Rick's. He was staring at me, my phone in his hands, held between his thumb and forefinger.

"It must be hard being away from your family," he said.

I nodded. "My mother hasn't forgiven me for leaving," I said.

He pursed his lips. I stared at them. Tiny white marks ridged their edges, like razor lines. He stretched out his hand, and I accepted my phone.

"Willie never forgave me for leaving," he said, smiling ruefully. His smile disappeared, and his face seemed to turn in on itself. "I cry for your country."

I thought he'd said "my country," and I wondered if he was crying for the Midwest he had pined after in our first class, if maybe he was crying for Willie. Then he said it again, "your country," and I blinked at him and then down at the picture on my phone, mortified by the face gazing back at me. It looked alien, arranged in an emaciated composure of earnestness, or was it naïveté, a pair of fleshy lips parted for the camera, smiling at god knows what.

I tried to think back to my life in Zimbabwe. We'd had the distinct honor of holding the record for highest inflation in the world. Our supermarket shelves had gaped empty. The riot police had thrashed marchers protesting against the food shortages, as though it were a crime to need food. Mama had cut her hair and dyed it a gorgeous blonde. It had complemented her smooth cinnamon skin. I'd attended weddings and laughed with friends and dated a knock-kneed, jade-eyed boy with a tousle of dark brown hair. His narrow face with its plump cheeks and bodacious smile had filled my world with joy.

I blinked at Rick and then turned away from him, only to catch Péralte looking at me. I held his gaze only briefly. What was that look? Was it pity? I could not bear to be the object of his pity. I inclined my head and slipped my phone into my pocket, and remained quiet for the rest of the class.

✳

A RIBBONED BOX arrived in the mail in the first week of October.

I tore the wrapping off, not even bothering to peel it. The only person who'd send me something was Mama. But what would she send? A care package? After all, I was the one who sent her things, not the other way round—a twenty-dollar bill here, a fifty-dollar bill there.

I gasped. Inside the box was a telescope. It was one of the newer models, a Celestron Schmidt-Cassegrain. It was short and wide, with a much larger lens, eleven inches and not eight like my father's Ultima 2000, and an auto guider port for astro-imaging and a thin, elegant eyepiece.

I fixed my eye to the eyepiece, my heart lurching in my chest, and then rummaged inside the box until I found a card:

*Every young astronomer deserves a new telescope. Your father and I saved for our first telescope in university. It changed our lives. Frank wielded that instrument like it was another body part—another arm or leg or a third eye; a second heart. His face would change moment to moment as he observed the skies—a slight furrow of the brow when he observed something he didn't expect to see; or he'd worry his lower lip with his teeth, lost deep in thought.*

*The most wondrous I ever saw him was when he glimpsed The Digging Stars in the sky in September. The whole of his face, from the ripples on his forehead to the sparkle in his eyes to the tautness of his cheeks, conspired in a childlike joy. The Digging Stars reminded him of his mother. After you were born, he said they mapped your little face.*

*Such an intense show of emotion embarrassed him, but he couldn't control any of it; his body seemed to be in communion with something beyond him. I hope this little gift ferries you to the stars, grasshopper, where you belong.*

*Love, Uncle C.*

So, Mr. C had gotten the letters I'd sent to his P. O. box address! I stood for a long time in my room, turning the card over in my hand. I imagined my father bent over his telescope, his pecan face the sky at civil twilight, his eyes lunar spheres above the pearly constellation of his teeth. My stomach lurched, making me giddy. I wished I had gotten the chance to experience my father this way. In a way, I *was* experiencing him, vicariously through Mr. C. I fingered the card, my chest swelling at the thought of Mr. C and the care he took with his memories of my father.

I sat down and wrote him a thank-you note, looping my letters carefully, in cursive, the way Grace Hendricks had taught us to do in etiquette class. Then I tiptoed down the corridor and into Shaniqua's room, and pilfered one of her pine-green envelopes and her Choctaw country stamps and slipped my letter to Mr. C inside. I tumbled down the steps two at a time and out of the apartment and down the street to the corner, where I slid the letter into the blue mailbox.

I began stepping out in the evenings with Shaniqua, who now spent whole nights cooped up in her biophysics lab with her beloved melanin molecules. The asphyxiating heat of summer had given way to a soothing autumn breeze—*fall*, as Shaniqua liked to correct me. The October sky was crisp and unsullied. I went up to the roof of The Program building. To my left protruded the dome that housed the observatory, like a great big nipple suckling the sky. I had with me my brand new Celestron Schmidt-Cassegrain and some art supplies—sheets of black sketch paper, my purse of pencils, a box of chalk, and an easel. I placed the sleek telescope carefully on the ground, near the edge of the roof, and angled its bulky tube up at the sky.

I set up a sheet of black paper on the easel and sharpened my white HB chalk stick. There was the moon, iNyanga, waxing gibbous. Magnified by the powerful lens of the Schmidt-Cassegrain, she was crisp and brilliant and beautiful, delineated in a way I had never seen before. Sunlight fell across her face, illuminating her as a bright and pearly spheroid. I began by sketching the part of her that was lit up, delineating it from the sickle-shaped westerly region that remained in shadow. Though in truth it was I who had traveled in an elliptical direction from the southern hemisphere to the northern and now stood "upside-down" on the Earth's crust, it felt as though iNyanga had spun one hundred and eighty degrees and now hung bottom up. Her basaltic seas, which had cratered her bottom during those pitch-black nights I spent out in Mama's backyard, now spilled across the top part of her luminous face.

From a distance, the basaltic seas were smooth, dark-colored patches, like melanated skin. I shaded them in, starting with the patchy lava floors of the Sea of Serenity in iNyanga's northeasterly region. Next, I contoured the low mounds ridging the darker basaltic bed of the Sea of Tranquility below, where Neil Armstrong had landed in 1969 and planted the United States flag. Farther east lay the diamond-shaped patch that made up the Sea of Fertility. Its rugged, uneven surface appeared in my sketch as a series of streaks, like a bout of acne.

Next, I sketched iNyanga's ivory-colored impact craters using my white 2B chalk stick. I started with Tycho, which appeared through the telescope as a luminescent pit crusted by a gray dusty rim. It, too, was upside down, on iNyanga's bottom and not her top. It looked like a navel. I sketched this ivory umbilicus and then traced the lavish streaks webbing it like adolescent stretch marks. They were hardened remnants of the early crust that had been shattered by rogue asteroids millions of years ago and scattered across iNyanga's surface.

I imagined the asteroids ramming into iNyanga's soft, white, anorthosite crust, leaving large, gaping wounds. These asteroids had rammed into our planet, too, but had since been palimpsested by geological formations of mountain ranges and seabeds, leaving but a trace of this celestial hailstorm and its apocalyptic effects. It was iNyanga, with her gaping scars, who was left to tell this cosmic tale, which was our cosmic story, too.

I went up to the observatory again with my Schmidt-Cassegrain the following night, and the night after that, and the night after that, too. Each night, iNyanga unveiled more of her face. Drawing her upside-down rekindled my enchantment. I had to resist what I thought I knew of her, curtailing my hand's intuitive movements across the page. I marveled at how misleading intuition could be. Though I knew iNyanga was not round, for instance, but rather lopsided thanks to the compelling gravitational pull of our planet Earth, I couldn't help but revere her as I saw her in the sky, as a near perfect sphere. But this was only an illusion, for the Earth's pull had changed how iNyanga moved her body, so that in answering the Earth's call, she'd bulged out on either end and become an egg.

The Earth, too, in answering iNyanga's gravitational call, had also morphed into an ellipsoid. I thought of our planet as she had appeared to my father aboard the International Space Station: as a sublime, spherical illusion. What treachery of light! How endearing our folly, how enchanting our fragile, illusory human instincts.

✳

ON THE EIGHTH DAY, we all came out to watch the lunar eclipse. Our class huddled on the roof of The Program building, next to the domed observatory. We took turns glimpsing iNyanga through The Program's portable telescopes. Everyone jostled for my brand new Celestron Schmidt-Cassegrain. I made them line up and told them, in a reprimanding, superintendent's voice, that there was no need to act like ruffians, they'd all get a turn.

"Cool!" said Mausi, caressing my prized possession's sleek black body. "Where did you get this?"

"My father bought it for me," I said, beaming.

My gaze met Péralte's. My smile faltered.

"Come," I said, pulling Mausi by the hand. "You can go first. You'll love it. The images are super sharp."

Péralte came and stood next to me. "Seriously, though. Where did you get it?"

I could feel my face becoming hot. "Mr. C," I said.

"Say what?" he said.

"What?" I said, with a shrug.

"You shouldn't be taking things from that man."

"Envy doesn't look good on you," I said and gave him my back.

He turned and walked away and huddled with Bhaskor and Lisa around one of the old-fashioned observatory telescopes.

My posse and I took turns gazing at iNyanga through my mean machine, watching as she passed in the Earth's shadow. At first, iNyanga turned a peculiar pinkish brown, as though she were undergoing melanosis. And then, as the Earth's shadow seemed to elongate, refracting iNyanga's light, her color deepened, turning from a light brown to a dark pink. For a moment, it seemed as though iNyanga were withering under fall's glare, releasing anthocyanins, the phenolic pigments that give fall leaves their red and burgundy colors. But of course, these were my meager human efforts to give voice to what I saw, for iNyanga has no atmosphere and therefore no seasons, though, like a symphonic maestra, she conducts our seasons and crescendos our tides here on Earth.

I saw a strange object moving steadily across the sky with my naked eye. I turned to see if others, too, had seen it. It seemed they had, for they scrambled for the observatory telescopes. The object moved in a straight line, a strange, lonesome heavenly body, unfamiliar to us. Its shadow passed over the moon, becoming bloodied and mysterious. We could see its murky, winged outline.

My heart quickened in my chest.

"I call dibs!" I yelled, turning to my telescope.

Péralte shoved me aside and pressed his eye to the Schmidt-Cassegrain's eyepiece.

"Ouch," I cried.

"I think it's a satellite," said Lisa, who was hogging one of the observatory telescopes.

"What kind?" said Bhaskor.

"I don't know," she said.

"It doesn't look like any of the ones we usually see," said Péralte.

"What if it's a spy satellite!" cried Rick.

"Or it could be a piece of junk from space that's entered our atmosphere and is hurtling towards us at tens of thousands of miles per hour," said Chun.

They were working on a project called Dunk that Space Junk to clear Earth's low orbit of the thousands of pieces of debris and defunct satellites floating aimlessly up there like a disaster waiting to happen. They had created a space-cleaning gadget named Queequeg, after the character from the fictional island of Rokovoko in *Moby Dick*. It was a simple yet genius contraption, consisting of a harpoon and a net. With it, one could go "whaling" in space, fishing out the circuit boards and the stray gloves and the frozen propellant and the defunct satellites and all the other human shit that was floating up there in perpetuity, with neither oxygen nor bacteria to decompose it, turning space into another Pacific trash vortex.

The idea of a trash vortex in space the size of the Great Pacific Garbage Patch, which stretched all the way from California past Hawaii to Japan and could maybe fit a whole continent, made my heart stutter. I imagined low Earth orbit cluttered with a myriad of satellites belonging to governments and corporations and billionaires all vying for primacy in the heavens. Each proprietor would no doubt try to claim their own little res nullius, whether by tacit or overt means, recreating a little Earth up there, complete with its contrived, excisive borders.

Suddenly, space no longer seemed sublime but secular. At any moment, one could be beholding starlight from an exotic, mysterious celestial object that had traveled thousands of light-years to reach one, or one could be staring at mere sunlight reflecting off the wings of a two-year-old aluminum satellite costing some 50 million dollars or more.

"We're slowly making space into our own image," I said.

I sighed a sad, subdued sigh. There was something terribly banal and disappointing about it all.

"Some junk satellites have been up there since the sixties," said Chun, "and they're set to float up there for the next five thousand years or something."

"Welcome to cosmic time," said Bhaskor, deepening his voice, so that it sounded eerie and frightening. "Muahaha."

"Plastic in the seas, choking the fish."

"Plastic in our bodies, building settler colonies."

"Oh shit, that's a good one."

"What about them radioactive isotopes from all them nuclear bombs they been testing since nineteen-o-long," said Shaniqua, flicking her wrist. "I heard they're fucking up our teeth. And they're gonna outlive us by gazillions of years, y'all. Gag on *that* cosmic time capsule."

"Oh wow, so cosmic time is *in* us," I said.

"Welcome to the anthropoid revolution!"

"The plastic human?"

"The radioactive human. Ka-boom."

There was a group chuckle. It started from somewhere behind me, gaining momentum as it traveled up to the front where Péralte and I were busy jostling for my telescope. I couldn't help it, I found myself laughing, too. Péralte threw back that huge head of his and cackled like he was high.

"Hey, look!"

We gazed at the sky and saw the whole of iNyanga now suspended in Earth's shadow. Her cratered upper region was bright pink, becoming pale red in her mid-region and deepening to a soft burgundy around her navel.

The whole of iNyanga had become melanated.

The invitations to the space symposium arrived in the mail on a blustery Friday in the second week of October. They came in gold-colored envelopes, one addressed to Shaniqua and the other to me. The cards were black and glittery and felt expensive rubbed between the thumb and forefinger. They were embossed with the Infinity Inc. logo, their edges embroidered in silver:

YOU ARE CORDIALLY INVITED TO

INFINITY INC.'S PRESENTATION ON

THE SPACE FRONTIER AND OUR FUTURE IN THE COSMOS

WEDNESDAY, OCTOBER 31

11.00 AM—1.00 PM

GILLES CONFERENCE CENTER

CONFERENCE HALL 32B

RSVP BY OCTOBER 24

LUNCH | COCKTAILS | FORMAL ATTIRE

The rim of iNyanga's Shackleton crater ran across the bottom of the card in a chalky white streak.

Finally, I would get to meet Thomas Long! This was my chance to share my ethno-astronomy project on celestial objects and my ongoing attempts to decipher my father's treatise on Bantu geometries. Perhaps he'd offer to fund my work after grad school, or maybe even offer me an internship at Infinity Inc.

"Are you going?" I asked Shaniqua.

She grunted. "Chile, like . . . all this talk of new frontiers? The last frontier decimated my people."

I tried to look somber, though my heart was giddy.

Péralte called. He, too, had gotten the Infinity Inc. invitation.

"Not everyone at The Program received one, though," he said.

"Ouch," I said. "That must hurt."

"Yup," he said. "It's only the Thomas Long Fellows who got invited. Among the first years, that's the whole of our seminar with Dean."

"We're the creamiest of the crème de la crème!" I said, guffawing.

He became quiet. I cleared my throat and asked him in a more sober tone if he and his mother had kept anything from my father's work on Bantu geometries.

"Ooh, I've been wondering what'd happened to that paper! That was his last work before, you know . . ."

"Yes, I know," I said. "I have the paper."

"I'm sorry," he said.

"For what?"

"You know, 'bout how he died 'n' everything."

"Oh. It's not your fault."

"I know. But, you know. We've never really talked about it. I didn't know how you felt about it, if you'd be OK talking about how he died 'n' Mr. C 'n' everything."

"Mr. C?"

He began to stutter. "I don't mean to open old wounds. I miss Uncle Frank, that's all. I don't have anything from his Bantu project, and I doubt Moms has anything either, but I can check. And I'd love to work with you on his paper if, you know, you need another eye on it 'n' stuff."

"His writing is so convoluted," I said. "He's worse than Derrida."

Péralte grunted and laughed.

The following afternoon, I went over to his apartment with my father's paper. He let me in and told me to make myself at home and disappeared into the kitchen. I crept over to the alcove behind the yellow couch. The space suit wasn't there. There was a gaping space where it had been, the square where the glass box had stood rimmed by dust. I went back to the sitting room and sat down on the hardwood floor in front of the TV and spread out the sheets of my father's paper. Péralte shuffled back from the kitchen with two tumblers and sat beside me.

I took a sip from my tumbler—it was lemonade—and cocked my head and said, trying to sound nonchalant, "Where's the space suit?"

"Moms said to move it to the bedroom," said Péralte, raising his hands in the air. The lemonade in his tumbler sloshed and spilled onto his T-shirt. "She said she'll talk to you."

"I have nothing to say to your mother," I said.

Péralte regarded me, his lower lip tucked between his teeth. I averted my eyes and pointed vaguely at the papers spread before us. "Better get to work."

We worked throughout the afternoon, doing our best to decipher my father's cryptic equations. But they proved too complicated or were incomplete, the vestiges of a half-finished life. Péralte and I labored over loopy sentences and clunky mathematical proofs for hours.

He must have told his mother I was coming over or that I was there, because she Facetimed in the early evening and asked for me. I waved my hands at Péralte, mouthing "no, no, no," but he ignored me and switched on his TV and projected his iPhone onto the screen.

Candice popped up before us. Her was face eerily large. It filled the whole screen.

"You look just like him . . . The same lips, same nose, those eyes . . . ohmygod." She cupped her cheeks.

I blinked at her. For a moment I was a child again on Madison Avenue being coaxed into a Scotch frock and a hideous tan beret in one of the changing rooms at Saint Laurent.

I gaped at the TV, taking in the silver strands streaking across her hair, which was tied loosely on her head and looked like an unruly hat. She hadn't worn her hair out in New York. I would never have imagined the transformation garnered by shedding the suave, sheeny weaves of yesteryear and letting loose the thick entanglements that rose audaciously from her round head. Her face looked smaller, more vulnerable, friendlier, somehow.

"Hello," I mumbled, giving her a little wave.

"It's like looking at a replica," she said. "After your father's death, my thoughts were very confused. The same questions haunted me for a long time. Why him? Why now? Why like this?"

She held up a box of cigarettes. It looked oversized on the TV screen. I watched as she pulled out a cigarette from the cyan box with the tips of her fingers. There was a black, mystical Indian figure in a white headdress on the cyan box, puffing on his own cigarette. He was silhouetted against a bright red sun. I mouthed the words on the box: *Natural American Spirit.*

Candice slipped the cigarette between her lips, snapped a lighter with her thumb and brought the flickering flame to the tip. She began to puff-puff contemplatively. "Frank was everything to me," she said. "My companion, my colleague and my friend, the greatest lover I have ever known—" I blushed. "For a long time afterward, I would sit by the phone waiting for his call."

Péralte got up and said he was going to make us something to eat. I wanted to signal to him not to leave me alone with his mother, since she was gawking at me like I was an exotic star or a newly discovered asterism or something, and all I could do was stare back at her. He disappeared into the kitchen. I bared my teeth at Candice.

She puckered her lips and puffed a ring of smoke. "How's your mother?"

I mumbled that she was fine and looked away. I wondered why Candice was asking about Mama. She certainly hadn't asked about her in New York. Had I mentioned Mama in those dreadful emails I had sent her in my teens? I winced. My teenage rants to her had been overpassionate and probably childish. I had felt older than I had been and every feeling, from grief to self-pity to shame, had poured out of me, oversized and garish.

A child's face popped up on the screen. "Mummy, I can't find my skates," she said.

"Go check under the bed," said Candice, waving the child away. "Wait, say hello. Say, 'Hi, Athwa.' "

"Hi, Athwa," said the child. She waved shyly at the camera, the ribbons in her hair shaking in tandem.

I blinked at her. "Hi," I said.

A pair of jeans appeared on the screen, and then a set of large hands slid down and picked up the child.

"Sorry," I heard a male voice say, and then the child and the man were gone.

"Who's that?" I blurted.

"That's my husband, James, and my daughter, Frances," said Candice. She puffed on her cigarette, blowing spectral shapes in the air, her own wo(man) made pareidolia.

I licked my lips. So, Candice had a husband and a child. She had moved on. So much for her whole "Oh, Frank was the love of my life" spiel. I thought of Mama sitting with her album back home perusing photos of my father.

"The space suit," I said, leveling my gaze at her. "It's mine."

"Now, wait a minute," said Candice, raising her cigarette-wielding hand in the air. "Wait a minute—"

"I'm not asking," I said.

She sighed, and then began laughing softly. "You really are Frank's daughter," she said. "A real replica. I don't have anything from his Bantu paper, by the way. I wish I could help." She sighed. "Frank was excellent and everything but . . ." She frowned. She seemed far away. "His kind of excellence could be damaging."

I glared at her. "My daddy was a brilliant man."

"But that's exactly the problem, isn't it?" She looked incredibly sad.

"You always were jealous of him," I said. I had to bite my lip to stop from saying *and you took him away from us.*

"Oh?" said Candice, raising an eyebrow. "Perhaps you are right. Let us hope," she added, smirking, "that you are as brilliant as your father."

I scowled. "It was good talking to you," I said and cut the call.

Péralte appeared in the sitting room a few minutes later, two plates in hand.

"Why didn't you tell me about your stepfather and your half-sister?"
I said.

"What?" he said.

"I have to go," I said, getting up.

"I made us some dinner."

"I have to go," I said again and left.

I only realized once I got home that I had left my father's paper at
Péralte's. Should I go back for it? Or demand that he deliver it to me?
The thought of him alone with my father's paper made my chest hot. It
felt wrong, all wrong. Just like how he shouldn't have had the space suit
in the first place.

I was still trying to figure out what to do when he called the following day.

"I think I've made headway," he said. He sounded excited.

He didn't ask about the phone call with his mother or the way I'd
left, and I was glad. I thought of the man with the long legs and the
child with the pink ribbons in her hair. I would be glad if I never spoke
to Candice again. Péralte walked me through a parabolic equation in
my father's paper, explaining how he thought he might be able to simu-
late it on some software he was designing.

"Uncle Frank was very visual," he said, "I think being able to see
what he was tryna translate mathematically might help us."

There was something sweet about his effusiveness—he was the only
other person I knew who spoke about my father with such fealty. A
wave of tenderness washed over me, so strange and unexpected, and I
tried to shake it off.

First, he called about my father's paper, then he began calling me
about any random thing, whether to talk me through the latest sweet
potato pie recipe he was trying out or share some gaming idea that
involved a superhero symbiosis of Haiti and Africa. My phone would

ring at 5:00 a.m., at 1:00 p.m., at 2:43 a.m., and it would be Péralte, speaking like it was the most normal thing to do, to be calling me like that, at those hours. And I'd talk right back like it was the most normal thing for *me* to be doing, surprised by my pleasure at hearing from him, embarrassed by the joy I felt, my heart palpitating at the sound of his rumbling, basso cantante voice trundling through the airwaves.

"You owe me a gaming session," he said during one of his random phone calls.

"Name the date and time," I replied, cracking my knuckles. "I'm the undefeated champion of *Mortal Kombat*. I float like a butterfly, and I sting like Scorpion."

"Welcome, girl. I'ma whoop yo' Scorpion ass."

"Ooh. I really don't want to embarrass you."

"You mean *I* don't wanna embarrass *you*."

"Boy, I'm going to humble you the way Grandma Estelle humbled Carl in that parody video game of *Mortal Kombat* they played in that episode of *Family Matters*. What was the parody game called again? *Grandma Ninja*."

"Get outta here! You used to watch *Family Matters*? Like, back in Zimbabwe?"

"I can still remember that dork Steve Urkel making a fool of himself in front of the supercool Laura Winslow!"

Péralte was excited to discover we'd had similar childhoods, though he was also surprised. I didn't know why he should have been surprised; America was everywhere: on TV and in the magazines and in the stores and in our space fantasies and in our airwaves and in our governments and in our economies and in our food and in our fizzy drinks getting fizzier by the year and in our thoughts and in our nightmares and in our dreams.

We chortled over the age of the CD, mornings spent playing Rihanna's "Umbrella" (for him it was Ne-Yo), surreptitiously pressing the reverse button over and over on the CD player to relive a constellation of heady daydreams. We guffawed over afternoons spent perusing for the latest Beyoncé at the Music Box in midtown Bulawayo or a vintage Nat King Cole at Westsider Records on the Upper West Side of Manhattan. Tee-heed over first kisses tasted to the fervent proclamations of Usher, at lyrics scribbled in pink or purple ink in hardcover music books ("You also had a *music book*?"), the chiseled faces of Denzel Washington and Tom Cruise and Whitney Houston and Pamela Anderson cut out of *People* or the latest *O* magazine and glued lovingly over declarations of love or heartbreak.

When I mentioned *Little Rascals*, Péralte's voice began to boom throatily. I imagined him throwing back that huge head of his, and I threw back mine. Together, we began trumpeting the *Little Rascals* song: "too-ru-rou-rou-roo-roo-too-roo-ru-roo-ru-rou, too-ru-rou-rou-ru-too-rou-roo-rou-rou-ru." We were horribly out of tune, but it didn't matter; it felt nice.

"Remember Darla? She was my favorite rascal, so cute and pretty with her little curls and her song renditions of love and longing. Busy giving Alfalfa and Butch the run around. LMAO. I so wanted to be her!"

He became quiet.

"Hullo? Péralte? You still there?"

He sighed. "You know to be her, you'd have to be white."

It was my turn to pause. "You know I didn't mean it like that."

"How did you mean it, exactly?"

"Oh wow."

"It's just . . . just that . . . Never mind."

"No, I won't never mind. Just what?"

"Look . . . you wouldn't understand."

"Well, I want to understand. And how will I if you don't tell me?"

It felt, at that moment, like we were no longer standing on the same childhood Wonderland but light years apart, viewing the same thing but each from our own exotic little planet, exposed to different reflections of its light.

"There's just a lot of racist stereotypes going on with those kids, man. *Little Rascals* my foot. Buckwheat talking like a cotton-pickin' nigger from a Southern plantation, being told to go plant watermelon and the jokes about fried chicken and the bumblin' and shit. I mean, sure, the series was ahead of its time when it came out, during Jim Crow, there was nothing like it on TV, depicting the races together and all that, but there's just a lot of hurtful stuff going on there, the pretty girl always gotta be white, the bumbling fool gotta be black, there's the fat kid, the what-kid. Now we have a pretty black woman like you wishing she was white."

Had he said *pretty, black woman* or *pretty black woman?*

"I never wanted to be white, Péralte."

"Oh, no? Did you ever see no black Darla? You start aspiring to things that in reality you aren't, by things natural to you and out of your control, ever meant to attain, and it's that aspiration that keeps you dangling, like a damn fool."

I could hear the nastiness creeping into his voice. I remembered the time I had visited my father in New York as a child and how I had tried to be Darla for him, batting my eyelashes and twiddling my thumbs and smiling sweet-like so he could let me cook eggs for him, like I'd grown up seeing Darla do in the series to get her way. I resented Péralte for making me think of Darla as more than just Darla, spoiling the sweetness of that moment with my father.

"I was just a child, Péralte, filled with wonder. Is that so wrong?"

"Well, now you're no longer a kid. You gotta stop acting stupid and bring that interrogatin' adult lens to these 'innocent' depictions of the world."

"I'm not sure, but I think you just insulted me right now."

"Where is the lie?"

"You know what, you need to get your head out of your buttocks, you think you're so smart, busy going on about Haiti this and Africa that, well let me tell you, the Africa you keep going on about doesn't exist anywhere except in that big head of yours, it's got *real* people, not statistics, OK, Africa is not a *country*, like America, OK, we're a *con*—"

He hung up.

✳

I WANTED TO demand my father's paper on Bantu geometries back, but I didn't want to be the one to call first. I checked my phone constantly that week, my hand hovering over his name and then darting away. The truth was, I was simmering. I didn't want him to get it into his big head that he was somehow superior to me just because he'd grown up in this damn country and I'd only lived it through my father, fond memories he now sought to shatter.

But I couldn't stop staring at my phone. I missed him terribly. I was glad when Shaniqua asked me to accompany her on one of her mushroom picking errands that weekend. I needed the distraction and happily scrolled through the pictures she showed me on her phone of her biophysics experiments, though I didn't know what the hell I was looking at.

"I could stare at those little sausage-shaped molecules all day," she said, her voice all dreamy like. "They're the cutest thing."

"You find melanin molecules cute?" I said, trying to keep my face straight.

"Girl, don't start, I've seen you all up in your stars. Everybody's got their obsession!"

"Yes, but spectral light under a telescope and sausage-shaped blobs under a microscope . . ." I made a weighing motion in the air.

"Oh, please. Did you know melanin can conduct electricity?"

"Oh, wow, does that mean we have superpowers?"

"Now, now, let's not be getting wild ideas," said Shaniqua, chuckling. "But eumelanin—the type in our skin—has the potential to act as a conductor. With a li'l structure, those molecules could get zappin'. I'm practically sleepin' at the lab tryna figure this shit out."

"Get to working, girl," I said. "I want the zap. Imagine what I could do just with the power of my touch."

Shaniqua laughed. "Someone fucks wit' you—*ʒap*! A nigga wants to get fresh—*ʒap*! Barbie wants to get all mean gal on yo' ass—*ʒap*!" She chuckled. "But seriously, though. Melanin could be the future of bio-electronics." Her eyes sparkled. "Say hello to the future of Afro tech."

I squinted into the distance. "OK, I see it!" I said, nodding, and we laughed.

That Saturday, we set off with a picnic basket to a different forest a little farther out than the lumbered maple forest we'd first gone to. This forest was more lush, with an eclectic family of fiery maples and russet pines and yellowing basswoods. We trudged through it, foraging for Shaniqua's curly wood ear mushrooms and my veiny chanterelles. She also harvested this species with bright red caps dotted by white spots, almost like a ladybird. She crouched in the shade of a pine tree, where the ladybird mushrooms flourished, and held one gently by its creamy stem.

She looked up at me. "Wanna join me?"

My eyes widened. "You mean you want me to talk to the mushr— the nonhuman being?"

"You wouldn't know what to say!" she said, smiling a cryptic smile. "I'm inviting you to witness."

"OK," I said, wiping my palms on my jeans.

I crouched beside her. She clasped my hand and brought it to the creamy stem of the ladybird mushroom. I held it between my thumb and forefinger; it felt rubbery and cool to the touch. Shaniqua kept her hand over mine. She gazed down at the mushroom and murmured to it in Choctaw. Up close like this, the red cap was smooth and shiny, like a lollipop, the white dots crusty, like iNyanga's anorthosite rock. I lowered my free hand and caressed the cap with my thumb, gently, careful not to bruise it, soothed by the smoothness of its sheeny body, enjoying the bumpy feel of the white dots against my flesh.

Shaniqua exhaled and released my hand. Then, with her other hand, she brought a knife as close to the base of the mushroom as she could. Swiftly, she sliced the stem. She held the mushroom up to the light, twirling it around, and then, grunting, slipped it into a Ziploc bag.

"I feel so still," I said, blinking into the hazy afternoon light filtering through the trees. "It feels like time stopped there for a minute."

"Good," said Shaniqua, smiling.

"Are we going to eat those?" I said, eyeing the ladybird mushrooms in the Ziploc bag. They were bright and plump and juicy looking.

Shaniqua shook her head. "No, these are for my other project. I wanna run some experiments on the pheomelanin."

"*Pheo*-melanin," I mouthed.

"See them redheaded girls you seen on TV?" said Shaniqua. "They got pheomelanin in their hair. Just like these fly *Amanita* mushrooms here. It helps protect the mushrooms from toxins. I'm tryna produce a synthetic melanin powerful enough to flush out the toxins in our environment, and I'm hoping these babies here can help me out."

"Ah," I said, "you're making some Shani-melanin."

Shaniqua laughed and fluttered her eyes, and I laughed, too, surprised; I had never seen her looking so shy.

We must have trudged through that forest for hours. My feet ached. I was about to insist that we take a break when the trees cleared and we found ourselves standing before the muddy waters of the Mississippi River. A thick, dense, forbidding row of white oak and elm trees flourished on the other side of the river. A heronry of egrets was splashing about in the shallow waters by the bank where we stood, their long white necks and yellow beaks curved like question marks.

Shaniqua spread out an old, frayed plaid blanket on a patch of slightly damp, cool grass near the bank and laid out our picnic. I sat on the blanket with my legs crossed and began munching on the crackers we'd brought with us. I dipped them in a tub of hummus and stuffed them into my mouth and stared into the distance. A cerulean warbler fluttered past and perched itself on the branch of a white oak. It let out a rapid, staccato trill, puffing up the white and blue feathers on its chest. They shimmered crystal-like against the backdrop of the oak tree's white bark and bright orange leaves.

Shaniqua came and sat between my thighs, resting her head on my lap. We sat like that, in the splendor of the golden foliage. She didn't ask me to, but I began weaving her Afro into Alicia Keys cornrows.

"Where you grew up, y'all are Black?" she said.

"Well, we were colonized by the British," I said. "So, we have a white population in Zimbabwe. I went to a school where the majority of the kids were white. But where I live, we're black. Though that's not how we think of ourselves. Among ourselves, I mean. There are different ethnicities and clans and stuff."

"But your family, they're Black?"

"They're Ndebele."

She was quiet for a while. Then she said, "My ma's white."

I paused midway through a cornrow. "For real?" I said.

"Yeah," she said. "Part white, at least. What I mean is . . . sometimes she's white, depending on where we are. When we visit family at the Mississippi Choctaw Reservation, she's Indian. Grandma's real proud of ma's skin—she's the lightest of my aunties and uncles. You feel me? And I'm the darkest." She sighed. "You know why I love science?"

"Why?" I said.

"'Cause by learning about melanin, I get to learn about my own skin. Like, I get to love myself. Well, most of the time." She laughed.

Her voice went all dreamy, and she started talking about the ubiquity of melanin, how it could be found everywhere in nature, in plants and in other animals, too, birds and lizards, which had many uses for it, not as just protection from harmful levels of UV light but also for camouflage and preventing cell damage.

"Take these melanized babies, here," she said, shaking our Ziploc bags of mushrooms in the air. "You can find them growing in the extreme cold, I'm talking about some Antarctica typa shit. You can even find them deep under the sea, and in places where there's drought, and in acidic areas . . . you can find them damn near anywhere. They're some resilient motherfuckers. They been through so much, and yet here they are." She sighed again.

I gazed out at the landscape with its spectrum of red, yellow, and brown leaves. There was something enchanting about the variation of the colors, nature showing off its artistry, lavishing its extravagance upon the landscape. I thought of Mama and her smooth skin, the way it shined in the sun. After we saw the film *The Bodyguard* as a child, I told Mama all the time how she looked like Whitney Houston; . . . in response, she'd throw a leg in the air and laugh that sweet laugh of hers. And she did look like Whitney, especially when she relaxed her hair with *Dark & Lovely* and then curled it with these big rollers into a gorgeous, sheeny perm. We shared the same cinnamon skin, she and I, the same sparkling spectrum of light.

Something cinched my chest. We hadn't spoken much since my leaving. Maybe I really had been trying to get away, so I wouldn't have to deal with the fact that it was my fault Mama was the way she was. When The Terrors wouldn't stop assaulting me, she switched churches from Catholic to the Church of Revival, one of the mushrooming Pentecostal churches in town. She stopped perming her hair and soothing her skin with aromatic organic oils. The Terrors were all she talked about. The pastor at the Church of Revival made her stand before the congregation and confess her sins in order for me to be healed. She let it all out, her parties and her heathen life of fornication, the married men she'd had affairs with. The Church of Revival made her forsake her swanky clothes and her music. When that didn't heal me, the church ladies took to coming to our house to hold nightly vigils. They would form a circle and make me kneel in the center, and then start singing and praying, beating me over the head with their bibles, rebuking the evil spirits that had possessed me and imploring the Holy Spirit to take over me. I admired their passion and their verve, though I missed the old Mama.

Sometimes, when I looked at Mama, I felt spite rising in me. Maybe what I really despised was what The Terrors had done to us. But The Terrors were a part of me, and so maybe what I really despised was myself.

My head began to hurt. I looked down at the cornrows I was weaving down the length of Shaniqua's head and tried to think of something cheerful.

"Let's go see the mounds," I said, lighting up.

"What mounds?" said Shaniqua.

"There's an ancient place somewhere around here I read about in a travel brochure . . . Effigy Mounds, that's the name. It has these mounds shaped like birds and animals that were built by the Native Americans."

Shaniqua scowled. "I ain't ready for another history on the 'prehistoric' Natives. You'd think we'd gone extinct. I mean, they tried, damn, they tried. But here we are."

I averted my gaze, shame and embarrassment flooding my chest, making me feel hot.

"Whenever tourists would come to the reservation for the pow-wows," said Shaniqua, "my grandma would drive them to her house in her Jeep Wrangler for a tour of a 'real Indian home' and turn on the satellite news and serve them tea and biscuits on her Neiman Marcus china set. They'd bop their heads like headless little chickens and open their eyes real wide and hang their damn mouths like puppy dogs. You could tell they were looking for the teepees and the cedar canoes and maybe even a feather headdress."

"LMAO," I said. After a while, I said, quietly, "I didn't know Indians still existed."

Shaniqua curled her lips. "Well, there's America and then there's the Native American nations."

"There aren't any Native American nations on the map of the world. And I paid attention in geography class!"

"The reservations, chile. Places like the Mississippi Choctaw Reservation. Ain't you been listening to anything I been saying?"

"The reservations are nations? Sovereign nations?"

"*Yes.*"

"But inside the nation of America?"

"*Yesss.*"

"That doesn't make any sense."

"*YES*, it doesn't make sense, but that's how it is."

I paused. How could a country exist inside another country? Well, Lesotho was a country completely surrounded by South Africa. But Lesotho appeared as its own country on the world map. They had their own passports and borders and representatives in places like the United Nations, and other countries could trade with them. I'd even met Lesothoans at the World Youth Summit in Zurich. And I'd seen Lesotho competing at the Olympics. But I'd never seen any Native American nation on the world map or heard of any Native American nation represented at the United Nations or seen any Native American nation competing at the Olympics.

"Why aren't Native American nations part of the world?"

Shaniqua sighed. "Like I told you, they put us into them reservations and called us tribes and shit."

"We have reserves back home," I said. "Created by the British when they colonized us. They named them our tribal homelands."

"Oh wow," said Shaniqua. "Oh wow oh wow. The history's too close. It's too close, I'm telling ya!" She sounded excited, but in an agitated sort of way. "*Reserves. Reservations.* These mofos damn well created themselves some aliens."

"What?" I said.

"We were aliens, too, not so long ago. Now we got dual citizenship, in our nations and the United States." She snickered, and then, sighing, added, "But you still an alien!"

"I'm an *alien?*"

"That's the legal term in America if you ain't a citizen. *Alien.*" She let out a cackle.

I tried to laugh along with her, but only managed a halfhearted curl of the lips. My heart hammered my chest. I thought of all the alien movies I'd watched. The aliens were cast as crude, repulsive, and dangerous, and uncivilized even though they sometimes had superior technology—after all, it was they who had discovered the technology to bend space-time and travel hundreds and thousands and millions of light-years to reach us. But they were cast as savages, terrifying brutes who did terrifying things. I always cheered at the movie house, relief flooding my chest, when they were banished or crushed or exterminated.

My hands began to spasm. I lay back on the grass and breathed through my mouth, trying to quell my tremors. I could feel a Terror coming on. *Not now, you little fucks.*

"Are you OK?" said Shaniqua, sitting up. "Hon? What's going on? Is it allergies? Is there a needle I need to stick in your thigh or something?"

"I'm good," I mumbled. "I just need a minute."

"Yeah, don't you be dying on me now. I ain't finna carry your dead ass all the way home. I'll leave you for the bears."

I tried to laugh but ended up blinking back tears. Something in my chest hurt.

Shaniqua lay down beside me and held my hand. "You're shaking," she said.

"No I'm not," I said. "Just a stomachache."

She didn't say anything, just lay her head on my shoulder. We lay like that for a while. The silence sprawled between us, sweet and companionable. I was glad Shaniqua was there with me, that she didn't press me about why I was shaking, that she simply lay there and held my hand.

Slowly, the world came back to me. The red and yellow and brown colors of autumn came into focus. I looked down to find my hands had stopped trembling.

"You OK?" said Shaniqua, and I licked my lips and nodded and turned away from her.

We got up and packed our basket and grabbed our Ziploc bags of mushrooms and began our trudge back to the truck Shaniqua had borrowed from her vendor friend at the farmer's market. On the drive back, I lolled my head against the passenger window and watched the sun dipping beneath the flat, expansive horizon in the West, bathing the sky in an aurora of twilight colors. Yellows and reds seeped across the horizon like watercolors, merging into blue-greens and purple-blues. To my left, outside Shaniqua's window, the Earth had cast its shadow. It stretched as a dark blue arc across the eastern horizon. The sun cast the last of its rays, splashing a pink glow along the inner rim of the Earth's shadow. The glow spread across the sky like luminous fingers.

A nondescript object moved across the dimming sky as a steady band of light. It could have been a satellite or a rogue piece of space junk—or an alien aircraft. Across the land below, the yellows and reds and browns of fall cast mysterious, scintillating shadows.

I imagined seeing this kaleidoscopic play of light as an alien visiting Earth for the first time.

I t was the food I dreamt of all night.

I'd downloaded the exclusive menu for the Infinity Inc. event we'd been invited to at the space symposium. I googled the exotic foods I couldn't pronounce. That night, the night before the symposium, I tossed and turned in my sleep, drenched in a bed of perfectly seared foie gras rendered in its duck fat, and pink cutlets of rare-rare Wagyu beef still oozing blood, and roasted matsutake mushrooms served to me by a laser-wielding alien on a spaceship ferrying us from Earth to slavery somewhere in the Andromeda galaxy some two and half million light-years away.

The food was all I could think of the following morning as I got ready for the symposium. Imaginary pieces of Kobe beef melted in my mouth, succulent from the exclusive beer on which the cows had been fed and the professional massages their million-dollar thigh muscles

had received. By the time I got to the symposium at the Gilles Conference Center, gigantic apparitions of beluga caviar and bluefin tuna
were floating before my eyes, assaulting my tastebuds. My stomach
contracted in painful spasms. I blinked back tears.

Food was all I could think of as I waited for my classmates by The
Program's booth in Hall 3D at the symposium. All around me was a sea
of salmon-colored testosterone molecules of varied shades, heights, and
girths. They gangled past The Program booth in tightly fisted bands.
Some were weighed down by single-, double-, or triple-breasted suits,
while others ambled about in informal pants and *Star Wars* regalia. A
young man with a galaxy of angry pimples pockmarking his face broke
away from his cluster and approached me. He asked for directions to
the toilet.

I blinked at him. "I don't know," I said.

It took some blustering and stuttering to ascertain that no, I did not
work at the conference center. No, I wasn't one of the staff. I was an
astronomy student at The Program. The young man's pale, cratered
face reddened.

"I'm sorry," he mumbled, maneuvering a hasty, clumsy retreat. "So
sorry."

I watched as he stumbled away, suddenly self-conscious of my white
blouse, navy-blue skirt, and matching blazer. Did I really look like one
of the staff? The servers were dressed in smart, black tuxedos complete
with bow ties, even the women. I had assembled what I hoped was a
professional, academic look for the symposium.

Mausi arrived an hour later, followed by Lisa, whose eyes were glued
to her phone.

"Did you see the latest exposé in the *New York Times*?" she said
when she saw us.

I shook my head.

"The one about how Old Queens at Rutgers University was built in part by actual slaves," said Mausi.

Lisa nodded. "Yeah, this slave named Will laid the foundation of the building in 1808. Will, that's all they called him. That's all we know about who he was. That's, like, *crazy*."

"But it's not surprising," said Mausi. "I mean, New Jersey was one of the last states to give up slavery."

"It's depressing," said Lisa.

We loitered around The Program booth, watching as the final years set up some of their work, hoping to attract some of the investors or corporations or military contractors on the prowl. This would be us in a few years, I thought, my heart giddy, out here hoping to catch the interest of Infinity Inc. or Northrop or General Dynamics or some other company that had business in space.

Dean came over to our booth, a tall man and a little girl in tow. He introduced us as his "brilliant students" and then introduced us to the man, his husband, and the little girl, his daughter Zara. I looked down at the little girl and then at one of the posters plastered on our booth, of Dean and a smoldering, red exoplanet. The little girl was dressed in a floral red dress and matching sneakers, making her look like a Chianti sunflower in bloom, its wine-dark petals stark and bright in the light. I gazed at the exoplanet and then back down at her. She had, effectively, been immortalized. I eyed Dean wistfully. He looked at me and smiled, and I tried to smile back. The moment stretched, becoming awkward. I turned hastily to Mausi and Lisa and suggested we visit the other booths and exhibitions. We waved goodbye to Dean and Zara and the husband.

I glanced at my phone. It was only 9:00 a.m. Food would not be served for another four hours, after the Infinity Inc. event. There were so many military personnel at the symposium. I'd never seen so many military people congregated in one place before. They marched through the crowds, past us, conspicuous in their olive-green uniforms and their peaked caps and the colored bars on their jackets. I admired the American eagle flaring its majestic wings on the golden pins embroidered on their caps.

I ambled from booth to booth and exhibition to exhibition with a bottle of spring water in hand, raising it to my lips each time my tummy grumbled. I daydreamed about the Ayam Cemani I was going to cannibalize for lunch. It was a rare breed of chicken. I'd ogled it on Google the night before, stunned by its beauty. Its jet-black feathers and gleaming onyx eyes shimmered like crystal stone, its matte-black comb perked up on its head like a little Afro, the same tone of black as its beak and the wattles dangling from its chin. Even the meat on its bones was black. It glistened in a chicken broth dish I salivated over online for what seemed like hours, enchanted by its hyperpigmentation. I planned to wrap a glistening ebony drumstick in a napkin during lunch and gift it to Shaniqua for her melanin experiments.

It was while seated between Mausi and Lisa in one of the dark theater rooms, grappling with a pair of flimsy 3D glasses that kept sliding down the bridge of my nose, that I learned NASA's Kepler space telescope had run out of fuel the day before and would be retired. In its nine years in space, it had helped discover over two thousand exoplanets, helping humankind gain a greater understanding of the cosmos and bringing our species closer to one day making contact with alien life. The Kepler would be replaced by the powerful Transiting Exoplanet Survey Satellite, TESS, which had been launched into orbit earlier in the year.

*TESS*, I mouthed. What an unsexy, bureaucratic name. *Kepler*, at least, had a poetic ring to it, a history, named after the sixteenth-century German astronomer Johannes Kepler. *Kepler* sounded full-blooded, whereas *TESS* rolled off the tongue with cold, algorithmic precision.

"A salute to Kepler!" boomed the voiceover.

The Kepler telescope popped up on the screen. It was a peculiar, fragile-looking thing, a tube with a highly sensitive photometer wrapped in a sheet of aluminized polyimide, which shimmered like gold foil on the screen. It would be shut down and spend its days trundling in the universe, a lonesome, inert object floating in a swath of dark, velvety space. Perhaps, one day, Chun's Queequeg could fish it out of the universe and haul it back to Earth to be recycled or displayed in a space museum somewhere.

"To celebrate Kepler's astonishing successes," continued the voice-over, "we're going to look at its greatest hits, starting with the first Earthlike exoplanet it helped us discover in 2014, Kepler-186f."

The camera zoomed out for an artist's rendition of the planet floating in space. It looked slightly larger than Earth, with familiar brown patches on its surface and dull swaths of blue in between. It was the first Earth-sized planet NASA's Kepler space telescope had spotted orbiting its star in a habitable zone. A dim orange star popped up on the screen, scintillating in the distance behind the muddy-looking planet. Kepler-186f's opportune distance from its red dwarf star meant liquid water might very well gurgle across its surface. The possibility of water meant the possibility of life.

Something cinched my belly.

I wondered, my heart pitter-pattering, if this dull-looking, less-becoming planet-cousin might one day serve as a home for planet Earth's reviled aliens.

MY BIGGEST FEAR was running out of food while entombed high up in space on the Galileo. The theoretical space colony filled the humongous screen mounted on the stage in Conference Hall 32B. Thomas Long's voice boomed from a series of speakers arranged overhead along the walls, narrating the blown-up, high-definition visuals. His baritone

drawl lilted down to us in the red velvet chairs, compounding the soothing effects of the dimmed blue lighting of the hall.

The camera zoomed out, showing the Galileo's steel, globular exterior floating in space. It was propelled by two engines rotating along
its vertical axes, one at the top and one at the bottom. Fastened to
the axle, midway between the top engine and the globe, was a donut-
shaped sphere.

"This," said Thomas Long, hushing his voice, "will serve as the
Galileo's greenhouse, where we'll produce some of the freshest food
known to man."

The babble of journalists huddled in the front wings of the hall
cheered. The military men and women seated in the front middle rows
neither smiled nor clapped, maintaining their gravitas. From my seat
several rows down in the section reserved for the Thomas Long Fellows, I could see their olive caps bobbing as they exchanged clandestine
whispers with one another.

My stomach contracted. A greenhouse, sure. But would that sustain
the millions of inhabitants Thomas Long envisioned living on his steel
planet? What would happen when the food ran out? What would happen if the greenhouse malfunctioned?

"Nothing is impossible," boomed Thomas Long's handsome voice,
as though reading my mind. "There's no problem too big for an intelligence such as ours to solve."

"Except climate change and starvation and war," muttered Shaniqua
next to me, snorting.

The image on the screen zoomed in, slipping through the Galileo's
steel exterior to reveal what was inside. A whole world flourished in
there. Whereas we lived *on* planet Earth, humans in space would live
*inside* the Galileo, building settlements along its concave inner rim.

The camera zoomed in again on the futuristic world. It hovered above a couple gazing out into the distance, their blonde hair fluttering in the breeze. Uniform rows of corn stretched before them, punctuated by wood-paneled houses with rectangular chimneys and double-story mansions with classical white columns. A drone buzzed overhead, jetting convex sprays of water on the monocrops.

The camera zoomed in farther to show what the blonde couple saw. The landscape sped into the distance, only instead of disappearing over an asymptotic horizon as it did on planet Earth, giving the comforting illusion of flatness that had seduced Homer and the ancient philosophers, the landscape in the Galileo curved with the sphere, rising up, up, up, its trajectory hampered only by the screen, which cut it off abruptly.

The lens tilted. The Statue of Liberty came into view, holding her torch above what looked like the Hudson River. To the left of Lady Liberty, the Empire State Building shot out at an acute angle, almost perpendicular to the curved ground from which it sprouted. It looked, with its peculiar angle and its clean architectural lines and its stainless-steel spire, at once futuristic and nostalgic.

Once more the camera lens tilted upward, following the blonde couple's gaze. Directly above them, where one would expect to see a swath of sky, was Mount Everest. Its jagged, iconic peak hung suspended like a gigantic stalactite. I gasped. The audience broke out in chatter. The landmass, having been plucked from its icy range in the Himalayas and transposed into this sunny alien landscape, looked as though it would unhinge from its impossible upside-down position and crush the couple below. An upside-down brick colored dome of the Florence Cathedral flanked it on one side, a dense forest labeled THE AMAZON on the other. The houses overhead were also upside-down, as were the people and the bullet trains and the monochrome plots of red oak and yellow basswood and white pine.

"I won't bore you with the math of it," said Thomas Long, rolling his eyes to amused titters, "but what's really exciting is, Galileo's spin rate provides Earth-like gravity along its inner surface. That's why we can build anywhere along its surface, including upside-down. Gravity keeps the structures tethered to Galileo. Isn't science amazing?" There were cheers and murmurs. "Now, here's the really cool stuff," he went on, his voice at once spectral and mysterious. "As you get closer and closer to this axle"—the camera zoomed in on the spinning axle that ran through Galileo's center, its aluminum polyimide sheeting scintillating like gold—"there's less and less gravity. At the center, there's zero gravity, meaning you'd float. Yes, people, we'll be able to fly!"

The audience broke into a raucous cheer. I found myself cheering, too. Shaniqua shot me a dirty look. Péralte leaned forward on the other side of her and glared at me.

"What?" I said, shrugging. "It's amazing."

Shaniqua rolled her eyes. "Can't you see he's putting on a show? Just you wait, we're going to get to the real stuff in a minute."

"We won't have to rely on the Russians to give us a ride to space like we've been doing," said Thomas Long. "Everything will be *us*: the space rockets, the landing pads, the Galileo."

There was a noisy cheer from the military personnel.

The camera zoomed out again. Human figures popped up on the screen: men and women lounging on a sandy beach by a lake, their flesh a bronzed, healthy tan; men and women milling around a picnic table in a tranquil park, their pink faces gleaming. My heart fluttered when I noticed a coffee-colored woman with dreadlocks among the picnic crowd. She seemed oblivious to the golf shorts and polo neck shirts around her, her body captured in a perpetual gyration of the hips, as though she weren't at a picnic but at the club.

The camera zoomed in on the axle that cut across Galileo's center.

Men and women appeared on the screen, clustered around the axle, growing larger and larger as the camera zoomed in on them. They were suspended in the air, clad in tennis shorts and spandex pants and other leisurely apparel, cocktails and water bottles and lettuce sandwiches in their hands. The sun gleamed on their coral faces and their resplendent flying bodies.

"To the future!" cried Thomas Long, spreading his arms.

There was a resounding clap. People got up. To my left, Rick stood up. I stood up, too, and smacked my hands together in loud, painful thumps.

"Now, the big question," said Thomas Long, motioning for the audience to sit down, "is: How do we make this happen?"

The Galileo disappeared from the screen and was replaced by the moon, iNyanga. The camera began to orbit her, lingering over the cement-colored basaltic plains that cratered her surface. The visuals of the Sea of Serenity and the Sea of Tranquility were stunning, the mounds along their rims stark and delineated. The camera zoomed in on Tycho, iNyanga's navel, showing the sparkling detail of the radial rays scintillating around it like diamonds, their wondrous, star-spangled patterns crisp and fine-grained. I stretched out a hand, as though to reach out and caress them.

The camera zoomed in on each of the six American flags that had been planted on iNyanga's surface by the Apollo astronauts in the '60s and '70s. There was resounding applause from the military personnel seated at the front.

The simulated flags were shown fluttering in a majestic breeze, the red and white stripes crisp and sharp, the white stars twinkling in the iconic blue rectangle. I blinked rapidly, discombobulated; iNyanga had no atmosphere, so there'd be no breeze to gently whip the flags about. And the flags wouldn't retain their sparkling color all these fifty years later; they'd most likely been bleached by the relentless sunlight beating down on them for two weeks at a time. They were probably no more than limp, white rayon cloths now—peace flags.

"Space has unlimited resources," said Thomas Long. "Everything we need to build Galileo can be found up there."

"Isn't that what they once said about the Earth," whispered Shaniqua, snickering.

"We're going to start by mining the moon," said Thomas Long.

There was a collective gasp.

The camera zoomed out to show an Artemis space lander approaching iNyanga. There was a collective, hallowed hush. The oblong-shaped space robot flew past Tycho toward a desolate gray expanse. It was approaching Shackleton crater. Steel legs extended from its base. It lowered itself onto iNyanga's surface.

The robot began to move, rolling forward on thick rubber wheels. It came to a halt by the edge of Shackleton crater. There it bent its oblong head and peered its single eye into the dark depths below. A long laser beam, like a weapon, appeared from one of the flaps on its side. It was emerging for what seemed like a long time. It whirred as the robot lowered it into the crater. The camera zoomed in, capturing the laser beam as it cut rocks of what looked like ice out of the crater's walls and base. Three spiderlike finger probes protruded from the tip of the laser beam. They gripped the rocks of ice. The laser beam began to retract, whirring back to the Artemis robot idling on the edge of the crater. It deposited the rocks of ice into a transparent tank fastened to the robot's back.

The camera zoomed out. The screen went blank. The words INFINITY INC.—BUILDING THE FUTURE flashed in steel-blue, minimalist Centauri font.

The conference hall erupted in applause.

"I'd like to introduce you to the space leaders of tomorrow," said Thomas Long. "These incredible young men and women are recipients of fellowships from the Thomas Long Foundation. They're doing groundbreaking research that will help us realize our goals and catapult us into the future."

One by one, we stood up and shuffled out of our row and down the aisle and up the carpeted steps to the stage. Thomas Long stood on the top step, beaming down at us as we came up. We filed past him, shaking his outstretched hand. I paused when I reached the top step and smiled shyly. He was much shorter in person, about my shoulder height.

I gripped his hand and looked down at him and said, "I think you may remember my father—"

Chun bumped into me from behind. I stumbled forward, bumping into Thomas Long, who staggered but did not fall. The audience gasped.

"I'm so sorry—" I mumbled.

"Good job, good job," said Thomas Long loudly, slapping me on the shoulder and easing me forward. Leaning forward, he whispered, "Join the others on stage, sweetie."

I shuffled forward, my eyes on the ground, and joined the Fellows lined up on the stage. I stole a glance at the audience below. There were Shaniqua, Péralte and Mausi, still in their seats. Shaniqua was sitting with her arms crossed, while Mausi kept looking down at her lap, probably at her phone. Péralte was looking at me, his eyebrows raised. I loured at him and looked away.

"These are our future leaders of tomorrow," said Thomas Long. "I'd like to thank them for their work. I'd like to give a special thanks to this young man here—" He beckoned to Rick, who stepped forward, grinning, "—who's responsible for the visuals for our presentation today. He's one of our finest young minds."

Thomas Long hugged him and pumped his hand and then raised it in the air to resounding applause. I struggled to keep my face steady.

Rick's visuals were just OK. And he'd gotten the American flags on iNyanga wrong.

We posed onstage with Thomas Long and smiled for the cameras. They exploded one after another in our faces like supernovae. Then we filed down the carpeted steps and up the aisle and into our row, back to our seats.

Lunch was held out in the pavilion in the conference center's golf range. There, amid a crisp, impossibly green lawn, I swallowed mouthfuls of Kobe beef, which really did melt in your mouth, and Ayam Cemani, which really was jet black and tasted just like ordinary chicken.

I was wondering what the fuss over the Ayam Cemani was about when I spotted Thomas Long standing alone at the edge of the pavilion, fiddling with his phone. I saw my chance and shimmied up to him.

"I'm so sorry," I said, "about earlier. I think you knew my father, Frank."

Thomas Long frowned. "Frank?"

"Frank Siziba, you and he went to school together—"

"Oh, *Frank*!" said Thomas Long, his cobalt eyes lighting up. "Yes, yes. He was one of the most brilliant people I ever met."

"You were friends?" I said, beaming.

"I've never met a chap who loved to dance so much!" said Thomas Long, chuckling. "Every Friday night, we'd go out to the Steel Mill. After a few beers, Frank'd put a jazz song on the jukebox and climb the tables and start dancing. He'd shout, 'I can see it, Tommy! I can see the future! I'm inside my soul, baby, inside my soul!' He taught me a move or two."

With that, Thomas Long began swaying his hips from side to side. I smiled politely, too embarrassed to laugh. I couldn't imagine my father dancing. I couldn't imagine him laughing, or drunk, or just letting loose, like that. I couldn't imagine him as anything other the man who loved the stars, more than Mama, more than me, more than anything.

"I'm working on his project on Bantu geometries," I said, "his last work before he died. I'm also working on my—"

"Excellent, excellent," said Thomas Long, thrusting something into my hand. "Here's my card."

With that, he was swept away by a tall, sallow man in a military jacket with gold ribbons embroidered on the sleeves.

"Was that Thomas Long I just saw you cozying up to?"

I turned around to find Péralte standing behind me. We hadn't spoken for the past two weeks, ever since his phone foolishness. I had half a mind to shade him now. I imagined his chastising response to this: "That's terribly childish behavior. Where is the lie?" I laughed, in spite of myself.

"What's so funny?" he said.

"You," I said, poking him in the ribs.

He ducked, chuckling. I was glad to hear him laugh. "Are you coming to the party at my house tonight?" he said.

I pretended to sulk. "How can I, when I didn't get an invite?"

He looked alarmed. "Shaniqua didn't tell you?"

She had. "Why couldn't you tell me yourself?" I said, eyeing him out of the corner of my eye.

"Well, I'm telling you now. Come by. It's Halloween night. It'll be fun."

I shrugged. "I'll think about it."

I'd missed him terribly, though I didn't want him to know it, lest that big head of his get even bigger.

"Seriously, though," he said. "What was that with Thomas Long?"

"You know he was friends with my father," I said. "I was just saying hello."

"What did he give you?"

"His business card. Look, what's your problem?"

I stuffed a piece of foie gras into my mouth. Péralte watched as I ate it. He stared and stared at my mouth.

"What?" I said.

He had that same look he'd had when I'd had the episode of The Terrors in class, like he was going to kiss me. I tried not to blush.

"D'you know how they make that foie gras thing?" he said. "They ram pipes down the ducks' throats and force feed them. Even when they throw up, they don't stop, not until their livers are all swollen and fatty."

I began to retch.

"I hope you enjoy your foie gras up on the Galileo."

With that, he turned and walked away.

I gazed, glum, at the liver floating in an oily sea of duck fat on my plate.

For the party, I wore a boysenberry-and-lilac tie-dye dress I'd nicked from Mama before coming to America. Shaniqua draped herself in this gorgeous kente cloth she had bought at an insane price from an online African store, along with huge Bob Marley hoop earrings.

"I'm looking like a real African bad bitch!" she said.

"Yes!" I said. "We are some African bad bitches!"

Then, at the last minute, she changed into a black kanga, draping one end across her shoulder and tying it at the back of her neck. It was so she could match with this new boy she was seeing, I knew. His name was Moussa and he was from Côte d'Ivoire.

Moussa came by and we set off, all three of us, to Péralte's. All around us, porches had been decorated with torn, lacy material that looked like cobwebs and grinning pumpkin faces with eerie, glowing hollow insides and billowing white sheets with holes cut out for the eyes.

"That looks like Casper the Ghost," I said, pointing at a sheet billowing outside one of the houses we passed.

Shaniqua scowled. "It looks like the Ku Klux Klan," she said.

I squinted at the sheet and edged closer to Shaniqua. I clasped her hand and didn't let go until we reached Péralte's. He'd draped a torn mosquito net over the witch hazel tree next to the bird bath. A grinning pumpkin greeted us at the door.

We knocked and knocked. Finally, we heard footsteps, and then the door swung open and Péralte flung his arms wide and yelled, "Boo!"

I brought my hands to my mouth and tried to scream. Shaniqua groaned, and Péralte burst into laughter.

"Damn girl, you a bad actor!"

"You have to work on your scary, boo," I said.

We stepped inside. His apartment was empty; we were the first people there. I plopped on his couch and Moussa carefully lowered himself beside me, and Péralte and Shaniqua went to get some drinks. They returned with clinking glasses in their hands, a bottle of sparkling water for Moussa and a can of beer for me. I sipped the beer politely; it was an amalgamation of sweet and sour flavors. I couldn't tell what I was supposed to taste from it. After a while, I stood up and said I'd be back.

"The loo," I said, giving Péralte a little smile.

I ambled through the sitting room and down the corridor. I tried the doors to all the rooms. Péralte's room was at the very end. I slipped in, blinking into the gloom, and fumbled about on the walls for the light switch. Bright orange light flooded the room. The space suit was in its glass box in the corner, facing the queen-size bed, which was sheathed in a pistachio-colored quilt. I went over to the glass box and fiddled with the latch and swung it open. My breath caught in my throat.

A musty, acrid smell wafted from the space suit. It was propped up in the glass box, so that it looked like someone slumped forward with their head bowed. I stretched my hand and caressed a sleeve. The sheeny nylon material crackled between my thumb and forefinger. I slipped out of my tie-dye dress and unclasped the suit from the hooks in the glass box. It was heavy, heavier than I'd expected. I staggered under its weight but did not fall.

I hugged it. I imagined it was my father I could smell on there. But the faint sulfurous odor made my nose twitch. It took me a while to figure out how to put the suit on. I found a large opening, like the mouth of a sac, in the front. I slipped my feet through it and into the trouser legs, and then slid my arms into the arm sleeves. Then I hoisted the sac over my head and pulled it over my torso. Next, I flipped the transparent visor back and slid my head through.

I didn't know what to do with the open-mouthed sac, so I let it dangle over my abdomen. I stood before Péralte's full-length mirror opposite his bed. I slid the visor closed and placed my hands on my hips, swinging them from side to side. The open-mouthed sac slapped my tummy like excess skin. Save for my small brown hands protruding where the gloves should have been, no one would know it was me.

The rubbery material layering the inside of the suit felt alien on my skin. I felt different, like I wasn't in my own body. I felt extraterrestrial, like I'd gained superpowers or something, like there wasn't anything I couldn't do.

I trudged back to the sitting room to join the others.

"Whoa!" said Shaniqua when she saw me. "Where d'you get the space suit?"

"Happy Halloween," I said, spreading my arms. "I'm an alien."

"Hey!" said Péralte, thrusting a finger at me. "You shouldn't be wearing that! Moms says it's an art piece!"

I shrugged, trying to seem nonchalant, though inside I was seething. "It doesn't belong to your mother," I said.

Péralte averted his gaze. "Uncle Frank never let anyone wear it," he said.

"Well," I said, a hand on my hips. "He would have let *me* wear it."

A thick, suffocating cloud settled over us.

"OK, how about some music?" said Shaniqua, going over to the wooden TV stand and tinkering with Péralte's MacBook. "Everybody loves music."

Presently, an upbeat song started belting from a pair of Bluetooth speakers.

Shaniqua grabbed my hand and dragged me to the middle of the sitting room, where she began swaying from side to side like some lone, valiant dance warrior. I stood there, sweating in the space suit, and watched her. She grooved like a rebellious teenager, thrusting her hips from side to side, her long, athletic arms swinging with gymnastic delight, diamonds of light catching in the rich, cedar lushness of her trembling Afro.

"Shake that ass, honey-boo!" she yelled, motioning for me to imitate her movements.

I shuffled from side to side like I was ashamed of my body. Truth was, in that harsh and revealing light, she oozed a suppleness that both enchanted and embarrassed me, the kind mothers found sweet on clumsy, girlish bodies but wicked on teenagers who, too young to be aware of themselves, twisted their juvenile hips at family gatherings, making their buttocks twitch and their perky breasts shudder.

Shaniqua began grinding her hips against the air, against an imaginary crotch, out of time with the music, real slow and sensual, like she was selling something, like a ho, which was real entertaining and a little intimidating too in the carefreeness of it, the power of it, like a performance of something at once lusty and transient that collides with a pleasure deep inside you didn't know you were capable of feeling.

Her new boyfriend Moussa stood watching her from the sidelines, looking stiff and solemn, like an undertaker. He was dressed in charcoal trousers and an equally inarticulate shirt, his gorgeous, wine-dark skin glistening against the matte fabric. As a matter of principle, he wore only black, like he was making some sort of profound statement, whether about the world or the state of his soul or those unkempt spikes sprouting on his head, who knew. He was studying philosophy. I could see how he was the philosophical type, what with his dreary, funereal airs.

Beyoncé came on. Péralte joined us on the dance floor, thrusting his limbs with the joy of a child, a glass of gin in his hand. I hadn't seen him like this before, so unserious, so unself-conscious, so *free*. He always held his body as though it were a weighty and solemn object, moving through the world with a calculated deliberateness, a care.

I smized at him and gave him my back. I must have looked ridiculous, twerking in the puffy space suit, like that, with my head bopping like a chicken's in the globular visor. But I didn't care. There was something delicious about giving my body over to the spirit of Beyoncé. I felt my spirit levitating. I pressed myself against Péralte and gyrated my waist, grinding the space suit against his crotch. He obliged, thrusting his pelvis in tandem with my twitching buttocks.

"You go girl!" Shaniqua yelled. "Ooh, I didn't know you could back it up like that!"

Hell, *I* hadn't known I could back it up like that. I'd never shown myself like that, had never given myself over to metamorphosis in the light. I'd only let loose at the club back home, where I could shrug off my diffidence under the cover of a sultry, strobe-flickering dark. It felt liberating, cavorting with Péralte like that. I felt loose and free. Moussa cast his philosophical eyes on us, looking bored in his symbolic black suit, smiling arcanely as Péralte and I twerked to the floor and then twerked back up.

There was a knock on the door. Péralte walked over and turned down the volume on his MacBook and then went to answer the knock. I heard Lisa's cheepy voice pealing by the door, Mausi's shy voice and Bhaskor's grating laugh behind her.

"Hey, you!" said Bhaskor as he rushed in behind Lisa. He paused. "And what is this?"

"It's a space suit," I said, smiling sheepishly. "I'm an alien."

"Oh my, I like!" He tried to hug me, but his hands couldn't go around the space suit. I grinned and hugged him back.

Lisa brought her face close and smacked her lips against the globular visor. "That suit looks real," she said.

"It is," I said. "It belonged to my father."

Lisa's eyes widened. "Your dad was an *astronaut?*"

"Yes," I said, and then catching Péralte's eye, "I mean, no. He went up to the ISS with Thomas Long in the early aughts. As a space tourist. But he did some astronomy work when he was up there."

Lisa's jaw dropped. "He's friends with Thomas Long?"

"Your dad's a boss!" cried Bhaskor.

I didn't correct them, didn't tell them my father had died. Instead, I simpered. They were looking at me as though they were seeing me, *really* seeing me, for the first time. And yet it wasn't me they were really seeing, for I was an alien in a suit.

Péralte didn't correct them either. He mumbled for them to make themselves at home, and then went to his room and returned with a brown paper bag. He set it down on the low coffee table and sat on the couch. He unrolled a cigarillo, emptied the brown tobacco-paper of its contents, and lay it flat on the coffee table. Then he retrieved a tiny plastic packet from the brown paper bag and pried it open with his pinky finger. He emptied some of the contents, a dark, fine powder, onto the tobacco-paper. Then he rolled the cigarillo back into a skinny cigarette. He fumbled about in the brown paper bag until he found a lighter and lit the cigarillo.

"You want a puff?" he said, waving it in my direction.

"What's that?" I said, crinkling my nose.

"It's cohoba," he said, grinning. "I got it in Haiti over the summer. It's ground from the seeds of the cohoba tree. The Taíno folk used it for their spiritual ceremonies. I hear they gave Columbus a taste and he got high as fuck. Almost turned guy into a hippie!" He chuckled. "I see why he almost converted. I've smoked it a few times, and it's *wild*."

Between his prominent lips, the cohoba suddenly looked auspicious. He took several puffs, keeping the smoke in for as long as he could before blowing out rapid little puffs. He passed it to Shaniqua, who took several deep puffs.

"Ooh, I feel it," she purred.

Mausi and Lisa and Bhaskor joined them. Péralte lit a second blunt and passed it around. Very soon, the whole room was misty with smoke.

Péralte stretched out his hand to me, holding out his blunt, which was now a little stub. I stared at him and then at the blunt. Then I leaned over and accepted it, holding it suspiciously between my thumb and forefinger. I took a few shy puffs, and then inhaled deeply. We passed the blunts around, puffing spectral smoke into the air. I closed my eyes and tried to imagine the Taíno during one of their cohoba ceremonies.

The room began to spin. I lay down on the hardwood floor in my space suit and spread my arms. The ceiling plaster sparkled. Mausi came and lay down next to me. She mumbled something about quantum particles and Hopi astronomy and Einstein.

"Is a quantum particle a *particle*?" she asked, finally.

I squinted at the starry ceiling, trying to remember what I'd learned in undergrad in my space science class. ". . . They're fields of energy. We can't see them."

"Yes!" she said, thrusting a fist in the air. I had never seen her so exuberant. "When I speak Hopi, it's like I'm in this world, but in a different dimension? My body moves different. There's, like, a different vibratory motion? We have way more verb tenses than English, you know."

"That's rad," I said, and mouthed, silently, *ical*.

"Right?!" said Mausi. "It's like moving through spacetime, like Einstein discovered, and not a separate space *and* time. When I'm in Hopi mode, my world comes *alive*, man. It *moves*. It vibrates." Her voice reached my ears as a sweet, vibrating hum.

"Ooh, that's beautiful," I murmured, taking another puff of cohoba before passing the blunt to Mausi. "I feel it."

Mausi chuckled. She took a hit from the blunt and puff-puffed at the ceiling. Though the unruly behavior of quantum particles had confounded Einstein, she said, her voice quivering like a beautiful, taut string instrument, what Einstein called, eerily, their "spooky action at a distance," it made sense that two quantum particles affected each other's behavior across implausibly large distances. What happened here impacted what happened over *there*. Why the hell had that upset Einstein?

She took another hit and passed the blunt to me.

"Did Einstein want us to remain blobs of matter all our lives?" I said, glaring at the ceiling. "Didn't he want us to be *energy*?" Cohoba smoke spiraled from my nostrils, unfurling in languid tendrils. I handed the blunt back to Mausi.

Mausi made vague motions in the air with her hands. "The interrelatedness of everything isn't just some woo-woo ancient belief, but a science!" She sighed. "I hate going to conferences and having people eye me funny when I say this. Like, the world is messy, deal with it. There's no unified theory, no elegant equation that'll explain it all.

There's complexity and complementarity and fucking constant flux."
She inhaled deeply and held the smoke for a long time before hissing it
out. "I always worry that I'll be denied a fellowship or funding for my
research, that my work won't be taken seriously."

"That sucks," I said. My limbs felt weightless.

"It does!" said Mausi, thrusting another fist in the air. "And what's
so hard to get? Like, can you, by isolating a thing from its ecosystem,
honestly say you've come to understand that thing?"

"What is it to understand a thing?" I said and grinned.

"Right?! Can you separate the tree from the forest, the forest from
the Earth, the Earth from its galaxy, the galaxy from the universe?"

"We're star dust plus time," I sighed.

Mausi started talking about butterflies and creative evolution and
someone named Bergson. I hadn't heard of this Bergson, but the butterflies sounded beautiful. They fluttered out of Mausi's mouth and came
to life, first the spring butterfly, the *Vanessa levana*, with its translucent,
reddish-brown wings and black-and-white dots, and then the summer
butterfly, the *Vanessa prorsa*, whose bluish-black, melanated wings were
streaked with white lines.

Mausi said something about pupae and metamorphosis and the
environment. I stared at the butterflies and tried to follow the flapping
motion of their wings. She mumbled something about kinship. When
I grasped for the butterflies, they fluttered out of my reach and disappeared back into her mouth.

We stayed like that for what seemed like hours and hours, but when
we finally came to, only a little over three hours had passed. The ceiling stopped scintillating, becoming a dull matte again. I stretched and
yawned. I felt groggy and lethargic.

"What a trip!" said Shaniqua.

She was slumped over Lisa on the couch.

"That was a way better trip than Infinity Inc.'s presentation!" said Péralte.

"Don't even get me started," said Shaniqua. Besides the banality of that presentation, she said, and the utter lack of originality of the whole enterprise, it was the prospect of living inside the Galileo that irked her the most.

"Can you imagine living in a space that small?" she said. "Where you can see every corner of your world? Everywhere you look, you're met with the limits of your existence."

"I'd lose my mind," said Lisa.

"I'd slip into solipsism," said Bhaskor, "and eventually die from cynicism."

There was a collective chuckle.

"But what about the vision?" I said.

"What vision?" said Mausi. "Those were quintessential landscapes of the Western frontier. There was nothing on there we haven't seen or heard before. Just more settler colonial dreams of world domination— sorry, space domination."

"But wouldn't it be amazing to live in space?" I said.

"Why?" said Mausi.

"Because," I said, "it's space."

"But there'd be nothing new in space," said Péralte. "We'd just take ourselves and all our shit up there. And it'd be way harder living there than here. We'd need to manufacture *everything*. The air you breathe, the soil, the water, every damn thing we take for granted here."

"And who d'you think's gonna build all that shit?" said Shaniqua. "Who's gonna keep the air going? Who's gonna farm them little space plantations? 'Cause it sure hell wasn't masser who worked them here."

I shrugged. "Algorithms and AI machines?"

Shaniqua clicked her teeth.

"It's the moon he was always going for," said Lisa.

"Bam," said Bhaskor, thrusting a finger at her. "That's where the money is. That and mining asteroids. Bam!"

There was a knock on the door. Péralte stood up and went to answer it. We heard a commotion, then Rick pushed his way in.

"Happy Halloween!" he yelled.

"What the fuck?" said Shaniqua.

"Rick, no," said Lisa.

"What?" said Rick, spreading his arms.

He adjusted the feather headdress on his blonde head and moved his hips from side to side, shaking the plumed feather skirt fastened around his waist. Black briefs were visible underneath, hugging his skinny thighs. Red streaks ran down his pink cheeks.

"Man, what're you doing?" said Péralte.

"What? My great-great-grandpa wore this same outfit during the American Revolution, when we threw those chests of tea off the ships and kicked the British off our land."

Mausi got up and left.

"What! It's my family heritage!" cried Rick. He thrust a finger at me. "You can ask Rosa. The British colonized us, too. Tell them."

Everyone looked at me. I blinked at Rick.

"Tell them, Rosa!"

"That's not her name," said Shaniqua.

"What d'you mean, that's not her name?" said Rick.

"You should call her by her proper name."

"I thought her name was Rosa," said Lisa, speaking in a whisper. "Like, what other name does she have?"

"You don't even know her *real name*?" Shaniqua's lips were set in a firm line. "You gotta learn to say it. You gotta start calling her by her proper name. It's not that hard. Come, say it with me."

With that, she began saying my isiNdebele name, Athandwa, enunciating it slowly and letting it roll off her tongue. The sound of it in her mouth, entwined in her musical Southern drawl, felt intimate. One by one, the others began imitating her, trying to thread it on their tongues, as she was doing. The sound of my isiNdebele name bouncing around in the room in various, at times comic intonations, felt both charming and disorienting.

Rick, stuttering for the umpteenth time, said, "I think I'm just going to stick with Rosa."

"You can't even get it right," said Shaniqua, her eyes blazing at him.

"That's not fair," Rick said, adjusting the feather headdress on his head.

"I think we'd better get going," Lisa said, shuffling toward the door. "Bye, Rosa. I mean—sorry."

One by one, the Long Fellows shuffled out of Péralte's flat, waving and murmuring goodbye. I turned to Shaniqua.

"What did you do that for?" I said.

She raised her eyebrows. "Those are your classmates, but they can't even bother getting your name right? How's that work, exactly?"

It was true that no one in the Midwest could pronounce my isiNdebele name. We were almost at the end of the semester, and still, everyone tripped over the syllables.

"I don't mind being called Rosa," I said to Shaniqua.

"Of course, you don't mind. There's a lot you don't seem to mind. You don't seem to know where you are. Tell those folk to call you by your proper name, and to stop trippin'. They gotta learn to *see* you, all right?"

I told her my father had given me both my names and for this reason, I loved them equally.

She wrinkled her nose.

I told her my father had chosen my second name in honor of Rosa Luxemburg, the Polish Marxist, who had been a revolutionary woman, and that made it a revolutionary name.

"There we go, daddy again. Phew. All right. Whatever you say, Miss Jenny."

I plopped down on the couch, suddenly glum. The evening felt spoiled. As though he, too, could sense this, Moussa said he was calling it a night.

Shaniqua clasped his hand. "Can I sleep over at yours?"

I thought of sleeping all alone in our apartment, and I felt sorry for myself. I had been doing so well, these past weeks. The Terrors hadn't bothered me, and I'd attended all my classes. I didn't want to backslide. The thought of going home alone made me depressed. I wondered if the drugs Péralte had given me were intensifying these sensitive feelings. I asked to sleep on his couch.

"You take my bed, and I'll take the couch," he said.

I honestly didn't care if I slept on the floor. As long as I didn't have to be alone that night.

Moussa called an Uber. Péralte and I stood on his doorstep and watched as he and Shaniqua got into the Uber. Shaniqua raised a hand goodbye, her drunk, merry face pressed against the car window. I blew her a kiss. We watched as the car sped down the road and turned left, headed for Moussa's place on Court Street.

Péralte and I stood there for a while, the crisp fall air slapping our cheeks. Then, slowly, we turned and made our way back into the apartment.

Péralte and I sat side by side on his bed.

I stared at the walls, admiring their tasteful, muted pistachio hue and the way it matched the quilt on the bed. There was an oil painting of a man roped to a teal door on the wall above his bed I hadn't noticed when I'd come in looking for the space suit. The man was naked save for a white cloth around his midsection. His head was tilted to one side and his eyes were closed. There was a bruise on his left temple. He could have been sleeping were it not for the woman in a black robe and a white doek standing next to him, sniffling into a tissue or a handkerchief. A red and blue flag hung over the door behind the man.

"What's that?" I said, pointing at it.

Péralte looked up at it and sighed. "I'd better get going. I just came to get a blanket for the couch."

"OK," I said.

He didn't move. I took in the pimpled expanse of his face, his choc-olate eyes delectable delights glinting behind the panes of his glasses. His handsome nose protruded like a tubular West African fruit, flaring into mysterious hairy caverns. His fleshy lips were a titillating pecan tint where they met.

I wanted to kiss him.

I tried to think back to the last time I'd had sex. It had been with Rufus.

Before Rufus, I'd only had pretend sex in my teens, fooling around with a few boys, kissing and tonguing and rubbing and stroking, even pressing our pelvises against one another, our supple, youthful bodies thrusting and pumping through our clothes, until a holy spasming took over us. I'd been a young lustful thing, filled with heat and yearning, ashamed of my sprouting body yet excited by it. I'd known I was going to hell for indulging, and worse, enjoying the moist, ungodly delicious-ness. Sometimes, I wouldn't even be thinking about a boy or anything, only to realize my nipples were taut and I was wet.

At least, for all the kissing marathons I'd partaken in, I hadn't let anyone into my precious cookie, though one or two eager transgressors, pimpled with lust, their Adam's apples bopping with crimson tempta-tion, had tried. I hadn't wanted to be a full-blown sinner, especially after the church ladies from Mama's Church of Revival started praying for me to be healed from The Terrors. But my body betrayed me with its tremblings and its secretions, and Rufus and I started having sex. To my horror, I'd enjoyed fornicating very much.

I stared at Péralte.

I didn't want him to leave and go and sleep on his couch, not just yet, and so I started talking, just sharing the first thing that popped into my mind, which was a memory of the day Sarhann Hassim, an alumnus of my high school Girls' College, had visited the school and addressed us during assembly. I was fifteen. She was my classmate Nassim Hassim's older sister, and after her visit everyone wanted to be Nassim's friend, as though in this way, they would be closer to Sarhann and her aura. Sarhann was studying at Harvard, and a mature prestige emanated from the way she stood before us at assembly, neither squirming nor stuttering like the prefects sometimes did when they had to stand before us and make a speech or read from the Bible.

"I'm here to tell you that you can be absolutely anything you want to be," Sarhann said. She spoke loudly and clearly, with emphasis, gesticulating with her arms for effect. "Growing up, I was fascinated by the universe. Physics was a subject that fascinated me greatly. I got a scholarship to attend Harvard University and study astrophysics."

Here she paused, allowing our excited chatter to rise, crest, and break. We knew Harvard was an Ivy League university in America; a Hallmark of Excellence, just like Girls' College.

"It's also very important to give back when much is afforded you," Sarhann continued. "I teach classes to illiterate adults in a literacy program in America. I enjoy it very much. There is nothing as fulfilling as being able to inspire. I am also the captain of the Harvard women's soccer team."

"Wow!" we cried.

We could not contain our chatter, which spilled over and became a loud, thrashing thing, like a hall of pigeons trying to take flight.

"It has been my dream to go to the moon. Unfortunately," she said, lowering the pitch of her voice for effect. "In America, you have to be an American citizen to be an astronaut. So," here she smiled, "I shall be joining the Russians. I am going to be a cosmonaut."

We threw ourselves into the air and cheered. The sun beamed through the windows, hugging the ceiling with an unusual sparkle. That morning, we sang our hymns from the pits of our stomachs, just like Mrs. Smith, our music teacher, had taught us. We didn't slouch. We didn't lug our voices about like we were tired. We wanted to add to the magic in the air through the magic of our voices. We were singing not for Russia and its welcome of Sarhann as a cosmonaut, but for the excellence that was Harvard University.

"We were brimming with inspiration," I told Péralte. "It was a tingling feeling, like a tickle in your spirit that makes you want to jump and laugh, jump and laugh, and change the world."

Péralte was looking at me funny. "You romanticize America so much," he said. "You act like you're in a dream. Like this life isn't real."

I sighed. What were we here to do in America, if not romance?

"The history of this country is a whole messy entanglement, man. A lot of these prestigious institutions were built on Mayfair money."

"Mayfair money?"

He sighed and looked up at the oil painting of the dead man tied to the door. "I got that in Haiti," he said. "It was my first time visiting this summer. Can you believe it?" He snorted. "I always used to pester Moms. Even your dad asked her to go. But we never did. And then I finally decided to go by myself this past summer. I dunno. I guess I was looking for something, but not really sure what."

Péralte became quiet. I kept still, as still as I could.

After a while, he said, "Everywhere I went, when I told people my name, they'd call me Charlemagne. Charlemagne! They'd say. You're Charlemagne! Who the hell is Charlemagne? I asked Moms. She told me it was this hero my dad, my real dad, named me after. Charlemagne Péralte. This Péralte guy was a badass, like, he led a rebellion against the US occupation in Haiti. We'd freed ourselves from slavery a century before and he was having none of that bullshit. And you bet your ass they made him pay for it."

He frowned, just a slight furrow of his wide brow, but it was like a cumulonimbus cloud had dipped across the moon that was his face.

"The US Marine Corps dudes hunted him down and shot him. Put a bullet in his heart. Then they tied his body to a door and draped the Haitian flag over it, like in the pic there. They put him on public display in his hometown, can you believe that? Just like they used to do with the lynchings here. Look, here's another dead nigger strapped to a tree! They even took photos of his body and circulated them all around Haiti. Handed them out on the streets, put them up everywhere, dropped them from airplanes 'n' shit. It was crazy."

I looked up at the oil painting of Charlemagne Péralte. He looked, crucified on the door like that with the loin cloth around his waist, like a martyr, Jesus on the cross. Seeing the Haitian flag draped over the door behind his crucified body like that sent something cold and sharp down my spine.

Péralte clasped my hand. "I had that exact same feelin'. I was just . . . crushed, y'know? It's stupid, I know, but I was." He sighed. "So, I get back from Haiti, right. And I drive down to this little town about five hours away from New York. I had to go get some Taíno stuff for Moms she bought off Craigslist, this macuto, it's a handwoven basket made out of palm fronds, and a batea, this wooden tray thing she uses for her fruits and veggies. She's been reconnecting with her Taíno heritage and all that, so I did what good sons do and I drove the whole five hours there and the five hours back just to get this stuff for her." His voice had seeped into that place where I wasn't sure if he was still talking to me, or if he was somewhere else, deep inside himself.

"It was the stillest, greenest day you could imagine," he said, though his face was anything but still. "I had Nas on blast, the windows down, Doritos on my lap, Red Bull rattling in the cup holder. Yeah, sure, the music was a little loud, but so what, y'know? Then out of nowhere, these cops stop me." He squeezed my hand.

"I've been stopped by the police a few times back home—"

"Suddenly it hits me that we're in the fucking middle of Swamplandia. Just green wildness and ashy boughs on both sides of a single-lane road. The kind of place where you'd expect to find a little town that's not on the map with a Confederate flag draped across every porch."

"What's a Confederate fla—"

"It was that image of the flag that got me sweating. I felt that shit dripping down my back. And I tried to breathe, you feel me?"

"Yes," I said.

"I was glad to see one of the cops was black. I was like, *Hallelujah*. They were these big guys, with the Stetson hats and the visor-shades, and the white one was chewing gum, real slow, chew chew chew, his jaw going crunch, real loud. And I had everything, I had my papers, the car was registered, my shit is straight, you feel me?"

"I feel you."

"But now, they want me to pop my trunk. And I'm looking at the black officer, looking him straight in the eye, and I'm like, "But why, officer? What have I done?' "

I sensed that he wanted me to squeeze his hand, so I did, blinking at the furrows ploughing his brow.

"The next thing, there's a fucking gun in my face and the white cop is screaming, 'Show me your hands! Show me your hands and get out of the car!'

"Now, I'm yelling, 'What have I done, officer, I didn't do anything, officer!'

"He's screaming, 'I said show me your hands! Show me your hands or I'll shoot! I will shoot you, you hear me, boy? You hear me?'

"I look to the black cop and damn, mothafucka got his gun out, too! He's stepped away from the other guy, almost squatting, his arms extended, looking at me and then at his partner and then back at me, and I'm looking at him, and he says, 'Do as he says.' His voice is calm, he isn't shouting or anything like that, but he has the gun trained on me, and I can't get my eyes off that gun.

" 'OK, OK OK,' I say, and I'm shouting, my voice is shaking 'n' shit, I'm tryna open the car door, and the white police dude is shouting, 'I said get your fucking hands up, boy! Show me those hands, show me those hands!'

"And now I start crying, 'cause this mothafucka looks trigger happy, he's busy waving his gun all wild in my face, screaming at me, and I'm thinking, *Am I going to be the next Michael Brown? Am I going to go the way Eric Garner did? Is what happened to Charlemagne gonna happen to me?* So, there I was thinking I was going to die and shouting to the officer, 'Here're my hands, here're my hands!'

"'Get out of the car,' he shouts.

"'How am I supposed to get out with my hands up!' I shout back.

'You tryna be smart with me, boy? You tryna run your mouth?'

'No, officer,' I say. 'No, officer, sorry, officer, I haven't done anything, I don't wanna die, not today, officer, my moms is waiting for me, she's waiting for her boy, today's not my day to die, officer, see, I'm just gonna reach for the door handle real slow with my right hand, I still have my left hand up, see, I'm getting out, I'm getting out!'

'Get down on the ground, now!'

'But I'm out of the car, officer, see, I'm out and—'

'I said lie the fuck down! Now!'

'But I've done all you wanted, I've complied, I haven't done—'

'Lie down, son.' It's the black cop, now.

I look at him and all I want is to spit at him. I want to spit at his fucking orange face, I wanna shout, *I'm not your son.* I wanna cuss him out. I look away, dammit, my face is wet and I'm sniffling, my legs are trembling. Now, I'm tryna lie down, like they said, but the moment I lower my hands to get down on the ground, the white officer gets all rabid like and starts shouting, 'Did I not say hands up? You resisting an order from an officer of the law?'

'I'm just tryna get down, like you said—'

'Stop talking back to me! Stop talking back to me or I'll put a bullet in your fuckin' mouth!'

Now I'm straight out crying. I'm sure I'm gon' die and I'm praying to Charlemagne's spirit to help me, like, help a brother out, namesake, please, I don't wanna be no martyr. There's snot coming out of my nose, I'm tryna wobble down onto my knees and then throw myself forward with my hands still up, like the officer said, and my face smashes into the asphalt. It's a stupid thing to do, you feel me, but my face smashes into the asphalt and the pain shoots up my nose straight to my head. The mothafucka pounces on me, he grabs my arms and twists them behind my back, says I'm being hostile, says I'm not following orders, even as I'm down on the ground, like he wanted.

They leave me like that, sniveling and licking dirt, my face scratched and stinging, pressed into the ground, I don't dare look up to see what they're doing, I'm sure I'm gonna die. I can hear their feet going crunch-crunch around my car. They're opening my doors, they're rustling stuff, and then they pop my trunk, and it's just my moms' macuto and batea in there, that's all that's in there.

'Keep your head down!' shouts the cop, even though my head is down, my head is down, I'm not doing anything except lying there cuffed like he wanted."

I stared at Péralte's face, glistening from the effort of speaking, of expelling himself like that. I traced its pimpled expanse, his eyes wide, the corneas super white, nostrils flaring. He was scrunched up, his body no longer free like it had been as we danced earlier that evening, now a taut, constricted mass, as though he were trying to make himself small, as though he were trying to disappear. His large hand was crushing mine, making me wince, though I didn't cry out, I just swallowed.

I watched his wide chest heaving, counting the beats as it swelled, becoming a terrain terrifying and gorgeous, before deflating back into a decipherable mass. My own heart was beating fast and irregular, too, like it was trying to leap out of my chest. He released my hand. I brought it up to my chest and began gently massaging it. I didn't know what to do, so I placed my good hand on his shoulder. I kept it there. He didn't shrug it off, and I was glad.

"I'm glad you didn't die," I said.

I held his hand in both of mine and began massaging it. Then I put his finger in my mouth and sucked on it. It tasted salty. I gazed at Péralte. There was a look on his face. He leaned toward me. I uncoiled to meet him. His lips trembled. I sucked on them, the way I would suck on the ends of crushed chicken bones, slow and savory like. A million sensations prickled through me. I was hot. I was burning. He cupped my face, like he wanted to take in the whole of me and molded his mouth around my tongue. My cheeks felt warm and tingly in his hands.

I brought my hand down to his trousers. He pulled away.

"I'm sorry," I said. "I should have said at the beginning that I want to, I want us to . . . this is so difficult . . . I'm not used to having to be so direct, I mean, I understand it's the American Way, I just, oh, look, you're smiling, now I've gone and embarrassed myself . . ."

He gazed at me, but I could not read his expression. I felt a violent quopping between my legs. Leaning into him, I pressed my face into the pit of his arm and inhaled a heady scent, vinegary and sweet, like a mixture of sweat and cologne. He stood up and gripped the sides of his tunic shirt and lifted it over his head. He unbuttoned his trousers, letting them fall. They piled up around his feet. I averted my eyes for a moment, and then stared, not knowing what to do with his underwear sitting black and tight against his thick, shuddering hips. He slipped out of his undies in one go. Out sprung his thing, bopping with spry enthusiasm. I stared at it for a moment. And then I looked up at him. He was watching me, his hands on his hips, his head tilted to one side. He did not look at all shy, standing exposed like that.

It made me bold, seeing him naked before me, betraying his desire, heightening mine. I bent forward and slipped him into my mouth. He gasped, and I was afraid I had scraped my teeth against him, somehow; but he pressed himself into me, deeper into my mouth. I began to move down the veined, pulsating length of him and back up again. We continued like that, my mouth making a slobbering suction noise. He began to wheeze, his mouth open, making a guttural sound. It made me throb, hearing him pant like that.

He clutched me by the shoulders and pulled out of my mouth. My jaw ached. But I was pleased to see the glossy film over his eyes. He bent forward and began to fumble with the space suit. I thought, with dismay, how this, me huffing out the suit like some damn alien, was anything but romantic. Getting out of it was quite a mission. We got up, and Péralte helped me hoist the open-mouthed sac over my head. I slipped my arms, and then finally my legs, out of it. I stood there panting, feeling shy in my bra and panties. And then I sat down on the bed and hunched my back, though nothing could ever hide my big breasts. Péralte held the suit tentatively with both hands and walked over to the glass box in the corner and placed it inside. He hoisted it up slowly, carefully, fastening it back to the hooks in the glass box.

Then he turned and shuffled back to me. He stood before me, looking down at me. I fluttered my eyes at him and then looked away.

"Can I?" he said, placing a hand on my breast.

I nodded. He pushed me back gently until I was lying on his bed.

Then he pushed my bra out of the way, not even bothering to unclasp it, and molded his lips around a nipple. His mouth was warm, making a pleasant sucking motion. I moaned theatrically, like I remembered Catherine Tramell doing in *Basic Instinct* as Detective Curran kissed her all over.

Péralte slid down, planting a star of smooches over the soft roll of a love handle, and across my stomach to the other side. He slid down and kissed my dimpled thighs. His hand tugged my white cotton underwear to one side. The next moment his tongue was between my legs, a warm, flickering moistness. I had not expected that. No one had ever licked me down there before. The boys I knew hated the thought of it, saying women were dirty down there, blood came out of there every month, and it was humiliating for them to have their heads between a woman's legs. Though they had never minded being inside a woman's mouth. Oh. Péralte's tongue was warm and ticklish. My hips began to move, rising to meet his quivering tongue. I was overcome, with rapture, with rhapsody. It throbbed through me, starting from between my legs and spreading rapidly through the rest of me, an intense delight, making me hot, making me cry out.

I placed my hands on Péralte's head, trying to pull him up, wanting him inside me. Groaning, he rolled off me, pushing me away, and folded an arm across his face, covering his eyes. "I don't have any condoms," he said.

I whimpered. I was so hot I thought I would burst!

"I know," he said. "Me too."

"Just put in the tip."

"You know it never happens like that."

"OK, then you'll pull out."

"We're too old to be reckless."

"You're boring."

Slowly, we began to dress. I was feeling sticky. The brush of the lacy fabric of the bra against my nipples hurt. I could still feel the shadow of Péralte's lips around them, the way he had brought me into an intense communion with myself.

"I'd like to do this again," I said.

"Me too," he said.

"All right," I said, trying not to sound too pleased. And then, trying to sound nonchalant, "How many people have you been with?"

I had not expected him to look so annoyed. "What kind of damn question is that?"

I shrugged. "I've been with one guy. There. Now you know about me. So, I think it's only fair that I also know."

He frowned, studying his fingers. I saw he was counting. "Eleven."

"Eleven? Oh my, aren't we slutty."

"What's that supposed to mean? You wanted to know so you could insult me, or what?"

"I just . . . you don't look like someone who gets around."

"Are you saying I look like I got no game?"

"No, I just—"

"You've started again, running your mouth and talking shit."

"Oh wow. Really? Way to spoil a night."

"Are you sulking? I've never seen you sulk. You look really pretty when you do. Come on, sulk for me, now."

I couldn't help it, I burst out laughing. "If you continue like this," I said, wagging a finger at him, "I won't let you work on the Bantu geometries paper with me."

"Ooh! I'd like a spanking instead. Can I get a spanking? Come here, you."

The snow came without warning in the first week of November. Creamy vanilla fluff began falling mysteriously one afternoon. I watched it from my bedroom window, brimming with reverence. Emitting a dramatic little squeal, I sprinted out of my room and down the corridor and out the apartment door, bounding down the creaking steps two at a time. I burst into the cool air, which was crisp and offered a gentle bite. I stood in the street, my nightgown fluttering about my ankles like a cape, and stretched my hands out palm-up, trying to catch the wafting scoops. I was transported to a place childlike and distilled. I was the universe just before the big bang. I was a nucleotide. I was a glowing clump of helium-hydrogen, trundling along in outer space.

By the end of the first week, the streets and houses were palimpsested by snow. I was charmed by that blinding whiteness, the way it buried the landscape, obliterating everything. It rejuvenated me, this idea of being nothing, a blank slate.

I loved watching Péralte as he trudged through the snow toward my apartment. His knees kissed as he walked, his gait taking on a particular, bouncy rhythm, like he was attempting a cool step. I would wait for him on our front porch, just so I could take him in, enjoying the view as he came into focus.

Sometimes, his mind seemed far away, overcome by a shadow that muddied his beautiful, animated face. He would look up as he approached our house, and upon seeing me leaning against one of the peeling pillars of the porch watching him, his wide, sculpted cheeks would spread in a self-conscious smile. He looked so happy. I enjoyed this, seeing his usual braggadocious self become all vulnerable and shy. It was a tender part of himself he didn't reveal often. Maybe the other side of himself he liked showing me and the world, the hardcore, intellectual part, was tender, too, in its own way; a fierce kind of tender.

We'd started going on walks together. We were sleeping together, too. The sight of his sweat-beaded face twisting into a raw intensity as he heaved above me was as close to apotheosis as I had ever gotten. I was thrilled to get to know him so intimately, to let someone into the vulnerable parts of me and get to know theirs, acquainting myself with the seemingly infinite map of his brow and the colossal rumble of his voice, delighting in its spry timbre, worrying at its guttural notes.

We took our walks in the evenings on the days when the night sky was crisp. Hand in hand, we trudged through the snow down Dubuque Avenue, past Church Street and Brown, sloshing past these magnificent sorority and fraternity houses of a kind I had only seen in American college movies. Their trimmed lawns, which had been a sparkling, shamrock green in the summer months, now lay buried under piles of snow.

The lake came into view to our left as we sloped down the hill, look-ing shiny and bruised. We took a left onto Park Road and ambled past the bridge, and then turned left again, onto the walking trail. There we sat on one of the benches scattered along the lake.

"There's the Digging Stars," said Péralte, pointing at the constellation Pleiades, which was clustered like rowdy blue siblings in the northeast.

"My father also told you about the Digging Stars?" I said.

"Oh, you didn't leave Frank's study without an astronomy lesson on the Bantu and the stars!"

He became quiet. He seemed far away. I imagined my father had been the closest he'd had to a father figure as a child, before this James person his mother was married to came along. He never spoke about James. But his face would light up whenever he mentioned my father. For once, watching his wide brow crinkle and hearing his voice gurgle all nostalgic and soft-like as he gazed up at the Digging Stars, I did not begrudge him this.

We recited the star lore my father had taught us. We both knew the story of the Digging Stars, known by the Khoisan as "the Daughters of the Sky God." When their husband, that bloodshot Male Wildebeest star, Aldebaran, which we glimpsed shimmering south of the Daugh-ters, went hunting and shot his arrow at the Three Zebras—the hazy blob of stars the Greeks call Orion's Sword—his arrow fell short. He was afraid to retrieve his arrow thanks to the lioness—that fiery Female Wildebeest star, Betelgeuse—sitting watch over the zebras. And so, there hovers the Male Wildebeest star in the night sky still, unable to move forward or go back. This is why he's a bright, angry red star—he's bloodshot with fatigue.

"I never got why Aldebaran and Betelgeuse were called Wildebeest stars," I told Péralte, "not until one of Mama's lovers took us on a Safari in Mosi-oa-Tunya."

"Your moms had lovers?"

"Well, yes, when she was Catholic and only went to church every other Sunday. Then she joined the Pentecostals and became more devout than Jesus himself."

Péralte laughed. "OK, OK, we're not here to learn about your moms's lovers. Just tell me why they're called Wildebeest stars."

The Wildebeest stars usually appeared in the sky in the Southern hemisphere in the month of December, when wildebeest across the region birthed their young, all at the same time, as though they had colluded, eight months before, in a spectacular orgy.

"Isn't that beautiful?" I said. "And to answer the question you haven't asked but that I can see burning a hole through your provincial American mind: no, there are no wildebeest where I grew up in Bulawayo. . . ." Péralte laughed. ". . . I didn't grow up riding them, talking to them, picking ticks off their hides, or any of that Tarzan stuff. I only saw them when we went to the zoo for a school trip, and on safari with the Canadian guy Mama was seeing, and on *National Geographic* on TV."

"Moms says when the Three Zebras appeared in the sky at this time of the year, the Taíno knew the rainy season was coming to an end."

"This is too cool. My Bantu astronomy and your Taíno astronomy are having a convo right now."

When Shaniqua came stargazing with us on one of the evenings and heard us share our star lore, she pointed at the Digging Stars and called them Bagonegiizhig, "the Hole in the Sky."

I could see how the Digging Stars formed some sort of portal. We marveled at this, at how each of our people had always made use of the stars, and mourned the fact that we were only making this connection with one another now.

"Pa used to tell me how Sky Woman fell through Bagonegiizhig and brought the first humans to Turtle Island," said Shaniqua. "She came bearing gifts of tobacco, strawberries, and sweetgrass."

"Turtle Island?" I said.

"What the Europeans named America," she said. After a while, she said, her voice quiet, that she wondered what kind of America an origin story born of the Sky Woman, and not Manifest Destiny, would have birthed.

We were quiet for a little while, a somberness in the air. Then Shaniqua turned to me and said, her voice sprightly, "I been researching that reserves thing."

"Reserves thing?" I said.

"Remember when I told you about our reservations, you said y'all got reserves back in Zimbabwe?"

"OK, that's creepy," said Péralte. "Reservation. Reserve. The names are too close."

"I said the same thing!" said Shaniqua.

She told us how after much googling and perusing and many a night spent coughing in the dusty archives, she had finally found the connection in the history section of the university library, in a book that hadn't been opened since 1979. This was what the book said: In 1910, the apartheid government in South Africa had sent a delegation to the USA and Canada to study the North American reservation. They must have liked what they saw, because they borrowed this settler technology and went back to South Africa and created their own reserves.

"And then that dude, what's his name? The one who wanted to build a railroad across Africa?"

"Cecil John Rhodes," I said.

"Yeah, him!" said Shaniqua. "Him and his British South Africa Company built the same reserves in Southern Rhodesia! Wait, Southern Rhodesia's Zimbabwe, right? Or is it Zambia? Damn, can't remember all them names."

"Yes, that's Zimbabwe," I said. "Zambia was Northern Rhodesia."

"So you see?" said Shaniqua, her eyes sparkling. "We are created out of you, over there in Africa, and *you* are created out of *us*."

"This is crazy," said Péralte.

"How come we don't even know this history?" I said.

"We do now," said Shaniqua. "That gotta count for something."

"My father once called us 'colonial inventions,'" I said. "I thought he was just going off on one of his tangents, working through stuff."

"And Uncle Frank riffed off *a lot*," said Péralte.

I scrunched up my face. I didn't know what to do with all this knowing. It just felt so heavy. It felt as though there were already alternate versions of our lives going on here on Earth and there was no need to go in search of the multiverse. Like, in another life, history could have been different, leading us three to this moment, but a different kind of moment, where we were a different kind of together, twined by a more intimate knowing. Shaniqua came and wrapped her arms around me, pressing me to her bosom. She rubbed my back, her hands moving in soothing circular motions. I allowed myself to rest my cheek on her shoulder, my body going limp against hers.

"How about we build something together?" said Péralte, his eyes becoming lively, brimming things.

"Build what?" I said, squinting at him.

He shrugged. "I dunno. I mean, we've got all this star lore we didn't know about and then this history you guys didn't know you shared. I mean, we gotta do something with it."

"Maybe we could build a virtual world or something like that?" said Shaniqua.

"Now you're talking," said Péralte.

He could put the whole thing together on his gaming software, he said, and Shaniqua'd bring her biophysics work to the mix and I'd take care of the visual designs, seeing as I loved sketching so much.

"Hmmm," said Shaniqua, looking at us funny. "So lemme get this straight. You two want me to be the third wheel in your little lovefest, huh?"

"What? . . ." I said, trying to look confused, but she wagged a finger and laughed.

"Don't think I haven't seen you two," she said, and then, "Why didn't you tell me y'all are dating?"

Péralte and I exchanged a glance. For a moment, standing there watching the stars in the sky and their murky reflections glinting on the freezing waters of the lake, I had felt deliriously, unreasonably happy, and safe. It was this feeling in Péralte's presence I cherished, a beauty that felt at once sublime and mysterious, like the feeling you get when you behold a rainbow but know you can't ever touch it; it disappears over an asymptotic horizon when you chase after it, and that is its charm and its magic.

I didn't know how to say this to Shaniqua. I didn't even know how to articulate it myself.

Péralte said we'd better head back, and we began the slow trudge back to our apartment, all three of us hand in hand.

✳

I SUGGESTED WE model our virtual world on an exoplanet like Kepler-186f, Earth's first cousin. A planet not quite like Earth, but close.

"We still need to figure out how to map our world on the computer," said Péralte. "I wanna try and build some new software for it. Like, is it just going to be another replica of the same old shit we have here on Earth, or?"

"We could make a video game," I said. "Make our virtual world interactive."

"Ooh!" said Péralte. "Something cool, like discovering a new planet in the universe and having to make contact and build a life there."

"I love that," said Shaniqua. "And anyone who tries to pull some Manifest Destiny shit in the game dies and has to start from scratch. *Ka-pow.*"

"In this world, Sky Woman rules," I said, and we cheered.

"Yeah, like, I wanna put some landmarks from the Mississippi Choctaw Reservation in the game," said Shaniqua. "Sprinkle a little astronomy trivia here and there. We could all add to that. Like, if you know the history, you proceed to the next stage of the game or get points or something."

I loved dreaming up a world on an Earthlike planet that was not quite like Earth. It loosened something in me. I was awed by the vastness of our universe. As long as there was the possibility of water on Kepler-186f, there was the possibility of life. For all its variation and wonderful complexity, the universe is made up of the same basic ingredients. It was amazing to think how iNdonsakusa, with her gigantic size and gaseous interior, and iNyanga, with her anorthosite rock and basaltic craters, and Earth, with her rocky interior and plethora of life, all came from the same basic ingredients. It was amazing to think how we did, too.

Kepler-186f was no exception to this diversity. She took about half the time to orbit her dwarf star than our planet Earth took to orbit the sun, meaning we'd celebrate our birthdays there every six months. We'd be twice as old over there.

"Finally, humanity'll attain the secret elixir to long life!" I said, raising my hands in mock celebration.

Shaniqua chuckled. "Mercy, child. You're really dripping with the sarcasm, ain't you?"

"Is that a compliment from the Queen of Sarcasm?" I said, grinning.

We worked on our virtual world all through November. The crazier the weather got, the more I threw myself into it. The snow, which at first had charmed in its blinding white innocence, had turned deadly by December.

They called it the coldest winter in twenty years, so that even the veterans of this Midwestern college town stumbled across ice-slicked streets shivering in their puffy coats, eyes watery above cold-slapped cheeks. Seeing that others were suffering as I was gave me some comfort—a whole lot of comfort, in fact. We were cuddled in a communal victimhood at the hands of some enraged weather god, the combined efforts of Khione, Greek goddess of snow, and Shango, Yoruba god of thunder, et cetera, who together were taking pleasure in this damn shit visited upon us, this fucking crazy winter with the clouds pimpled and surly like the tumult of adolescence. The sun was cold-hearted even on the brightest of days. Not one ray of love.

I would wake up to weak rays of sunlight struggling through my window. I tried to blink them away, groggy with sleep. For a moment, I was on our imaginary Kepler-186f. I and planet Earth's other aliens had been beamed there, five hundred light-years away.

Eventually, I remembered where I was. I was beset by an odd mixture of grief and elation. It was as though, caught between sleep and wakefulness, my body ferried itself to that other dream world it now spent most of its waking days imagining into being and, once fully alert, mourned the rude thrust back into this world, the caress of the skin by this familiar air, the assault of the nostrils by these same smells, the fucking winter apocalypse threatening to annihilate us outside.

✶

TWO GOLDEN ENVELOPES arrived in the mail in the second week of December, one for Shaniqua and one for me. They were offers to intern at Infinity Inc. part-time the following year. The internship gave access to their groundbreaking research and their state-of-the-art facilities to further our own projects. The letters had been signed by Thomas Long himself. I traced his squiggly signature with my fingers, my body trembling. I felt faint. I could barely contain my elation. I already saw myself high up in space aboard an Infinity Inc. ship. Or perhaps even living on the Galileo. Perhaps, one day, we'd build a spaceship that could travel at the speed of light and thrust us out of our solar system into other planetary systems in the Milky Way and, eventually, planetary systems in other galaxies. Reaching heaven, wasn't that the dream? And what could be closer to the proverbial heavens than the stars? It was as close to the sublime as any one of us was ever going to get.

Péralte, too, had received a golden envelope in the mail. He called for an emergency meeting at his house. We sat on the floor in a circle in his sitting room, a brown paper bag between us.

He rolled a cohoba blunt, lit it, and took a drag. "So what y'all think about this whole Infinity Inc. thing?" he said, passing the blunt to Shaniqua.

Shaniqua accepted the blunt, tilted her head and took a nice long drag. She passed it to me. Puffing on the blunt, passing it between us in the communal spirit of blunt-sharing and watching the smoke spiral in the air, the world felt mellow. I liked the way this particular batch of cohoba made me feel, the way I became loose and lazy and sleepy, the way Péralte's wide face began to float hazy-like before my eyes.

I said, passing the blunt to Péralte, that this internship would get me close to an accomplishment like my father's. Eventually, I'd go to space. Maybe I could even reach heaven one day.

Shaniqua started laughing this high, lethargic little twitter. I wondered if she was high already. She said, puffing on the blunt, that she was never going to work for Infinity Inc. She, Shaniqua, working to make Thomas Long richer than he already was? In what universe did that make sense? All the work we did over there would belong to Infinity Inc. We'd basically be giving away our best ideas.

"And what will happen to our Kepler project?" she said.

I tried to keep a straight face. Who the hell cared about our fake Kepler? I wanted to go to space.

Shaniqua dragged on her blunt philosophically. "This is the time to do our own shit," she said. "We're never gonna be as free to pursue our own silliness as we are now."

"Damn, it's gonna be the nine-to-five grind after we graduate," said Péralte, beckoning for Shaniqua to pass the blunt.

Shaniqua snorted, handing it over. "Chile! We're gonna be at places like Infinity Inc. helping them gentrify space 'n' shit, *or*, we'll prolly end up working for Northrop Grumman helping them make space missiles or General Dynamics helping them make weapons systems satellites and all that shit. And you know they'll make insane profits dropping those babies on some Iraq or some Syria or someplace like that. Like, that's the extent of our dreaming?"

"Didn't you see the space materials division on the brochure?" I said. I was feeling itchy and hot and sore. "They're testing melanin to see if it can shield humans in space from radiation. Don't you want to be part of that?"

"I ain't helping folk wear black face just so they can go to space," said

Shaniqua. "Do they got respect for the melanin right here on Earth, first and foremost, that's the damn question. That Galileo shit didn't even bother pretending to be speaking to people like us."

"What do you mean, people like us?" I said.

She gave me that tragic look I'd gotten used to. "You Black, ain't you?"

I said I didn't know.

"You don't know?" she said, breaking into a little titter. "Girl bye! What d'you mean, you don't know? Péralte, talk to your girl. I seriously can't."

"Well, at home I am Ndebele. Then there are the Shona. Then—"

"Here in America, you're Black," Péralte said, giving me this impenetrable look.

I fell silent.

"Promise me you won't go and work for that man," said Péralte.

"Why not?" I said.

Shaniqua began to laugh, though her laughter was without warmth, without humor. "Oh Lord," she said.

"What?" I said, glaring at her.

"Promise me," said Péralte, sitting up.

I rolled my eyes. "Negro, please."

"*Negro, please?* When the hell did you start talking like that? Girl, you're doing way too much. You're gonna trip yourself up on these streets and hurt yourself."

"I've heard you say it. And Shaniqua calls you 'negro' all the time."

"Right. 'Cause everyone wants to be Black America cool, but nobody wants to be an ally, and remember actually being Black."

I didn't know what to say. I just looked at him.

"Busy going on about 'I don't know if I'm Black,'" muttered Shaniqua, settling back down on the hardwood floor. "Girl, bye!"

"'Girl bye' to you, too."

"Péralte, you better talk to your girl, 'cause she's making me seriously upset right now."

"Everything we've been talking about," said Péralte, "I told you 'bout Haiti and what happened to me on that trip to get the stuff for my moms, like, you don't get it? You don't see me at all?"

"I just want to go up to space, that's it," I said.

"All right, go on and be a house nigger then," said Shaniqua, puffing on the blunt.

I knew enough from her tone that she didn't mean the N-word in a cool way, the way Lil Wayne and Rick Ross and Nicki Minaj and all those American rappers who had made the N-word cool the world over meant. No, she didn't mean *nigga*, but *nigger*. And a *house nigger* at that, which although I wasn't exactly sure what it meant, I was sure must have been way worse than just being an ordinary nigger for her to use it on me like that.

Péralte nudged me and motioned for the blunt. I took a small puff and handed it to him. I found I couldn't look him in the eye. I sat there, unable to look at them both, feeling bruised.

"I think I should just up and leave America," said Shaniqua.

"Leave America?" I said, frowning at her. "Where are you going to go?"

"I don't know," she said, shrugging. "Africa. I could move to Côte d'Ivoire with Moussa after he graduates in the spring."

I watched her, trying to keep my face straight. "Why on earth would you want to do that?" I asked. I was still stung by the way she'd been talking to me.

"I'm tired of this shit," she said. "Tired, man. Tired of them cops tryna kill us, tired of being told I'm extinct, just fuckin' tired. They got Black and Indigenous folk in Africa, don't they?"

"Like I already *told* you," I said, barely keeping the irritation out of my voice. "Back home, you don't have to think about being black. Not like here in America. That's not how we think."

"Yeah, well, I'm going to move there."

"Move there and do what?"

She took a drag from the blunt. "Moussa's a prince back in Côte d'Ivoire, y'know. He's the son of a royal over there. He's always telling me about his family and this magnificent royal compound they have at the foot of Mount Niénokoué that looks out over the stillest lake you ever saw. In the mornings, it looks like it's reflecting the sky, complete with the patterns of the clouds. Now, who wouldn't wanna live there? I'll prolly live better there than I'm living here! Africa, baby! Woo!"

I couldn't help it; a snicker escaped my lips. Moussa, a prince?

"Stop it, you two," said Péralte. He looked checked out, stretched out on the hardwood floor with the blunt now dangling between his lips.

"What?" said Shaniqua.

"Nothing," I said, in a way that implied there was clearly something.

"You obv got something to say, so just say it!"

"I just . . . you don't need to lose yourself in a man like that, Shaniqua. It's just plain desperate. It doesn't look good on you. . . ."

It felt good to have one over her, for once. I thought maybe she'd step up to me and get all up in my face, like she liked to do whenever she was mad. I intended to put on airs and keep calm throughout, which would infuriate her even more.

Instead, she threw back her head and started laughing, swaying like the laughter was so abundant it was going to demolish her. I chuckled uncertainly, not sure what was happening.

"'Don't lose yourself in a man, Shaniqua,'" she said, her voice rising to a whine, certainly not sounding like how I talked, her tongue thickening the syllables, a parody, dragging out the *T* and the *S* in her speech. "Says the gal who goes on about her daddy like he's Barack Obama or something."

We both fell silent. It was as though the air were being sucked out of the room.

"My father was a brilliant man."

"*He left you*," she said, thrusting her face into mine, her dainty hands fisted by her sides. "Don't you get that? He left you in goddamn Africa to come chase the 'American Dream.' " She rolled her eyes, making quotation marks in the air.

My eyes began to flutter, like I'd been slapped. For a moment, I was at a loss for what to do. Then something cold and surgical surged through me. "You mean *your* father left *you*," I said. "And now, because you don't even know where the hell he is, you're throwing yourself at some shady boy who's feeding you shit."

I wanted so much to hurt her. Instead, she threw back her head again and began cackling. "At least I've got no illusions about *my* daddy. I don't go around talking about him like I'm goddamn two years old, acting like he was a god or something. Men are trash. You hear? Men are trash, *and so was your daddy*. At least I know mine left me. You don't seem to know yours did! He left you, you hear? *He left you.*"

"No, he didn't," I said. "He didn't. He died. He just died. But he loved me. My daddy loved me."

" . . . "

"___"

" . . . Oh!" Shaniqua's voice was all soft now, her face crumpled, no longer a twisted, horrible thing. "Honey boo. Oh, I'm sorry. I'm so sorry, baby, I didn't mean . . ."

I didn't understand what she was doing, why she had approached me and was trying to press me to her bosom. There must have been a look on my face. Embarrassed, ashamed, confused, I didn't know what I was feeling, I pulled away from her and got up and stumbled to Péralte's room. I slammed the door and turned the key and threw myself on the bed and squashed my face in my hands. I found I could not cry.

I didn't know what was happening, why we had said those things to one another. I ignored first Shaniqua and then Péralte's soft rat-a-tats on the door, their voices calling out my name, my isiNdebele name, the first name my father had given me, unbearable in its tenderness.

The exposé on my father was published on Christmas Eve in the *New York Times*.

I woke up to weak rays of light filtering through my window, casting a hazy, ephemeral glow on the framed photo of him aboard the International Space Station. I blinked at the photo, groggy with sleep. The naked branches of the hackberry tree were thumping against my window. It was a light tap-tap sound, like a knock. The branches were laden with snow. It held them in its icy grip, tracing every contour and every ridge, right down to the spindliest twig. The fresh snow that was yet to turn into ice spilled to the ground with each tap. It looked gelid and seraphic, each particle identical to and yet distinct from the next, like the fungal DNA Shaniqua was studying for her biophysics experiments. Maybe that was why the particles became luminescent and sibylline when they coagulated, like they had come together to create a life force.

The article popped up in my inbox. I saw my father's name and clicked on it. For years, read the article, my father had been working for the weapons manufacturer and US military contractor Xylus in exchange for funding for his astronomy projects in Africa and the Caribbean. His university seemed to have known about my father's compromised work and may have even encouraged it. In return, the university had received funding from Xylus for its observatory and its laboratories.

According to university records, my father and his university had accepted a grant from Xylus to design and build a multispectral detector that could capture distant celestial objects in the sky at a more refined spectrum—and also distant military targets on the ground. The heat sensor technology had been used to build the Sativat V satellite and the Habar drone, which had been used in military strikes in Afghanistan and Iraq and, more recently, by the Assad regime in Syria. The *NYT* had come into possession of top-secret documents that proved that both my father and the university had known what the technology he was building would be used for.

His former students were up in arms. They had worked with my father on both the Sativat V and the Habar drone, which they had been told would help responders identify victims of natural disasters and transport medical supplies. Current students were calling for a strike and an investigation. Antiwar protests had broken out outside of the campus gates, spilling onto the main thoroughfare.

A photo of my father's face appeared at the end of the article. In it, he was staring, unsmiling, at the camera. It looked like a mug shot. Beneath it was a series of photos of the antiwar protestors waving their banners:

SPACE IS FOR PEACE NOT WAR

THE BOOMERS ARE KILLING OUR PLANET

**WHAT DOES THE MILITARY WANT IN SPACE**

**STOP HURTING THE MOON**

**C———— UNIVERSITY OWNED SLAVES**

**OUR PROFESSORS ARE KILLING US**

**JUDGMENT DAY IS HERE**

**MAKE LOVE NOT WAR**

I read and reread the article. Then I got up and got dressed carefully, like I had somewhere to go. I slipped out of the apartment, stumbling down the steps two at a time. The early morning winter air lacerated my throat. I walked with my head hunched in my coat and my hands in my pockets.

I wandered down cobbled streets. I took slow, deliberate steps. All around me, Christmas decorations spiraled around snow-laden, juniper-colored trees, blinking against the pale early morning sky. The landscape nictated in schizophrenic bursts of color.

The road ended, and I found myself standing before a small park. The trees were denuded of their leaves, groaning under piles of snow. Gray wooden benches with ornate legs were arranged along the stone paths crisscrossing the park.

How enduring the park looked, as though it had always been there. Gazing at it, with its piles of snow and its manicured trees and the majestic little pavilion crowning its center, I was overcome with transcendence, a sense of unsullied beauty. I chastised myself for feeling this way. There was something banal about the feeling. How could I know if I were experiencing an authentic emotion, culled from the very depths of my being, or if I were performing a memory of a manufactured past, miming an emotion I'd seen others perform countless times, on television or in the books and magazines I read? I thought of Shaniqua and the prairies and marshes she said had once made up this place.

A man and a child, a little girl, emerged from the pavilion in the center of the park. The girl was perched atop the man's shoulders. She gripped the top of his head with her gloved hands. Her laughter filtered through the air in sweet, lilting bursts.

I thought of Rufus and the Rogerses' farm and the one trip my father and I had taken together to his ancestral home. My father had stood before that farm and said, his voice bunged up, how he wished he'd known in which mass graves lurking somewhere on this land his parents had been buried, if they'd been buried at all, or if the government soldiers had come in the '80s and done what they'd done and then left their bodies out in the open to be picked at by vultures. He needed to know. There must have been a way to know. How could he know?

"Do you think there is a way to find out?" he'd said.

"Yes," I'd said, because I hadn't known what else to say.

Something in his voice had made me frightened. It was the only other time I ever saw him as anything other than my father.

The little girl lifted her gloved hands from the man's shoulders and raised them above her head. She opened and closed them, trying to catch the falling snow. Her hand managed to clamp around a fluffy pellet. Her face lit up. She giggled, and the man dropped her into his arms and buried his face in the scarf around her neck.

I turned around and began walking again.

HE BOUGHT ME a plastic globe, once. I must have nagged him for it. It arrived unexpectedly in the mail one summer morning, in January. It was light, made of some sort of durable plastic, but huge, so that my hands, which held it in a bearlike embrace, couldn't meet. I set it down in Mama's living room and studied it. I caressed it, marveling at the oceans and the seas and the rivers with their shimmering shades of blue, at the green and brown landmasses.

On this inflated wonder, the earth ceased to be flat, ballooning into an illusory spherical shape. Africa swelled at the sides, so that my finger had to curve as it traveled through the continent, following an imaginary aeronautical chart across the ultramarine Atlantic toward America.

"You are up, up, up!" I said to him that afternoon on the phone. "And we are down, here." My voice took on a low, disappointed pitch as I said "down."

"There is neither up nor down," he said. "It's an optical illusion. The sky is above us, as well as below us."

I felt compelled to grunt in agreement. But any sensible person knew the sky was above us and the ground beneath us!

As though he could read my mind, he said, "I want you to go outside and look down at your feet. Are you listening? Imagine you could bore a hole into the ground, right through to the other side of the earth. What would you see? You would see the sky, on the other side, through that hole. Because the earth is round. Do you understand?"

"Yes," I said, though I didn't understand.

"Learn to question your habits of thought," he said.

After our call, I went outside and stood facing our cottage. I looked up. It was the height of summer, and the sky was a concave, searing blue. I turned around and followed that hot blue with my eyes, all the way to the horizon. I was no longer looking up but straight ahead of me, into the distance. The sky dipped beyond the cluster of houses and trees dotting the horizon.

Any sensible person knew the sky was up, because wherever you went, there it was, above you and not beneath you.

I dropped my gaze to the ground. Stomped my feet, provoking a cloud of rust-colored dust upward. Any sensible person knew that if you dug deep enough into the earth, you would eventually reach hell, or a searing olivine mantle, whichever came first. Just like if you soared high enough, you would reach heaven, or America.

I stood still for a while, my face creasing and uncreasing. And then I marched over to the tool shed behind Mama's cottage. There, I retrieved a hoe and dragged it all the way back to our front yard, where I had been standing.

It was this way Mama found me, sweating and grunting in the ineffectual little hole I had managed to excavate.

"What are you doing?" she said, her hands on her hips. "That tool is not a plaything!"

"I am looking for the sky," I said.

She raised a hand to her face, cupping it over her forehead like the bill of a cap, and gazed up at the sky.

"Father says it's below us," I said, giving her an *I know* look.

She threw back her head and laughed. She laughed long and hard, so long and so hard I thought her face would burst. I watched her, sullen.

When he called that evening, I heard her say, "You will never believe what I found your child doing today."

And there it was again, that laughter, this time echoed by a throaty, basso cantante chortle coming from the phone.

✶

WITHOUT REALIZING IT, I had made my way to The Program building.

It loomed before me, all two stories of it. A triangular piece of snow-laden lawn sloped at an obtuse angle up the incline that led to the first part of the building, whose wood-paneled walls stood blushing in a coat of ruby paint. To my right, the newer brick-and-glass wing distended from the older structure. Someone had built a lopsided snowman on the lawn. His smile slid down one side of his face, so that he looked like he was scowling.

There they stood, appendaged to one another, the old building with its filigreed Greek columns that spoke of a classical history, and its sleeker, modern counterpart promising future innovations. Their gravitas seemed to cast an accusatory shadow on me, becoming colder and more menacing the more I stood there staring at them.

The front door was locked, though there was a side door that was sometimes left open by grad students who'd spent the night cooped up in there, trying to meet a deadline. I went around the side of the building; it was unlocked. I slipped inside.

I made my way to Dean's classroom on the first floor and stood before the *Allegory of America* print that hung on the wall. There was Amerigo Vespucci with the brass astrolabe in one hand and the banner of the Southern Cross constellation in the other. Behind him, to his right, was the ship. He wouldn't have stumbled upon the shores of Turtle Island without the largesse of the governments of Portugal and Spain, who'd made his scientific expeditions possible. He wouldn't have made it without his knowledge of astronomy and his nautical instruments and the stars to guide his way. I gazed at the astrolabe in his hand. He'd had to use it to determine his latitude at sea. I imagined him dangling his astrolabe from a piece of rope and pointing it to the sky and rotating the alidade and coming across four new stars that glowed like a kite but that must have looked to him, with his Catholic sensibilities, like a crucifix. He simply named them "the Four Stars." They were dubbed "the Southern Cross" by subsequent European explorers.

I gazed at the bare-breasted young woman in the drawing. I took in her feather headdress and matching skirt, her hand raised toward Amerigo as though in supplication. I read the inscription *A M E R I C A* back to front, as it curved toward the woman.

Amerigo. America.

America. Amerigo.

Something cinched my chest.

I pictured my father in his lab working on his multispectral detector to capture distant celestial objects. Ever since he was a boy, he had looked up at the night sky, hungry to commune with it. That was all he'd cared about—his precious stars. Always looking out, never looking in or down, where I sat, wrapped around his legs, watching him, waiting.

Had he thought about it, the way the multispectral detector's atomic speed would lock in on a target and its laser precision guide a kinetic missile, shredding a body to its molecular composition—not quite to star dust, but close? Had he thought about his mother and father, my gogo and khulu, sprawled in some mass grave somewhere near the Rogerses' farm? Or had he been too enamored of the stars? High on all that light?

It could make you drunk, just looking at it.

I thought of how the human eye bends light, transmitting images upside down to the retina. It's the brain that flips the images back the right way up. I thought of how planet Earth seems flat from our limited point of view, how it isn't even the near-perfect sphere we see from outer space. I thought of the satellites orbiting Earth, the Sativat V among them, winking down at us like stars. I thought of the treachery of light.

Perhaps where I had thought my father extraordinary, he had merely been an ordinary man, his ambitions shaped, like other men, by the everyday brutalities of the world.

The stone path leading up to Péralte's apartment glistened with salt. To my right, the bird bath was partly submerged, its copper-colored bowl piled with snow. It looked like a cake on a cake stand. Next to it, stray tufts of golden leaves sprouted here and there from the spindly branches of the witch hazel shrub.

A Christmas wreath hung on the front door. I shoved it aside and knocked. No one answered. I began to bang on the door, one rapid rap of the knuckles after another. Finally, it swung open. Péralte stood there with his hands on his hips. His red-and-white robe fluttered in the wind, revealing a pair of cotton pajamas with Christmas trees patterned on them. When he saw me, his gaze softened.

I plowed past him into the house. A dwarf fir tree stood in front of the curved window of the tower appendage to my left. It was wrapped in blue and red lights. Ribboned boxes were piled beneath it; I caught sight of a box with my name on it.

"Did you know?" I said to him.

He shook his head, his eyes wide. "I knew about Mr. C," he said. "Not this."

"What about Mr. C?" I said.

He looked at me and said nothing.

"Mr. C is like a father to me," I said.

Péralte cringed. "Let me call Moms," he said, fumbling about in his pockets.

He retrieved his phone and began scrolling through it.

"I don't want to talk to your mother," I said. "I'm talking to you."

But he had already dialed her number. She answered after only a few rings. Though she had a night bonnet on her head, bunning her hair to one side, her face was perky, if a little tired.

"Did you know?" I blurted.

"I'm sorry," she said. "I'm just . . . I just . . . " She pinched the space between her eyes.

"She keeps asking about Mr. C," said Péralte.

Candice looked alarmed. "That man," she said, and then seemed to stop herself. And then, "He's not your friend."

"He was friends with my father," I said.

Candice snorted. And then, her voice softening, she said, "The world your father grew up in was very complicated. Very difficult. Do you understand? African nations were gaining their freedom and struggling to define what that freedom meant. And then it turned into a nightmare."

"Thanks for the history lesson," I said, rolling my eyes.

She inhaled sharply, but I didn't care. Her breath made a loud, sucking sound. Then her chest heaved, and she seemed to relax, her small breasts shuddering beneath her nightie.

"The leaders began looking out for themselves at the expense of their own people," she went on. "The postcolonial genocides and ethnic cleansing reminded your father of the Crusades in the twelfth century, when Europe spread its doctrine of conquest across North Africa and the Middle East in the same way. We were repeating history, he said, reenacting its nightmares. And that broke his heart."

"OK, and so?" I muttered. I didn't know where the hell she was going with all of this. I felt sorry for her students, having to listen to her ramble like this in class after class. "What does Mr. C have to do with any of this?"

Candice sighed. "I tried to warn Frank against C, but he wouldn't listen. He knew C did clandestine work for your government. He had been doing it since their university days. But Frank insisted there has to be a liminal space where a man can exist as neither this nor that, where he can escape the boxes created for him by others and belong to himself. This is where he believed he and C could reside, outside of work and sinister politics and obligations, in this sacred space of friendship, of love. He forgot how jealous and all-encompassing a nation can be.

"I begged your father not to come down and collect you. His government had been hounding him for years. They wanted him to work for them. I didn't know why he mattered to them so much, then, but it all makes sense now. They must have known about his work for Xylus, and they wanted access to it. They believed he should be doing it for Zimbabwe and not America.

"I didn't know about any of this. I thought Frank and I were building something together. He said we were building a new world. He said—" She cupped her mouth, blinking rapidly. And then, frowning at something I couldn't see, beyond the screen, "I told him, you can't go back. It's not safe. But he wouldn't listen. He said he had to do this, that you were his kid and he had to come talk to your mother and bring you back with him."

A cold crept through my fingers and up my arms, searing my chest with its hypothermic touch.

"I got you," said Péralte, rushing toward me.

He tried to wrap his arms around me, but I shoved him away. I blinked at his wide, blurry face, so close to mine, and then at his mother's compressed on the phone screen.

"What are you saying?" I said.

"I'm sorry," she said.

"It was an accident," I said. "I know there were whispers as a child but . . . Everyone always says that about accidents at home. But it was an accident. He had an accident. . . ."

"I think they just intended to scare him," whispered Candice. "Maybe they just intended to run him off the road or something. I don't think they intended for it to happen that way. After all, they wanted his work.

"Your father had barely landed in Harare when C showed up at his doorstep in New York demanding to see his papers, demanding to go through his things.

"I laughed and said, 'Let's call Frank, I want to hear it from him.'

"He said, 'I'm sorry but Frank is dead.'

"I slapped him. What a cruel thing to say! I cried. I slapped him again and told him to leave.

"But he said Frank was dead and that he was sorry. He kept saying this over and over, 'He's dead, I'm sorry, I'm so sorry.' He claimed Frank had said he should take his research for safekeeping if anything ever happened to him. But I knew Frank would never have done that. He hadn't trusted the man with his work when he was alive, for goodness' sake!

"I said, 'How could you know Frank is dead? How could you know before us, before his family? How could you know before anyone else?' I refused to give him your father's work. He tried to threaten me. I had to call the police to make him leave."

"You are lying," I said to Candice. My voice was hoarse. "Mr. C would never do that. He loved my father."

"Oh, my darling," she said.

"I am not your darling."

"I'm sorry. I thought you wanted the truth."

"My father was a great man."

Candice clicked her teeth. "Stop acting like a child," she said. "You're not the only one who's hurting. He betrayed me, too, you know."

"You bitch," I said.

"I won't have you talking to me like you were raised in a tree."

"You bitch," I said again, and hung up.

I meandered aimlessly. I didn't know where to go. I found myself trudging past the public library, and then past St Mary's Church, whose steeple was piled with snow. The world began to bend and crest. Stomp-stomp-stomp I went, stumbling down the pavement, past the newspaper building that housed, below its offices, Devotay on one side with its fine wines and paellas, and Bashu on the other with its chow mien and mapo tofu.

I sloshed past glittering mounds of snow. They proliferated everywhere, slithering across the ground, creeping up the trees, covering the roofs, obliterating the landscape.

The winter air fisted my face. I struggled to breathe. I found I couldn't lift my arms. I looked down at my hands. They had dislodged at the wrists and hung suspended in the air, making rapid, frenetic motions. The air shredded my cheeks. I lobbed myself down the street. I ran as fast as I could, faster than I'd ever run in my life. I hadn't known I could run like that. And then I slipped, or my body crumpled, or both of these things happened, and the next moment I was spasming on the icy ground, and all around me was a profound, blazing darkness.

✳

THE DAY OF my father's funeral, I saw the grief almost topple Mr. C.

He was helping the pallbearers carry my daddy's coffin from the Doves Funeral hearse to the grave, that ivory box whose embroidered edges caught the glint of the steel-blue clouds, clouds so resolutely steely that when you stared at them your eyes hurt, almost as if you were look-ing into the sun. He was helping the pallbearers and taking the weight of my father in one hand, the other stretched out for balance, when he peered into the grave, and what he must have seen there, that oblong hole in the ground in which my father was going to be entombed, over-whelmed him (it must have been a terrifying vertigo, the kind that has assaulted me time and time again over the years) and his Kenneth Cole shoes lost their grip on the soil. There was a moment when he seemed to be slipping into that frightful hole.

In all of this, he did not let go of the coffin. He held on to it. His grip was determined. A look of dread overtook his face, the kind of dread that evades language, that, like all highs and lows of human emotion in their purest form is so genuine as to be terrifying. It was very brief, that peculiar dread on Mr. C's face, but in that moment—probably less than a second—I recognized in it something close to what I felt and had been feeling ever since I had learned of my father's death but did not have, in the way of children, the vocabulary to articulate it, only a numb, overwhelming dumbness.

Watching Mr. C teeter at the edge of the grave, as though flirting with death, a fist of heat clutched my chest. It was as though I were wit-nessing my father die, as though he were dying all over again, perform-ing death before my very eyes by succumbing to that dreadful hole. I was overcome by a profound Terror. My hands dislodged at the wrists and hung suspended in the air. Gasping, I tried to lob myself into the grave, almost knocking Mr. C in with me. But Mr. C regained his balance, pulling me back with him, saving me, and it was as though I had almost fallen into that frightful burial pit and not tried to jump in.

And then the moment had passed, and some of the Ladies of Roma, who were dressed in the chocolate skirts and tortilla blouses of their Sunday uniforms, with their matching Catholic berets angled carefully on their heads, smiled relieved smiles. Their voices tintinnabulated in that death-still afternoon, seeking those soprano peaks and contralto watersheds and tenor valleys, relentless, relentless. They dragged out sorrow as though it were death that had given them the wisdom to mine our deepest pits of woe and reflect them back to us in songfuls of unbearable feeling, imploring us nevertheless to bear it. And it was beautiful to hear, and awful, too, so very awful.

I broke into a fit of coughing, I couldn't help it, and Mr. C rubbed my back and pressed me to him and held me close.

✳

SOMEBODY HAD CALLED an ambulance.

At the hospital, the doctor asked me if I was aware that I was seeing her for the second time, exhibiting the same psychosomatic symptoms. She was going to run some tests, she said. Meanwhile, I should fill out the admission paperwork.

I glared at her. I wasn't going to be admitted to anywhere, I said. I just wanted to go home. She ignored me and ordered the nurse to do a battery of tests. The nurse came and drew my blood and then accompanied me to the toilet and waited outside as I peed in a plastic container. The pee wouldn't come, and I squatted over the toilet seat for a long time and plotted my escape. Then it came, and I straightened up and put the plastic container in a Ziploc bag and handed it to the nurse and followed her back to my hospital bed and waited.

The doctor returned after a few hours. She said the tests had come back normal, just as they had before, and that she was referring me to psych. The psych ward at the university hospital was full, so I would be going to the one at Mercy Hospital nearby.

It was a much better ward, she said, for women only.

Two chiseled paramedics tried to womanhandle me. I struggled against them, trying to pry myself out of their grip. I didn't want to go to Mercy or be admitted to any psych ward. I just wanted to go home. Frowning, the doctor said if I became violent, she was going to have to call the police. Talk of the police scared me. I remembered what they had done to Péralte. I smiled at the doctor, suddenly meek. I thanked her and thanked the paramedics and thanked everyone who talked to me, nodding yes, yes, yes, to whatever they were saying, whether it was a question or a comment or a suggestion, yes yes yes.

I climbed back into the ambulance with the chiseled paramedics.

At Mercy Hospital, they asked me if I was lucid, and I said thank you, yes, yes, yes. They asked if I agreed to be admitted. I thought of Shaniqua and thought of Péralte and tried not to think of Mama all alone back home and said thank you, yes, yes, yes. Sure, why not. I said it like that, "Sure, why not?" *Why not?* They made me sign some forms.

I blew a kiss at the handsome paramedic who had brought me in and then followed the nurse up to the second floor. There, she handed me over to another nurse, who had me fill out more forms. She had a flat, sallow face, the forgettable kind, the perfect extra on the TV series *Grey's Anatomy*. She smiled at me, the way actors with minor roles do, meaning neither this nor that. I, too, gave her a blank smile. I was tired of the signature chirpiness of the Midwest.

The nurse stripped me of all the meagre markers that made me who I was in this world; my black leather belt with the silver butterfly buckle; my Africa bead necklace dangling around my neck like a talisman; my floral scarf I'd bought at a market in Zimbabwe for my trip abroad; my brand new boots I had bought online on Artemis; my ivory bracelet and silver earrings; my winter coat, my jeans, my top and all the layers I had underneath; even my bra; my Samsung phone. In exchange, I got a generic hospital dress that was like a gown worn back to front and that left your backside exposed. They also gave me two pairs of baggy trousers, which I took gratefully. I asked for another hospital dress and wore it the proper way you would wear a gown. Lastly, the nondescript nurse handed me several pairs of socks. They were all yellow.

"What about shoes?" I asked.

"Shoes aren't allowed," she replied. I pointed at her clogs. Her smile waned.

I suppose I was being a smart aleck, demanding more of her than her role as an extra in this seminal film called *Life* required. After I slipped on a pair of socks, she held my arm and clasped a FALL RISK tag around my wrist. She instructed me to keep it on at all times.

"Thank you, nurse," I said meekly.

The extra led me down a hallway with gray carpeting to a dim room, motioning first to my bed, which faced the door, and then to my toilet and shower wedged in a crescent-shaped silver cubicle to my right. Then she disappeared. I stood for a moment, appraising the two single beds in the room, one hugging each wall. A form rose and fell gently on the bed to my far right. I appraised it for a moment. And then I crawled into my bed. Its white sheets were crisp, the way hotel sheets felt. My tummy grumbled, reminding me that I hadn't eaten all day. I wondered if I could get the extra to bring me something to eat. Then I hugged myself and tried to fall asleep.

I could feel, all around me, my American Dream crumbling. I had no words for the grief swelling inside me.

I woke up the next morning to find a woman sitting on top of the frumpy white sheets and pewter blanket on the bed opposite, hugging her legs to her chest. She rocked to and fro. Her long, gray hair covered her face and fell almost all the way down to her waist.

"Hullo," I said, but she neither replied nor stopped rocking.

I figured she must not be from around these parts, to be so glum and unreceptive to my acquired Midwestern chirpiness. I surveyed the room. We each had a chair and a bedside desk drawer next to our beds. I got up and went to inspect the bathing area. I was glad to discover that we each had a half crescent to ourselves, with its own shower the shape of a Reuleaux triangle and a tiny stainless-steel sink and a matching toilet bowl. Satisfied, I returned to my bed, pulled the covers up to my chin, and faced the wall. I tried to console my grouchy tummy.

Later that morning, a young woman dressed in mint-colored scrubs and a white coat breezed into our room. She smiled, flicking pheomelanated hair out of a pair of teal eyes. I knew she had to be the lead doctor, the Meredith Grey of my own personal *Grey's Anatomy*.

"I'll be with you in a minute," she said, nodding in my direction, before pulling a chair up to the other bed.

I resolved to be a good patient for Meredith Grey, better than the sulking woman. The woman with the gray hair rocking herself to and fro like she needed somebody to hug her told Meredith Grey she wanted to be moved out of her room. When Meredith Grey asked why, she cast her eyes on me, like I had done something, and said she didn't want to share a room with a nigger.

"You're the nigger," I said.

She jerked her head at me. You could tell nobody had ever said that to her, called her a nigger. You could tell it landed on her with a painful weight, heavier than a slap, a punch in the gut that nobody could see, that left bruises on the inside, and not the outside, of the body.

"Am I a nigger?" she said, raising her hands to her face. She turned to Meredith Grey. "Oh God, am I a nigger?"

"You're not a nigger," I said.

She looked at me and smiled. "I'm not?"

"Yes, you are."

She began to sob.

Meredith Grey began speaking to the woman in hushed tones, telling her to "Shush, Rose." Whatever she said must have worked, because the woman quietened down. Though I strained my ears and tried to eavesdrop on their conversation, I couldn't make out the rest of what they were saying. I was convinced Meredith Grey must be a pro to be able to conduct a conversation so discreetly in such an intimate space and continue talking consolingly like that to the nigger-calling Rose-woman who had put us all in this intractable situation.

Meredith Grey finally came and sat by my bed. She introduced herself as Sophia, a resident on rotation from the Carver College of Medicine.

"You're Meredith Grey," I said.

She laughed, a high-pitched little tinkle, like she was flattered to be Meredith Grey.

I told her I was also a student at the university. "I'm at The Program," I said casually, waiting for her eyes to widen in admiration, the way people's eyes around here always did when they learned this piece of information.

Meredith Grey, despite being Meredith Grey, was no exception. "The Program, huh?"

I returned her illuming smile, even though what I really wanted was to ask her what she meant by "huh," like she didn't believe me.

"I have the director on speed dial," I said.

She didn't respond to this, but just continued flashing her Colgate teeth at me. She looked down at her clipboard and ran an amethyst-colored nail down her notepad and said, "Do you know why you're here?"

I pretended to give this a think. When I continued to frown but offered no response, Meredith Grey said, "It says here, on my chart, that you suffer from psychogenic symptoms."

My heart began to hiccup. "I don't know," I said.

"You don't know?"

I shrugged, suddenly sullen. "I'm starving," I said. "The extra forgot to bring me supper last night."

"Well," said Meredith Grey, flicking her wrist, though she wore no watch. "I think breakfast ends at ten. Why don't you go and eat, and you and I can talk later? Is that OK?"

I nodded shyly, suddenly feeling meek.

Breakfast turned out to be in the communal area just down the hall-way from our room. There were round tables in the middle of the room, where other patients sat, dressed in the same hospital garb I was. They were congregated rather haphazardly, with only two or three people at each table.

There was something eerie about the communal area. It made my hands tingle. It was nothing out of *Girl, Interrupted*, that was for sure. There was nothing decidedly devilish about it, no barred windows or the promise of an electroshock therapy machine wheeled out by an eager, dumpy nurse. What it was, I realized with surprise and confusion and an odd feeling of insult, was terribly childish. It was as though it had been designed to regress us into our childhoods, or imagined versions of our childhoods, what the quintessential American childhood was supposed to look like, which, I guessed from the scene before me, was all color and fluff.

A table of crayons and neon pens stood to my left, separating the TV area from the rest of the room, laden with sheaves upon sheaves of blank paper, presumably on which to reanimate our childhoods. Next to the paper was a stack of games, Pictionary and bingo and Chutes and Ladders and several puzzle sets. Colored beads were arranged on a desk rammed against the window.

The TV area of the communal room was made up of an impres-sive twenty-four-inch TV sitting atop an ornate chest of drawers with golden handles, like nineteenth-century door knockers, and dainty matching feet. Presently, it was switched off. On the floor by the chest of drawers, lined up along the gray carpet, sat cute little penguin dolls and several miniature Sesame Street Big Birds and some teddy bears and a whole assortment of other fluffy toys.

I felt like I was in a crèche.

Breakfast was stashed in rows of trays in a giant trolley on wheels to the right of the neon, crayon, and puzzle table. To my left were two

computers, sitting on one end of the bead-and-card desk by the window. Hugging the wall to my right, next to the corridor that led to our
rooms, was a table littered with bowls of fruit and cartons of juice and
slabs of energy bars and tubs of yoghurt. This we could have at any
time of the day, I would learn later.

I walked up to the giant trolley and appraised the trays. They had
different assortments of food. I wondered if I was allowed to take more
than one tray. I was so hungry. My eyes surveyed the room, eyeing
the nurses' station behind me, near the TV area, where two nurses
stood behind the counter. I felt them watching me, ready to pounce
and make an example out of me should I dare take more than my one
allotted tray.

I looked around me. The other patients were bent over their food
or otherwise slouching in their seats, spooning cereal and eggs and
some other stuff I couldn't make out into their mouths. I peered back at
the nurses, then at the trays. Then I pulled out the cereal, boiled egg,
bacon, muffin, and coffee tray, grabbing a fistful of celery sticks from
a neighboring tray and tucking it into my hospital gown as I turned to
make my way to the tables. I glanced over my shoulder. The nurses
were still behind the nurses' station to my left, on the phone or otherwise just chattering with one another.

My eyes settled on Rose, who sat sulking by a table to my right. I
went and stood next to her. She neither raised her head nor stopped
prodding her bagel like she was digging for treasure. Maybe she had
forgotten I was a nigger. I moved on, shuffling to the next table, where
I plopped myself opposite a swarthy girl who was about my age. Her
hair was shaved on one side of her head, like a half-mohawk. She looked
ghastly. The shaved part of her head was slathered in tattoos, a skull
and an oversized knife and a penis running through a heart.

Between me and the girl sat an older woman who had her hair piled

dramatically atop her head, like maybe she was making a fashion statement or something. I waited for them to say hello. But they didn't. The
girl continued slurping her cereal, her eyes fixed on her plate. The older
woman sort of raised one corner of her mouth at me, and then gave
up midway, like maybe it was too much effort. I took their cue, and
together we ate our breakfast in silence.

When the orderlies came to collect our trays, they brought a food
menu for us to look over and choose what we wanted for lunch and
dinner. I frowned at it in great concentration, making sure to read each
food item carefully before settling for what seemed like the biggest portions, a burger and fries for lunch, and a meatloaf for dinner. It seemed
to me that this place wasn't so bad, what with being given a menu and
choices and everything, like important guests.

After breakfast, I resumed my session with Meredith Grey. I thought
she would start asking me again if I knew why I was there, and I greeted
her with a steely expression. But she didn't. Instead, she asked me to
tell her about my childhood. She told me not to inhibit myself, to tell
her whatever I was thinking as I was thinking it. I wasn't thinking any
damn thing except how soon I could get out of there. But she had one
of those faces, the kind I'd seen countless times on TV, that inspired
confidence. Before I knew it, I was pouring my heart out to her. She
wanted to know about my mother, my father, about being an only child,
whether I had been neglected ("My daddy loved me! It's just that he
died! He died! But he loved me!"). She wanted to know about the time I
visited New York as a child, every nitty-gritty, scribbling ominously in
her notebook. She smiled and frowned and nodded in all the appropri-
ate places, even going so far as to blush when I told her about my adolescent love affair with Rufus. I was charmed by her open yet strangely
controlled display of emotion, and flattered by her interest in me and
my life. No one had ever asked me so many prying questions before.

Finally, she snapped her notebook shut and said we would stop there for the day.

I watched her gather her things and waved goodbye as she left, smiling as hard as I could. I wanted her to like me.

Afterward, I went to sit by the computers. They were dusty, like nobody ever used them. Well, I had no interest in playing with the childish toys. The computer would be my plaything. It went onto Google all right, but when I tried opening Gmail, it said *site blocked*. I tried to punch in my Yahoo Mail, but same thing. It wouldn't even let me log onto Facebook. I glared over my shoulder at the nurses sitting by their station, probably chattering away on Twitter on their phones. If we couldn't get onto Gmail, or Yahoo Mail, or Facebook what was the point of the damn computers? They had even taken away my phone! I began to feel like I was a sinister thing, surrounded by sinisterness, cut off from the outside world. At that moment, I felt, with all my heart, like Susanna Kaysen in *Girl, Interrupted*, like I'd been imprisoned in Claymoore and they had no intention of ever letting me out.

I began to wheeze.

And then I remembered my university email. I punched in *Microsoft Outlook*. There, it popped up. Ha! The dumpy nurses hadn't thought of everything, after all. I bet they didn't even know what Microsoft Outlook was. There, I had my portal to the outside world. I hunched my back, trying to shadow the screen with my body so the nurses or any other snooping busybody wouldn't be able to see that I'd managed to breach the wall against communication, that I'd set myself free, freed my mind and my spirit and couldn't ever be brainwashed, like poor Susanna.

I decided to write Dean. Surely, he would be wondering where I was and what had happened to me.

"Hey Dean," I wrote and then deleted this and wrote, "Dear Program Director . . ." I told him I was suffering from a terrible cold and had been ordered to bed rest by my doctor and didn't want to be disturbed. He mustn't try to call me or contact me or look for me or anything. I signed *Warmly*, thought better of it, then typed *Sincerely*.

Next, I decided to write Shaniqua. I paused, thinking of what to say. I typed short, clipped sentences, letting her know that I had been admitted at Mercy Hospital—after a while I went back and added, the *psych ward* at Mercy Hospital—where I was getting the help I needed. I didn't know what help I needed or what I was getting. Then I added, above this, that the doctors had said I would be released in a few days. I didn't know when I would be released, but a few days sounded like a comforting, assuring amount of time for someone to be away in a psych ward.

I asked her to please *please* not tell anyone I'd been admitted, not to say where I was, and not to try and contact my mother or tell our fellow Programmers or Dean or anything like that. Then I thought of Péralte. It would be best if he didn't know I had been sent to a psychiatric ward. I wrote that Shaniqua was to absolutely, under no circumstances, tell Péralte where I was or what had happened to me. I held my breath, and then pressed send. Then I shuffled to my room and stretched myself out on my stomach on the pewter blanket covering my single bed. I buried my head beneath my pillow and cried and cried.

One of the nurses, a different one from the one who had admitted me two nights before, came and told me I had a visitor. I followed her, pleased that someone would think of coming to see me, though I had no idea who it might be. I wondered, thrilled, if I had a secret admirer.

There was Péralte, seated by one of the round tables where we ate our meals, which also served as recreational tables, where some of the patients spent the afternoon playing cards and board games and scribbling on blank paper. The tables also served as the visitors' section. I hadn't expected to see Péralte seated there. So embarrassed was I to see him that I froze. The nurse who was walking behind me crashed into me.

"Ouch!" she cried.

"Sorry," I mumbled, turning to give her a remorseful smile.

When I turned back around, Péralte's large eyes were cast on me. Dammit. I had planned to slip away back to my room and tell the nurse to inform him that he was mistaken, no patient by my name was incarcerated in this institution of the insane. I gritted my teeth, thinking how Shaniqua had told him, despite my express instructions that she tell no one where I was. I didn't want Péralte to see me like this—I didn't want anyone to see me like this. I, myself, did not want to see myself like this.

I felt like I was in a dream, watching someone who looked like me act out an incomprehensible part.

Forcing a smile, I walked over to him and took a seat at the round table. We eyed one another. Then he got up and came around the table and hugged me, wrapping his stocky arms around my shoulders and burying his face in my neck. It felt good to be hugged. I inhaled the musky scent of his cologne. His cheek was bristly where he had shaved. He kissed me on my forehead. I was suddenly self-conscious. I watched him as he dragged a chair over and sat beside me, planting his bum on the edge of the seat and leaning forward to take my hand in both of his. I fondled the lush hairs proliferating on his knuckles, as though of a strange, glorious mammal.

"How are you doing?" he said.

"I'm great!" I said.

I realized I was shouting. I didn't know why I was shouting. I hadn't brushed my teeth that morning, and I wondered if my breath smelled.

"Yeah? They're treating you OK?"

"Yes, everything is fine! Meredith Grey is my doctor!"

"Who?"

"Meredith Grey!"

He paused. "I see."

"You have to play along, or it won't work!"

"What?"

"You have to play along! I am seeing Meredith Grey!"

He paused. "That's nice."

I tried to think of something useful to say. "How's school!"

He smiled this sad little smile. "Don't worry about any of that," he said. "You just focus on getting better."

Smiling still, I leaned forward and whispered, "You've got to get me out of here."

He blinked like he hadn't heard me. "Say what?"

I leaned forward again, baring my teeth, and said, "You've got to help me escape."

Péralte's lips twitched. "All right," he said, getting up. "I have to go. You take care, OK?"

My smile widened. I winked at him. He bent and kissed me on the forehead again, said he wished I would get better soon and promised to come again. I told him I loved him, because I wanted to tell somebody I loved them and hear them say they loved me back. I watched him go, his buttocks bouncing with the funny way he walked. He paused by the exit, turning to wave goodbye. I blew him a kiss. And then he was gone. There was an odd sensation of grief in my chest, as though I would never see him again. I felt a deluge of panic rise in me. I tried to swallow it back down. I smiled at the nurse behind the nurse's station and thanked her for the visit, as though she was somehow responsible for making it happen. Then I got up to go to my room.

The Terrors came, quick and abrupt, like a menace that had been hiding in my blind spot and now saw the opportunity to pounce. My legs turned into porridge. I tumbled to the ground. A parching heat flooded my chest. It felt as though I were in a really hot furnace. My vision began to blur. The seizures crept up on me. They started at the tips of my fingers and crawled up my arms, like ants, making the small of my back wet. I began convulsing, like I was being taken over by the Holy Spirit, just like it had taken over Mama's church ladies, spasming their bodies and channeling its mysterious tongues through their froth-ing mouths.

Faces pooled above me. They frowned and mouthed things, but I could no longer hear them. They seemed so far away. It felt like I'd fallen through a very deep and very dark hole. I saw Meredith Grey's pretty face coming closer, getting bigger and bigger, and I tried to smile, to let her know I was glad she was there. She placed a hand on my forehead. I saw her placing it, but I couldn't feel it. I could only see her face, coral and blurry, becoming flushed. Her honey-red pony-tail flicked over her shoulder as she turned and shouted something to someone, her mouth widening in slo-mo, like she was trying to swal-low the world.

A stretcher was wheeled in, and a bunch of people struggled to get me on there. I was getting fat in America, I thought wryly, fatter than I had ever been, fatter than I had ever thought possible in this world. I was finding myself in places I hadn't known could exist, in worlds more exotic than iNdonsakusa, stranger than iNyanga or even our imaginary Kepler-186f.

A portal had opened up inside me, lobbing me into another dimension.

I stopped convulsing. The seizures crept in and crept up and crept through me. They were finished with me. They had finished me. But now, I couldn't move my body. It felt like the world was on top of me, trying to slip through the same hole I'd slipped through, crashing on top of me. Crushing me.

The stretcher began to move, Meredith Grey alongside it. We went down a brightly lit hallway and entered a huge elevator. The steel walls made it seem like we were in a fridge. I wanted to hold Meredith Grey's hand. My brain commanded my arm to move, but it didn't budge. And then the stretcher was rolling again, and we were under more bright lights. They wheeled me down a corridor and into a room and the room was cold. Meredith Grey said something to someone, moving her head from side to side and then up and down. She looked, in the muted blue light, extraterrestrial. Globules of spit leapt from her mouth and began their long descent, like they never wanted to reach the ground.

*Neither did I,* I thought snarkily, *but here we are, friends.*

Meredith Grey began to move away. A warm, wet panic welled up in me. I yelled for her to come back. But my lips and my voice rebelled against my mind, and she disappeared through a swinging door. Even though there was a man in a white lab coat with me, I felt all alone in the world.

I began to cry, but inside, because even my tears had abandoned me.

✳

THE MAN IN the lab coat slid me into a cold white machine shaped like a donut. He said, cheerfully, that it was called a magnetic resonance imaging machine, or MRI, and it was going to take a scan of my brain. It felt like entering a spaceship. And then the machine started making all these strange, cosmic sounds: a beeping and a terrible squawking, like a bird in distress. There was a disconcerting pinging followed by an abrasive sound unlike anything I had ever heard or could imagine. It was the sound of the universe thirteen billion years ago, banging rudely and gloriously into existence.

I felt like I was being atomized. I began to scream for somebody to let me out. But the scream remained imprisoned inside my head, and my body remained perfectly still, like I was in a coma. And then the thing stopped making its terrible cosmic noises, and the man in the lab coat pulled me out of that black hole into ambient blue light, and I felt like a miracle.

Somebody who wasn't Meredith Grey came and trundled me away to another room, where they latched me onto an EEG machine. Afterward, they took me to another floor and drew my blood. I was sweaty and bright-eyed and still aflush from my galactic journey in the MRI pod, so much so that I tried to get up and walk on my own, but the nurse wouldn't hear of it and insisted on pushing me around in a wheelchair.

"Where is Meredith Grey," I said.

The extra bent forward over my wheelchair, proffering her ear. "Who?"

"I'd like Meredith Grey, please."

". . . You mean, like, from the TV series?"

I sighed. "You're ruining everything. Dr. Sophia. I'm talking about Dr. Sophia."

"Oh! She's gone for the day. But she'll be back tomorrow."

I was sad to hear Meredith Grey had already left. I was disappointed she hadn't stayed to see how I was doing. But I was glad to return to my room and sleep. By then, it was late afternoon and a winter gloam had spread across the city. Blocks of pale-orange light winked at us from the houses across the street.

I slept and slept. I slept through a cognitive therapy group exercise, and I slept through dinner, even though an extra came and tried to force me to get up and eat. I wouldn't, or couldn't, but she kept pestering me. I snapped at her, but all that came out of my mouth was some indeterminate mumbling, which was all the same to me, because eventually, she left me alone.

The next morning, I woke up to find I had developed a stammer. Meredith Grey came in to see me. She sat patiently by my bedside, listening as I tried to explain to her that I had never stammered before. She looked like she didn't believe me, so I told her, slowly this time, trying to measure my breathing, that I had been the president of both the debating team and Toastmasters in my high school. I was an orator, like President Obama. She laughed, and I felt relieved, like maybe I'd communicated something substantial to her.

She began asking me questions about my medical history, scribbling in her notebook as I spoke.

My tests from the previous day had all come back normal, she said.

I wanted to jump and shout "Aha!"

That meant I was exhibiting psychosomatic symptoms, she said. She thought I might be suffering from pseudodementia. It wasn't really dementia, she said, but "depression masquerading as dementia."

All I heard was *dementia*.

Meredith Grey said she wanted to start me on some medication for the pseudo*dementia*. It would help with the pseudoseizures. I nodded, trying to keep my face calm. I licked my lips and then sucked on them and licked them again.

Shutting her notepad, Meredith Grey appraised me, her teal eyes scintillating as she gazed steadily into mine, the way she did with her patients at Seattle Grace Mercy West Hospital on *Grey's Anatomy*.

"Yesterday, you asked for me by my real name, Sophia," she said.

I fluttered my eyes at her, suddenly feeling sheepish. "The nurse didn't know you were Meredith Grey."

"Well, that's good. It tells me that you don't have a thought disorder, and that you're consciously entering a fantasy world and are aware, at least to some degree, of the boundaries between reality and fantasy. Usually, regression into a constructed inner world happens when we don't feel safe. It's a way to create a safe space. I'm trying to figure out what's making you feel unsafe."

I paused, considering this. I told her I had been thinking a lot about my father. Thinking about him took me back to my childhood. It made me feel like a child. I liked this childlike space it allowed me to inhabit.

It was a space of innocence, filled with beauty and promise and devoid of sorrow. Perhaps I held on to this state of childhood because it had felt so simple, so pure. So easy. It was a state of probity from which I wished never to wake up.

"Do you think," said Meredith Grey, "that maybe your quest for accomplishment, your various trips to conferences abroad, your making it into a prestigious institution such as The Program, working so hard all the time, in essence almost working yourself to death, are all a substitute for your father?"

I thought about this for a moment. I didn't know what to make of it. I just stared at Meredith Grey.

"Let's talk about The Terrors," said Meredith Grey.

I squirmed. I didn't want to talk about The Terrors.

"You're good at describing the physical sensations of them, but I'd like to know, from you, what you believe is happening to you."

"Ecstatic moments of pain—"

"OK, but what does that mean?"

I paused. "A feeling of death—"

"Use your words. It's OK. Breathe. Try and describe to me in concrete terms what has been happening to you."

I blinked at her. How did The Terrors feel? They just washed over me as a series of confusing, overwhelming sensations, agitations over which I had no control and which perplexed and vanquished me, causing me pain. Not physical pain but a . . . *pain*, somehow. My body kept reliving catastrophe or trying to safeguard itself from catastrophe. The Terrors felt like a visceral, repetitive form of self-destruction, a terror of destroying others or of being destroyed by others.

I didn't really have a language for The Terrors. And because I did not know how to give them a language, it was easy to pretend, when everything was going well in my life, that they didn't exist, that they weren't a part of me. Each episode of The Terrors almost felt like it was the first.

"I feel betrayed by my body," I said.

Meredith Grey was quiet for a moment. She scribbled something on her notepad. She said, not unkindly, "Maybe it's trying to tell you something. Maybe it's trying to help you heal. What would happen if you thought of your body as trying to help you rather than working against you?"

I paused. I hadn't considered this. I'd just been trying to get through life. I thought about Mr. C and the things Candice had said. Each time I tried to make sense of it, a bile-like taste flooded my mouth. What the fuck was I supposed to do with the things she'd told me? I thought I was going to be sick, or die.

I thought of the *New York Times* article on my father. My mouth felt dry. I swallowed and forced myself to stay with it. I went over each paragraph in my mind, pausing over the unsmiling image of him at the bottom of the article. Something seared my chest. But I stayed with it. I stayed with it, and came to a terrible understanding: my father, had he lived, would not have been the same father I had known, the father of my childhood memories which I had played over and over and pearled in my mind. No, he would not be the same father, and I was no longer the same daughter.

Barricaded from the wintry night by the wide floor-to-ceiling windows on the second floor of Mercy, the snow looked harmless, falling in delicious white fluffs, like candy floss. Even though we were in the third week of January, Christmas decorations still glittered everywhere. At night, the Christmas lights blinked brightly at an inky night sky, a Morse code to other galaxies.

I was charmed by the world before me. Everything was eclipsed by snow, the unfenced, single- and double-story houses lined up along East Bloomington Street, the hulking cars parked next to the sidewalks. At night, their laden roofs seemed to emit a phantasmagorical fluorescence, beacons in the pale darkness.

Nurse Johnson's trolley squeaked across the floor, bumping against the computer desk. I turned to her and opened my mouth wide. In the early evening light, she looked, with her slightly bent posture and her hips filling out her blue uniform, like my grandmother.

"There you go, darlin'," she said, picking up a miniature cup from her trolley.

It was like a measuring cup for medicine, the kind that used to come with cough mixtures when I was a child. Nurse Johnson upended it on my tongue. Then she handed me a tumbler and watched as I drank the water. She waited for me to stick out my tongue so she could peer down my throat and make sure the pills had gone down the way they were supposed to.

I liked having Nurse Johnson feed me the pills rather than having to take them myself. She didn't do this for every patient, making me love her even more. I wondered if I reminded her of someone in her life, too. She kept asking me about Africa, wanting to know if I lived in a hut and whether I could see the lions and the cheetahs out on the plains near my house. I laughed each time and told her she would love my family rural home in Empandeni where my father had grown up, among the dusty plains and scraggly bushes and gurgling streams and the kudus of southwestern Zimbabwe.

"I'ma come with you one of these days," she said with a chuckle. "We did one of them DNA kits, and it says our ancestry's from West Africa."

I told her I'd been to Nigeria once, which was in West Africa. This seemed to please her, like maybe it made our meeting here, in this out-of-the-way place in America, more than just serendipitous. Nodding goodbye to Nurse Johnson as she trundled past with her trolley of medicines, I turned and faced the window and gazed at the world outside.

I felt like a shadow, like I was trying to flesh out different parts of a partial sketch to bring out the color and make a hollow whole. I was overcome by the sensation of being unmoored, of being taken over by the deception of language and the disintegration of meaning. Failing to reconstruct signs and words and signals the way they needed to be reconstructed. Failing to acquire meaning.

I had started dreaming of my father in my sleep, though I hadn't told Meredith Grey or anyone. The dreams were illogical in their beauty, for they were of things that couldn't have happened, making them even more exhilarating, charming because they were fanciful, as though with death so dies time, the revolving wheel of grief spinning off frivolous reels of memory, so that it was as if I were there with him, my father, growing up in Empandeni village, the fourth of nine children, sprouting under my gogo's unyielding grip as she dunked him and scrubbed him and baptized him in rivers of water.

In my dreams, I see my gogo polishing him, my daddy, lathering him in the sacred oils of Vaseline petroleum jelly until his gangly limbs glisten like a pecan in the sun. He tries to scamper off, this svelte young Horus. He's ten. His heart beats wild in his chest. She grips him, my gogo, grabs his arm, even as he tries to wrench himself free. She tugs him toward her and holds him close, and if he continues snarling and gnarling like a crazy thing without a mother's guiding hand to instill some ubuntu, some love, she's not above unthreading him with a slap that I can hear ringing—*pa!*—in that tranquil afternoon of my father's youth, double-ringing—*pa! pa!*—in my ears in my father's ears, stopping me stopping him dead in our tracks, me trembling from the shock of the vividness of it, he no longer trying to run, although his gaze upon my gogo is fierce even as he never dares do to her whatever impiety the passions of youth are imploring him to do. He begins to cry. I begin to cry. I sniffling abashedly, he bawling ashamedly, burying his eyes in the pockets of his fists, shaking, whether from the shock of her slap or the force of his passions. Those deep-throated, heart-slitting wails make my gogo laugh even as she holds him close and even as he tries to turn his streaked face away from her, yielding eventually to her embrace.

He lurches suddenly, ducks and manages to slide out of Gogo's grip, laugh-crying as she yells for him to stop, hey, wena, stop, mani, come back here, if I catch you, I'll . . . it fades, Gogo's voice, to a whisper as he scampers off. He's laughing now. His laughter swells in the still afternoon air, swelling the heart that hears it, this unruly croak of a boy teetering into adolescence, boisterous and yet unsure. He slinks off to the River Tati, all gangling pecan limbs, ashy cedar at the elbows, darker at the knees, those knobby knees bunched up like fists, ready to punch the ground where he crouches by the riverbank, squinting at the verdant bushes teetering on the banks opposite, threatening to dump their wine-dark berries into the water, their roots all tripped up by the sedges that sprout indiscriminately from underground rhizome colonies and cling to whatever offshoot they happen to curl around. There he raises his long face to the sun, which shines flame-hot and eggshell colored, and I imagine he imagines we imagine I can taste he can taste we can taste those plump berries bursting warm and wet in my his our mouths.

✳

MEREDITH GREY SAT on a chair by my bed, a slight furrow on her brow. Her lips were slightly parted, and the tip of her tongue was moist and visible, a distinct strawberry color, like she'd been sucking on a sherbet.

I told her I finally understood why it was that Americans kept referring to Africa as a country. It was because they, themselves, the Americans, had gotten so big as an Empire that they had stopped referring to themselves by their proper country name, USA, and instead had taken on, for themselves, the name of a whole continent, the Americas. This was why everything was so big in America—the food, the cars, the egos. Having lost a sense of proportion of themselves, they no longer had a sense of proportion of the rest of the world.

"That's why to them Africa is a country—like America."

Meredith Grey thought this terribly clever. I beamed at her.

She dropped her teal eyes to her notepad, and, as if in mockery, or honor, of the joke I had just made, she started asking me about my perilous escape from Africa, and about the things I'd told her during our sessions, the food shortages and the money shortages and the fuel queues and the hyperinflation I had experienced during my teens.

Meredith Grey's questions made me feel very depressed. Her unwavering gaze and the way she prodded me about my life in Zimbabwe, wanting to know about the things I had suffered, made me depressed.

I told her how I had always admired America from afar for the way it seemed at once innocent and wise. I, myself, perhaps, had always wanted to remain in a state of innocence about my life, a perpetual childhood, if you will. I had always thought of America as a chimera forever allowing one to luxuriate in that state of innocence. In innocence, I could cling to my father as I remembered him, as I loved him; I could remain childlike. But that idyllic innocence had turned out to be an illusion. It was now forever shattered.

I mourned my America, mourned the things I now knew were not real but that had a visceral power over me, nevertheless.

"Why can't you let them go?" asked Meredith Grey.

I tried to think about this.

"Because," I said slowly, my heart succumbing to dread, "letting go of them would mean letting go my cherished vision of my father."

I knew, as I said it, that it was true. I had clung, all my life, to the towering, infallible figure he'd been. I had found in him when he was alive and in his letters after his death an intellectual peer, someone who could have understood the person I was, my desire to live inside my mind. I liked to think he would have encouraged my juvenile excursions into astronomy and my philosophical ramblings.

Though Mama was loving, she had morphed, after my father's death, into a practical woman, cautioning my desire to flap my wings and soar when experience told her this world was brutal and expedient with our lot. She hadn't always been this way. She had been vivacious in her youth, embracing possibility. And then The Terrors began terrorizing us, and home became a terror of its own. Mama became what I feared to become, a small woman, and visions of my father what I feared I would *never* become, large and terrifying and gorgeous—something that awed the mind but sometimes hurt the heart to see.

I looked up to see Meredith Grey gazing at me with so much tenderness I began to cry. I covered my face with my hands. I was shaking. I couldn't help it. It was awful. Meredith Grey tapped my arm and handed me a tissue. I bawled, bubbling tears and snot into it until I could no longer breathe. My chest began to hiccup.

"I'm really happy we've gotten here," said Meredith Grey, handing me another tissue.

I glared at her, sullen. "Gotten where?"

"To a place where you can express some deep-seated emotion. Where you can let it out. I think we're finally breaking down those walls. Hmm?"

She tilted her head as she said this, and at that moment she looked incredibly old, and wise, like maybe she knew things I didn't.

"I don't want to be a trauma story," I said.

Was that what I was? I had seen "Africa" trauma stories on TV, fly-infested faces gouged out by famine and swollen, ribbed toddlers gazing expressionless at the camera, branded by WHO and Red Cross T-shirts. They never seemed fully human, always trapped by the camera and the narrating, twanging voices in one perpetual film of suffering, like that was all they were, like they never laughed or fell in love or had dreams or ambitions. They didn't look like any person I knew or would ever want to be. I felt myself morphing before the power of Meredith Grey's gaze, her eager questions about the things I had suffered in my life flattening me into a trauma story.

Even if something was wrong with me, I said, even if I needed help, I just wanted to be a person.

Meredith Grey nodded gentle-like, and then she did something she had never done before. She leaned forward and hugged me, enveloping me in a caramel-scented embrace. Then she leaned back, like the moment hadn't happened, back to her psychiatric ways. She picked up her pen, frowned at her notepad, and asked me to tell her what I did in the days following my father's death.

I told her how I had spent inordinate amounts of time hunched over the computers at school, away from Mama's censorious gaze, googling death. I had wanted to understand how a person died.

*How, exactly, does a person die?*

*Up to seven minutes for the brain to shut down. Those valiant cells of the body acting as soldiers, fighting for the nation that is the brain, tumbling one by one under the rifle of that notorious assassin, Death. Or perhaps the cells, shorn of the superheroic, are closer to the civilian, the pedestrian, the human. They rupture to form a messy terrain of remembrance, a bloody torrent of memories that flood the prefrontal cortex.*

Did he think of me as he died, my father?

Delirium. Disorientation. Liquid flooding the lungs. How was it, when a man died? Did the fading light lap like a postcard sunset at the fading consciousness? Trapped in hypnopompia—the state leading from sleep to wakefulness—did the dying victim, *death's* victim, fight the current, dragging himself toward that beach of wakefulness, wrestling against death's tide, trying to cling to the solidness of the world he had always known? I hoped my father hadn't died this way. I hoped his experience had been closer to hypnagogia—the slipping from wakefulness into sleep—inspiring little resistance. What could be more beloved than sleep? To be dazzled by random speckles and geometrical shapes, all in mosaic, shifting colors. These, surely, would have offered something pleasurable as he went under.

I pictured him dying. Having driven for almost four and a half hours, something he wasn't used to, he would have been absorbed by this activity he'd just been performing, mercifully prevented from realizing what was happening by the illusory feel of the upholstery of the Mazda 323 warm against his bum. The smell of a lemon-scented carfreshener, this, surely, would have been preferable to the rusty smell of blood. Perhaps, taken over by hypnagogic hallucinations, he heard, once again, our very last conversation, which we'd had a few hours before, just after his flight landed in Harare, when he'd promised to see me soon, his voice thick with fatigue. His features spread and tightened. Perhaps, affected by synesthesia, the last thing he saw before he died was the proverbial streak of blinding, celestial light.

And somewhere in all of this, maybe, my face.

started by sketching our Kepler-186f's dwarf sun, which appeared in my Keplerian sky as a large red ball, much larger than our sun appeared in ours. Next, I shaded in my white sketch paper in light red strokes, just as I imagined the world on Kepler-186f would appear to anyone living there or visiting for the first time—as a world perpetually bathed in sunset hues, thanks to its dwarf sun's dim light.

Shaniqua began playing around with possible bioorganic life on our imaginary Kepler-186f. She helped me sketch the plant life on the planet. We dreamed up these large leafy plants and trees as tall as mountains. Shaniqua imagined the wood would be light and airy, like balsa, allowing the trees to tower over our Keplerian landscape without sinking into the ground, their roots shooting deep down into Kepler-186f's mantle to steady their massive girths, just as with our mountains here on Earth. I outlined the foliage on our Keplerian landscape in white, shading in the leaves of our gentle giants and the plant life flourishing beneath in

darker shades of red. It was strange, imagining trees and plants as anything other than the green color of chlorophyll that was so natural to
our planet. But Kepler's dwarf sun released a steady stream of red pho-
tons, meaning its plant life could very well be red and not green.

"Will we have melanin?" I asked.

"Oh, we'll need plenty of it," said Shaniqua. "The dwarf sun emits
some major UV light. You bet those red plants and them red humans
living on there are gonna be pretty melanated. Melanin over there could
also be red! Imagine that, a world of red, cherry, scarlet, rose-colored,
candy-colored, and mahogany humans."

I had spent about six weeks at Mercy, from the end of December to
early February. We were now in mid-March. The day I was discharged,
I sat in my room and stared at the photo of my father high up in the
International Space Station, Mr. C's birthday cards piled on my lap.
I read each card, pearling over the snippets of my father. Mr. C had
always etched him in such a dignified light, a delicate eulogy. I finally
cried, reading those birthday cards. Hot, angry tears spilled down my
cheeks. I could not disentangle myself from Mr. C. I would always have
these snapshots of my father, and Mr. C would always be the one who
had given them to me.

I scribbled him a letter. I couldn't stop my hand from shaking. I
wrote one question, squiggling crooked capital letters across the page
in black ink: *DID YOU KILL MY FATHER?* I knew, as I wrote the
P. O. box address on the envelope and trudged down the street to the
blue mailbox and slipped the letter inside, that I would never hear from
Mr. C again.

Shaniqua and I showed our sketches of Kepler-186f to Péralte. We
were in his gloomy apartment, haloed by the red light emitted by the
LED bulbs behind his huge flat-screen TV like a bunch of extraterres-
trials. We huddled around him as he uploaded our sketches on some

gaming software he'd been developing. I placed a tentative hand on his shoulder, but he shrugged it off. I pressed my lips together and tucked my hand behind my back.

The visuals popped up on the TV. Even blown up on the screen, looking heavily pixelated, they were really good.

"I've got a surprise for you," said Péralte.

"Oh, what is it?" I said, taking the opportunity to tilt my head and gaze at him.

He stared levelly back at me. Then his eyes softened. Not so long ago, I would have snuggled in his arms and stared into his eyes and felt the world dilate in there. I smiled, feeling wistful. His eyes darkened, becoming glinting pools, and he turned away from me, back to the keyboard on his lap.

Shaniqua pretended not to notice, and I sighed and looked up at the TV.

Péralte opened a file and uploaded one of our sketches. It was a landscape drawing, with Kepler-186f's dwarf sun shining red in a pink sky and gigantic cherry-colored mountains in the distance. To the left was a candy-colored waterfall. Mountain-sized balsa trees and a cluster of plants that, with their reedy stalks and drooping panicles, resembled wild rice but Shaniqua called, cheerfully, *large-leaf leather-roots*—"the extinct natives of the prairie"—filled the foreground.

Péralte punched a bunch of keys and ran a program. All at once, our sketch shifted from a three-dimensional representation running along the $x$-, $y$-, and $z$-axes to a conical view. It was strange to behold, as though we were encountering the dwarf sun and the cherry mountain and the candy waterfall and the balsa trees and the large-leaf leather-roots for the first time. Our waterfall seemed to "come alive," as did the mountain in the distance and the dwarf sun in the sky.

"These are your father's Bantu geometries," said Péralte to me. Then he turned to face Shaniqua on the other side of him. "See? The world feels different. The view changes depending on what you're interacting with at any given moment. It changes when you're interacting with the waterfall and also when you're using the dwarf sun as your point of reference, for instance. See?"

"It's almost like, almost like the sun and the mountain and the waterfall are alive!" I cried.

"Well, what it is, is that we now see them," said Péralte. "They're no longer abstract, disembodied lines on a flat surface."

"How did you do it?" I said.

"I didn't," he said. "Your father did. I used his equations. If there's anything you should emulate from him, it's this precision."

His voice was soft. I squeezed his shoulder and fought the urge to hug him. He didn't shrug off my hand this time, and I was glad.

"What I wanna know is," said Shaniqua, her eyes flitting to my hand on Péralte's shoulder, "what will the aliens on Kepler look like?"

We exchanged a glance and burst out laughing.

"You're gonna put yourself on there, aren't you," she said.

"And you!" I said. "And Péralte, too. I mean, we're aliens here, aren't we?"

"Well, I got US citizenship, so technically I'm not an alien," said Péralte, raising an eyebrow.

"Oh shush," said Shaniqua. "You're such a showoff. Like, do you wanna be part of this world or not?"

"I mean, I could do dual citizenship?"

"LOL." I glanced at my watch, and then straightened up. "I have to go."

I felt Péralte stiffen.

"Bye," I said, but he didn't respond.

"See you later, hun!" yelled Shaniqua.

I flashed her a grateful smile.

I left and trudged down the street, through the snow, to the bus stop on Dubuque. It was evening, and the night sky was a deep and beautiful dark, crisp and bottomless-looking. I had to wait only for a few minutes, and then the bus came. I now knew the ride by heart—I would ride for about thirty minutes, and then the bus would drop me off right outside the fenced cluster of white buildings.

I caught up with Chun and Bhaskor just as they were alighting from Chun's car in the parking lot. Together we made our way down the parking lot, round a fountain ringed by golden lights, up some steps and through a set of revolving doors.

The night guard waved us through the body scanner by the entrance, and we walked briskly across the marble floor, past a white statue of a man holding a planet, the logo INFINITY INC. towering beside him.

My heart lurched in my throat. Péralte's eyes had glazed over when I told him I was taking up the internship at Infinity Inc. He'd bit his mouth and licked his lips and said, fixing his eyes on something just above my head, that it was best he and I take a break.

"It's just for one year," I said, trying not to let my hurt show.

Still, he refused to look at me.

"I'm not my father," I said.

His face became contorted, then, the wide map of his brow rippling, his facial muscles spasming, making his eyes small and indiscernible.

I had tried to explain to Shaniqua how I thought I could do some good there, how there was something to be said about trying to change things from within. She laughed, though her laughter wasn't unpleasant, even if it wasn't warm, either. I was taken aback. I'd expected her, and not Péralte, to be the one to bite my head off.

"Things are different," I said. "With the whole thing about . . ." I gulped, and let the word *father* hang in the air between us. "I came back out different," I said. "From Mercy. I . . ."

"I know," said Shaniqua. "But you're curious, and maybe a little too ambitious. You want a taste of that fancy tech they're using over there at Infinity Inc."

"It's just for a year," I said, and then, "They're going to cut into the moon whether I'm there or not. Maybe I can go in there and . . . help change things."

"Yeah," she said. "Maybe you can go to space and change things."

I gazed at her, my heart hammering my chest. "I need you to trust me. *Please*." And then, "Imagine humans on the moon playing our Kepler."

She had pinched my cheek, a strangely intimate gesture. I had held her hand there, pressing it to my cheek, grateful for this little bit of grace.

Chun, Bhaskor, and I made our way to the elevators. They stepped inside, and I waved goodbye and continued walking. They were headed to different floors, Chun to the technology department, Bhaskor to the microgravity manufacturing section. I was headed to one of the buildings at the back. It was as large as a hangar and housed a prototype of *Project Lunar*, a long, white, tubed vessel with spherical protrusions on each side. It was set to land on iNyanga in the next five years.

I gazed up at the sky. There she was waxing gibbous. Her westerly region was cast in shadow, her easterly face bathed in light. From this distance, the Sea of Serenity and the Sea of Tranquility were dark patches, like melanated skin, on her luminous, rocky pearl surface.

## Acknowledgments

I am deeply indebted to the Lannan Foundation, especially Martha Jessup, for its generous support of my work through a Lannan Foundation Fiction Fellowship. Thank you for the support I received at the University of Houston Creative Writing Program through a Dissertation Completion Fellowship and an Inprint Fondren Foundation/Michael and Nina Zilkha Fellowship, which enabled me to complete an early version of this book. Special thanks to Margot Backus, Sreya Chatterjee, Ann Christensen, Sally Connolly, Chitra Divakaruni, Allegra Hyde, Onyinye Ihezukwu, Auritro Majumder, Isle McElroy, Maurine Ogbaa, Chinelo Okparanta, Kavita Singh, Alexander Parsons, and Peter Turchi.

I am indebted to Sam Chang and the wonderful people at the Iowa Writers' Workshop for their boundless support. I am profoundly grateful to my literary agent, Samantha Shea, for her excellent edits, her unwavering support, and the meaningful conversations we had about this novel; to my wonderful editor, Alane Mason, for her incisive eye and her boundless enthusiasm, and for teasing the best out of me and this work; to her assistant Mo Crist, for their generous eye; to my copy-editor, Ashley Patrick, for her superb edits.

A special thank you goes to Alexia Arthurs for her brilliance, patience, and generosity; her wise eye and trenchant feedback were invaluable to the culmination of this work. Our countless conversations and her read-throughs challenged me to write the best version of this novel. I am grateful for your boundless support of me and my work.

A big and heartfelt thank you to the Indigenous peoples of North America, whose history shaped, informed, and challenged this work. Engaging with this history informed my own engagement with my Indigenous history in Southern Africa. Thank you to the countless thinkers, writers, and philosophers whose knowledge and wisdom made this work possible. Ngiyabonga.